Catch a

Ris DUE

Catch a Rising Star

A Novel

Tracey Bateman

FaithWords

New York Boston Nashville

This book is a work of fiction. Names, characters, places, and incidents are the product of the author's imagination or are used fictitiously. Any resemblance to actual events, locales, or persons, living or dead, is coincidental.

FaithWords
Hachette Book Group USA
237 Park Avenue
New York, NY 10017

Visit our Web site at www.faithwords.com.

Printed in the United States of America

First Edition: July 2007
10 9 8 7 6 5 4 3 2 1

The FaithWords name and logo are trademarks of Hachette Book Group USA.

Library of Congress Cataloging-in-Publication Data
Bateman, Tracey Victoria
   Catch a rising star : a novel / Tracey Bateman.—1st ed.
      p. cm.
   ISBN-13: 978-0-446-69893-1
   ISBN-10: 0-446-69893-8
   1. Actresses—Fiction. I. Title.
   PS3602.A854C38 2007
   813'.6—dc22
                                          2006037375

*Dedicated to my fellow Drama Queen
and friend of more than twenty years, Angie Shivers.
It's only fitting I should write a book about a soap star
and dedicate it to my Days-watching buddy and forever friend.*

Acknowledgments

Rusty, you think it's sooo funny to watch *Days* with me and laugh at the storylines. So, laugh if you will, but all these years of "research" have finally paid off, buddy—this book is proof! Thank you for being my hunky hero. I'm so glad I'm going to grow old with you— yes, I really am. You have no choice! ☺

Kids, you rock. Every day, you make me so happy to be your mom. My two driving teens, Cat and Mike—how did that happen? Yesterday you were in diapers—okay, not literally, thank goodness!! But you two, behind the wheel of a car? Be still, my heart. And Stevan in junior high? All those honors classes . . . you have your work cut out for you, my little overachiever. (You're just like your mom—only a lot smarter.) My baby, Will, already a third grader and sooo smart. Where have the years gone? My honorary girl . . . Robyn. You make me so proud every day. You're growing into a beautiful, godly young woman. Keep up the good work!

Big, *big* thanks to Nancy Toback, extraordinary writer and critique partner. You know what they say: you can take the girl out of New York, but you can't take New York out of the girl. Thanks for helping me keep this book real. I'm blessed to have a real New Yawkuh for a pal.

Debra Ullrick, you read and send me happy thoughts. I appreciate you more than I can say.

As always . . . major thanks to my best friends—Chris, Susan,

Susie, and Rachel, for instant prayer covering, constant friendship, and unconditional love and support.

My editor Anne Goldsmith: once again, you set high standards and challenged me to meet them. You're a true gift, and I'm learning so much from you. Thanks to the rest of the team from FaithWords who work so hard to help my books succeed from packaging to promotion. Heidi, Jana, Brynn . . . I really like you guys!

Steve Laube, you have the golden touch when it comes to my career. I'm so glad God put you in position to keep taking me to the next level. Thank you for sharing this journey with me and for seeing potential—even when I don't.

Catch a
Rising Star

A girl should always count the cost before diving into blind dates, suspicious-looking sushi, and/or rabbit suits.

Especially rabbit suits. Well, especially weird sushi, but the rabbit suit is an incredibly close second. Case in point: at the moment I'm squirming around in itchy fur and sporting long, black whiskers that twitch when I talk and tickle my nose like crazy. Plus I think I feel a sneeze coming on.

My inner voice warned me, "Call in sick," and I completely ignored it because, you know, a girl has to make a living. Although, I should point out that some jobs are better than others. A great job, for instance, is a starring role in a highly ranked daytime drama. That is, until a person gets unjustly canned—like a poor dolphin—for being in the wrong place at the wrong time.

But, oh well. I'm over it. You know . . . mostly.

Which brings me to the opposite of a great job—dressing up like a rabbit and getting ready to read to all the kids lining up outside the bookstore's children's section, for instance. Yep, there must be a hundred of them (or maybe twenty or so) just waiting for a big furry bunny—a.k.a., me—to thrill them with a stunning tale from the Beatrix Potter collection.

I'm trying to psych myself up for the ordeal, but honestly? All I want to do is run away from the impending and inevitable humiliation. I stare at my muted reflection in the glass display window. The case holds a first edition copy of *Charlotte's*

Web and a few photos of my manager, Mary, standing next to various famous authors like John Grisham and Stephen King. I usually pause for a moment of respect when I pass the case, but right now I can't concentrate on anything but the need to get out of this suit. Gee whiz, if real rabbits itch this bad, it's no wonder they're always hopping.

I yank on the fur at my neck and rake my paws across my collarbones, hoping for relief. I mean, sure, I make an adorable bunny. But that's not the point. This thing is murder.

Teresa Shewmate, our resident—and self-appointed—room mother, slides across the floor with all the grace of a ballroom dancer. If I'm not mistaken, she's got donuts in that bag. My donut radar rarely fails. And it truly has nothing to do with the fact that she brings Krispy Kremes every Saturday.

"Morning!" she says a lot more cheerily than anyone has a right to on Saturday morning when her friend is wearing a suit like this one. But Teresa's such a nice lady, I instantly smile.

She raises the bags. "Food!"

My stomach responds like Pavlov's dog and lets out a growl. Due to a faulty alarm clock, I had no time for breakfast, so I'm starving and I can't fight the magnetic pull of all those carbs. True, the treats are technically for the kids. But, I ask you, do they *really* need all the sugar? And besides, a nibble or two isn't going to hurt me and as a matter of fact might actually help the situation. I mean maybe if I feed my brain . . . Plus, I think I deserve a bit of chocolate since I'm stuck in the itchy suit from you-know-where.

I know I probably shouldn't complain. Acting is my life, is it not? So, I can *act* like I'm having a good time. True, I didn't attend NYU as a drama major with the lofty ambition of playing a bookstore reading bunny, but you know . . . it's a living.

And there's something about wearing a bunny suit that sort of reminds me of my dad.

I can't help but smile at the thought. Dad has called me bunny since the day I made my first appearance in this world. He says it's because he was fixated on my pink ears when I was a baby. Mom says it's because of the way my nose scrunched up right before I let out a loud wail. Whatever the reason, I have a soft spot for the animals. And for Dad.

The cow suit, on the other hand, was a completely different story. There are no fuzzy memories, nor is there a smidgen of affection associated with the thought of wearing that humiliating thing. Mary tried to get me to wear it last week, and I was forced to put my foot down. No way was I sliding into that thing and parading around in front of a room full of kids. The big pink udder was downright indecent, if you ask me, and not entirely appropriate for children.

Oh, brother. This darned suit is really starting to get on my nerves and, oh, please help me, Lord, is something crawling up my leg?

The curse of having a creative mind is that . . . well, it doesn't take much for your imagination to run away with you. In my mind's eye, I see little spider legs inching along my skin. The itsy bitsy spider . . . *Stop it, Tabby.*

Teresa taps me on the shoulder, effectively pulling me out of my arachnophobic panic. "What's wrong with you?"

"What do you mean?" I fire back, slipping one hand out of my paw and snatching a treat from the box.

Teresa gives me her slightly crooked smile and opens the box of donuts.

"You're squirming like a three-year-old waiting for the potty."

See, words like *potty* are what separate the thirty-year-old mommies from those of us who haven't taken the maternal plunge—for one reason or another.

"I can't help it," I whine grumpily. "It's a lot itchier than Mother Goose or the dog suit. Another hour in this thing and I'll be a raving lunatic." I give a shudder. "I think something's crawling up my back."

Teresa snickers.

I chomp on my donut, and something about the sweet taste of fried bread smothered in chocolate frosting helps me see the humor of my situation. I toss a napkin at her and grin. "Sure, you can laugh about it. You're not the one dressed like Bugs Bunny."

"You're adorable," she soothes, scratching my back—although I can barely feel the blunt nails (another sign of motherhood) through the fake fur.

"Thanks."

"But you might be having a slight bunny identity crisis." She gives me a pat. "You're Peter Rabbit, not Bugs."

"Oh yeah."

Teresa pushes another napkin-wrapped, glazed Krispy Kreme at me. "Here, sweetie," she says with the kind of sympathy that makes me feel totally sorry for myself. I choke back tears for a couple of reasons . . . one, I really don't want to ruin my bunny makeup, and two, the first donut simply whet my appetite for this one, and I can't eat and cry at the same time. Any other day I might cry first, then eat, but I only have a few minutes before the kids come rushing in. So of course, I pick the donut. Who wouldn't?

Just as I maneuver a bite around the whiskers, my two co-workers, Janice and Kristin (picture Cinderella's wicked step-sisters), enter the reading room. I bristle at the sight of their wrinkled smirky faces looking on in amusement as though I dressed up like this for their entertainment. I really hate them sometimes. I know, I know. Christians can't hate, and as a matter of fact, you can't be a Christian at all if you hate people. So I don't hate *them*, I just hate their smirky faces and snotty attitudes that make me feel stupid and so much less than them. What is it with women like that? And why do the rest of us give in to the low self-esteem? I mean, we know they're doing it on purpose. And still they enter the room, and my self-worth takes a hike.

Teresa nudges me and whispers, "Hey, aren't you three supposed to take turns dressing up?"

That's another thing I hate . . . the way those two always weasel out of the unpleasant tasks around here and leave me to do everything they wouldn't be caught dead doing.

"I think you and I are the only ones who remember that part," I say ruefully.

"Why don't you say something?"

Maybe she's right. Maybe I really should pull Mary, my manager, aside and say, "I'm not going to take this anymore, Mary. Now, maybe you haven't noticed, but I seem to dress up in these extremely uncomfortable and slightly humiliating costumes an inordinate number of times compared to the rest of the staff."

That's it. I'll complain with sophisticated words like *inordinate*, thus intimidating Mary into seeing things my way.

What is this stirring in the pit of my stomach? *Oh, I remember, God.* I'd love to complain, truly I would, but after a certain spiritual epiphany last night, I'm turning over a new leaf, and the new me is trying to get along with my fellow workers—the women who live to make my hours at work a living you-know-what.

My life would be a lot easier if God would consider talking

to a few other people around here. You know, give someone else a spiritual epiphany like mine. I know He didn't ask my opinion. I'm just saying . . .

Okay, I know I need to relax. Because the truth of the matter is that God is in control—at least that's what we talked about last night—me and the Almighty. All about how my life stinks and maybe it's because I've been trying to run things my own way (thus the spiritual epiphany). Who knew?

Mary pokes her gray head around the corner into the kiddie room. "Are you ready, Tabby?"

As ready as I can be. I fake-chomp my big fake carrot. "Bring 'em on, doc."

Mary gives me a frown like she doesn't get it. "You do know you're supposed to be Peter Rabbit, not Bugs Bunny, right?"

"Yeah, I was just . . ." Uh, trying to make a joke? My face burns. "Never mind."

Her frown deepens, and she walks away, shaking her gray head. That woman has no sense of humor. I swear. Hello? I'm a rabbit. I say "doc." That was worth a little bit of a smile. But no such luck. I just can't win.

"Forget her," Teresa says. "The woman's made of stone."

"Tell me about it," I mumble, eyeing the donuts and seriously considering snagging another one.

But it's too late. Teresa nods toward the door. "Here they come."

Deep breath. Happy place. Find the happy place.

But it really is hard to find that place when Janice and Kristin keep smirking. And they both seem to get a kick out of the fact that I was once a glitzy red-carpet-goer, and now I'm reduced to this.

Okay, I can rise above this even with a slight touch of donut-induced heartburn. Just my luck.

"Children," Mary says, putting on that happy face I know is totally for the sake of all the mothers in the room who will most likely leave the store in an hour carrying a bag of books—including the one we're about to read. The smile to launch a thousand dings of the register. "Give a big hand to Peter Cottontail."

This is it, Tabby. You're on. Time to get into character. Discover the bunny. Be the bunny.

I *am* the bunny.

"Hello, children," I say in my perky rabbit voice. I throw in a couple of hops just to make the character more real. "Who wants to hear the story of Peter Cottontail?"

A rather unenthusiastic whoop goes up into the air. I have to say their lack of exhilaration doesn't do much for my bunny confidence.

"Oh, come on," I prod. "Peter Cottontail? I'll tell you all about how I—you know—" What did Peter do? Get thrown into a briar patch? Turn left at Albuquerque? Wait! He lost a mitten. Shoot, no that was the kitten, wasn't it?

"You can't be Peter Cottontail."

In the midst of my brain-wracking, I look down until I find the source of the first annoying comment of the day. Less than a minute into the story hour. That's got to be a record. The little girl has blue eyes, curly blond hair. Honest, she looks like a child actress. But she's not acting very sweet, I must say.

I draw in a long, steadying breath. Perky. Stay perky.

I give another couple of hops. "Of course I am."

"No, you're not." She puts her chubby little hands on her chubby little hips. Clearly a challenge.

My teeth grind. I feel myself sliding to a bad place here. But wait. I mustn't argue with the children. I replay Mary's words from the last time I entered into a "discussion" with someone under nine. "One more time and we're going to have to let you go." True, this isn't much of a job. But it gives me the hours I need and pays—well, pretty poorly, but it does pay. I force a smile. "What makes you think I'm not Peter Cottontail?"

"You're a *girl*," she says matter-of-factly and with all the wisdom of a know-it-all twerp. "Peter Cottontail is a *boy*."

I look down my black bunny nose at her and focus on being condescending—one of my better acting traits if I do say so myself. "Maybe I'm in touch with my feminine side. Ever think of that?" Oh, I probably shouldn't have gone there. I glance guiltily around and kids are staring, maybe a little fearful of the crazed bunny.

The hideous child folds her arms across her chest and gives me a smug stare down. "You're still a girl. And you don't even know the story of Peter Rabbit."

"Yes I do. I just don't want to brag."

Okay, that was bad even for me. The kid gives me a know-it-all sneer. Suddenly I realize who she reminds me of. "Didn't you play the little girl in *Interview with the Vampire*? You know, the one who gets burned up in the sunlight while clinging to her mother-figure?" The little bloodsucker.

The child's blue eyes widen in fright just before she runs away, and I realize she might have been scared by my reference to vampires or possibly the mental image of flesh turned to ash. Shoot! Why do kids have to be such babies? This is why I never babysat as a teenager. Oh darn! Now she's coming back over here with someone who looks like a ticked-off mother.

Grown-up blue eyes flash before me. I give the woman a good sizing up. She's a larger version of the child. Pretty, petite. Blond. I wonder if I could take her if things get ugly, or should I be prepared to pull a Forrest Gump and run away? She doesn't look that big. I could probably hold my own.

"Did you just tell my daughter she looks like a vampire?" she demands.

"Of course not." Backpedal, Tabs—backpedal fast! "Um . . . I was just thinking how much she resembles Kirsten Dunst as a child. And I couldn't remember any movie except that one. I—uh—didn't even think about her being afraid. Your daughter is so pretty, you should consider getting her some auditions."

"Really?" The woman's face brightens, and I know my work here is done. Catastrophic firing from job is once more avoided. Now to drive the nail home.

"Of course—I used to act on a soap opera," gotta get that little plug in—I'm so weak, "so I know the type of children they scout around for, and your daughter definitely has the right look." I glance at the little girl, who is still glaring at me. Obviously all the flattery hasn't made a dent in her armor.

She stomps her patent leather shoe. "You still can't be Peter Cottontail if you're a girl."

Irritation creeps back up. What is it with this kid? "Oh yeah? Watch me." Shoot. That's arguing, isn't it?

"Of course Tabby isn't the *real* Peter Cottontail." Mary walks into the room and immediately order is restored. She gives me a one-eyebrow-raise in passing. Doggone it. I realize she's heard enough of my conversation to figure out that the kid and I weren't swapping recipes. She skewers me with a glance that no one could possibly have caught but me and continues on like she's one happy camper. "Let's just pretend."

How does she sneak up on a person like that anyway? She just appears, like a . . . Well, I'm not sure if I should say this but . . . If anyone's a vampire . . .

Vampira's giving me that "get on with it" glare, and I know I'd better start reading . . . or else.

Thirty grueling pages and a gazillion kiddie interruptions

later, I bid Teresa good-bye until next week, then go to the ladies' room, zip out of the bunny suit, peel off the whiskers. I stare at my pitiful reflection. My face is blotchy red from trying to get the whiskers to let go and from scrubbing off the makeup. Hideous. But what's a girl to do? I pack away the suit. And let me tell you, this is absolutely the last time I'm wearing that awful thing. After tucking it away in the costume closet, I walk to the counter, ready to face the music. I try not to be too scared since I'm sure God is directing my steps here. Surely He's going to reward me for the first half of the day when I was so good about surrendering to Him. Even when I got cut off on the highway. Not only didn't I flip anyone the bird, but I waved and acted like it was my idea to let the guy over.

Mary smiles at a customer and hands her a bag. "Happy reading."

Then she looks up and sees me standing there. Her smile fades fast like I sucked the happy right out of her. She gives me the evil eye, and I know I'm a goner.

I wonder if I should ask for a reference.

By the time I make it home, I'm trying to shove the hideous day aside and focus on my big plans for tonight. My parents are coming over for dinner at the apartment I share with my two best friends, Laini and Dancy—only they've decided to be absent. I honestly can't say that I blame them. I'm not all that crazy about the idea myself, but you know, it's all about dinner with the folks. A necessary part of every adult's life. At least every three months or so, I'm obligated to invite the parents over. Otherwise they start to imagine I have something to hide, and once their minds go there, short of marriage to the man of their dreams, there's no convincing anyone I'm A-OK and not hopping from party to party with Paris or Lindsay.

Anyway, I figure Mom and Dad will shove off by nine, and I can curl up with my new copy of *Soap Opera Magazine*. Or better yet, read while taking a bubble bath. It's my night for a long soak in the tub. Rule number four on our door: One person per night is allowed a long bath in the tub. First of all, because three women sharing an apartment can't possibly all soak each night, and secondly, because we have water pressure issues, and it takes as long to fill the tub as it does to soak away our troubles.

Laini is the official—and self-proclaimed—rules person. Being an accountant, she's big on lists and organization. She works for ACE Accounting. And—not to brag or anything, but—she's the aciest of all the aces there. A real hotshot with numbers. We'd never get all the bills paid if she didn't keep track of things.

Some of the rules are only posted "just in case." For instance number two: Men are not allowed in the apartment after midnight. Okay, honestly? I can't remember the last time either of my roommates had a date—unless you count Floyd Bartell, the guy Dancy's mom is dying to have as her son-in-law. It's really a curious thing, if you ask me. I mean, they're both attractive, smart, nice. All the attributes that should act as bait on a hook. But unfortunately, my two gal-pals aren't getting so much as a nibble. As a matter of fact, the only nibble I'm getting is from Brian Ryan, a total mistake. A guy I went on a blind date with and can't get rid of. I'm sure he's harmless. Well, almost sure.

Sooo, back to this evening. Everything has got to be *perfect*. Otherwise I'm going to have to hear about it from my mom. I hurry home to the two-bedroom apartment where Dancy and Laini graciously allowed me to crash when I lost my own place three years ago—after I was canned from *Legacy of Life*. That day still haunts me. The day I realized that after paying off most of the debts I incurred when I thought I had another three years on the show (per my contract—apparently they could terminate if story line necessitated—whatever!). I had two choices: Go home and live with Ma (kill me, please, for even thinking of that as an option) or beg my friends to take me in. After all, I don't take up a lot of room.

Not to be a snob or anything, but I had a condo in a high-rise with an elevator, doorman—swanky digs if I do say so myself. Now I live in more of a Sarah Jessica Parker, *Sex and the City* building. But it's nice too. I'd never complain. Only, well, the other one *did* have a doorman.

Regret—just a twinge, mind you—pinches me. And immediately I realize that the new Tabby who is giving it all over to God has no reason to feel regret. But then . . . I can't be too hard on myself. After all, Rome wasn't built in a day.

It's not easy to take the high road though. It's quite a comedown going from a soap opera diva to a reading bunny. I love acting, and darn it, I just want to do something more meaningful with my talent than dressing up for the bookstore. I mean, I still audition from time to time and have an acting coach, who incidentally always smells like a brewery and has more love scenes for me to practice (with him as the male lead, of course) than really seems necessary. But there hasn't been a lot of time for auditions between working two jobs.

My whole life I've wanted to be an actress. NYU, extra acting classes, auditions. Finally, after tons of rejections and a few embarrassing Tampax commercials, I landed a recurring role on *Legacy of Life*. A character that the fans immediately took to—and begged to see more of. A role that turned into a five-year run.

I really was on the fast track to stardom until I had a sort of fling with the head writer's husband. In my defense, let me be clear: I had no idea he was anyone's husband, let alone Julie Foster's. She uses her maiden name. He didn't have on a wedding ring—believe me, I checked. The producer's house, where we had the now infamous Christmas party, was enormous. If I had married a man with a roving eye, I'd keep him on a short leash—wouldn't you? So as far as I'm concerned, it's partly Julie's fault that I ended up wasting my entire evening chatting with her husband.

I truly thought I had maybe found Mr. Right. I mean, we had a lot in common, talked for hours about family (mostly mine, come to think of it), goals, hobbies, and—long story short— Julie caught him just as he was about to move in for a kiss. Not that I blame her, given the circumstances, but she caused a big fat scene. I tried to explain, and Mr. Definitely-Not-Right even took up for me . . . which I think actually made things worse. But despite my insistence that I was innocent, no one sympathized with me because everyone assumed my shock and dismay were just good acting. After all, I *was* nominated for an Emmy once.

Julie had the last word when she concocted a story line whereby two months later my character was killed in a fiery inferno. And the powers that be let her get away with it. Can you believe that?

I tried to make amends, but she didn't believe my innocence. Within a week she had thrown her husband out of their condo and started dating the director of the sitcom three sets down from ours. So much for true love. Again, not that I blame her. But she could have taken all that woman-scorned fury and done something a little more constructive with it than kill off the most popular leading actress on the show. And not to brag, but I was. My portrayal of Felicia Fontaine got me that Emmy nomination in the last season I was on the show. I mean, come on. How could they just let that go? But they did. And now I wait tables and dress up like various animal characters to make ends meet. Well, I did anyway.

I swear, when is Prince Charming going to take me away from it all?

2

Why can't my mom get it through her head that Brian Ryan is *not* my Prince Charming? I just hung up the phone with her. Here's how the call went.

Me: "Hello?"

Mom: "Hello, dear."

As soon as she called me "dear," I knew something was up.

Mom: "Your father and I are bringing a guest, so be sure you have plenty of food."

Sinking feeling in stomach because she said "guest" with a lilt.

Me: "Ma! You tell me two hours before dinner? I've been planning this for two weeks. How am I supposed to ord—uh—fix more food on such short notice?" (Okay, Mom didn't have to know I called for Chinese—but in my defense it's the good Chinese place and not the cheap one that was recently closed down for a week after the health inspector found a cat in the freezer. And let me just say—well, no, I'd better not go there.) Back to why my mom drives me crazy.

Mom: "You've had two weeks, and you didn't plan for extra company?"

See? It's that attitude. *Have you learned nothing from me? You're such a disappointment.*

Me: "I was just really hoping for time alone with you and Dad."

Totally not true. I dread every second of it. But if there's any chance . . . any chance at all that my mom will consider recanting her invitation to whatever unsuspecting male she's planning to inflict on my life, I'll do or say anything. I know it sounds selfish, but Brian Ryan is a prime example of why I don't trust my mom's matchmaking skills—or the lack thereof. Oh, lightbulb moment . . . and this is truly a horrific thought. What if she . . . ? *No!* Surely she wouldn't . . .

Me: "Ma! You're not bringing Brian, are you?"

Mom: "And what would be so terrible about that?"

Me: "Do you want the list? Mother! You're killing me here."

Mom: "Lands, Tabitha, the way you carry on, you'd think he's a troll. Brian's a very nice young man. Very handsome and interested. And in case you haven't noticed, you're not exactly getting any younger."

She paused, and that's where I should have jumped in, but outrage and dread combined to render me completely speechless, thus opening the door for Mom to continue.

Mom: "And you know, he's very successful in the restaurant business."

Why was it that all of a sudden Mom's words sounded something like *wa-wa wa-wa*. Like every adult on the *Peanuts* cartoons.

Me: "Oh, Ma! I mean it. Call the funeral director because you're sucking the life right out of me."

There was slight whinage to my tone, I am ashamed to admit. But gee whiz. The guy just doesn't do it for me. And I don't care what my parents think, he's not that great of a catch. It has nothing to do with his choice of profession either. I mean I'm the reading rabbit, so who am I to look down my nose at anyone's job? But the restaurant business? Hello? He manages a steakhouse franchise with sirloin steak on the buffet. Not exactly a five-star anything. I probably get more respect wearing the rabbit suit.

Mom: "Don't be dramatic, Tabitha. We'll discuss it later. I have to run and set your father's clothes out for him to wear tonight or heaven only knows what he'll wear."

Me (stupidly): "Sure, Ma. Because heaven only knows how he dressed himself the thirty years he was alive before you took over the responsibility."

Mom: "Sarcasm isn't becoming, young lady."

Me (suddenly I'm ten years old): "Sorry."

We hung up not so pleasantly.

So here I am pouting about my mother's inviting Brian along to my dinner and seriously debating the spiritual damage it might do to me if I were to suddenly come down with a case of Asian flu, when Laini rushes in after work. "I know your parents are coming. I'll be out of here in two seconds." She buzzes right past me and into the bedroom we share. (Dancy gets the private room. We don't mind—most of the time.) I follow Laini because I need a shoulder to cry on.

She starts pulling clothes from her drawers as I plop down on her bed. "Mom's bringing Brian," I say glumly.

Laini stops perusing the clothes she's just taken out and stares at me, her big blue eyes beneath a pair of Ralph Lauren glasses going wide. Then she frowns, scrunching the freckles on her nose together. Laini looks like a redheaded Meg Ryan—before Meg cut her hair—more like in *When Harry Met Sally* than, say, *You've Got Mail*.

She shakes her head and plops down beside me on the bed. "What kind of a jerk moves in on a girl's parents?"

"The kind without caller ID block on his phone." I give her a sheepish grin. "I ignore his calls. But don't sell my parents short. It may not have been Brian's doing. He was probably sitting at home ready for a night of popcorn and *Star Wars*, minding his own business."

"You think your mom called him? Just like that?"

"Oh yeah." I'd be surprised if she hadn't.

Laini checks out her image in the full-length mirror hanging on the wall and rakes her long fingers through her shoulder-length curls. "I'm glad I'm not going to be here to witness the fiasco."

In a rush of panic, I grab Laini's arm. "You can't leave. Stay, please. I've ordered Chinese."

"You invited your folks and ordered in?" Another disbelieving shake of the head. "You're incredible."

Somehow, I know that's not a compliment.

"I worked all day. No time to cook a proper meal. Besides, Dad adores Chinese, and Mom never lets him have it."

"That's because it's loaded with sodium, and your dad's blood pressure worries her."

I throw myself back and lay across the bed, staring at the ceiling. "She nags him all the time."

Laini gives me a pat on the knee and grabs her purse off the bed. "She loves him as much as you do, my friend. You really should give her a break."

"No. No. No." I shoot up so fast, Laini jumps and loses her grip on her purse. In a flash I take her upper arms in my hands. We are almost nose to nose as I search her startled face. "You can't be on her side. Even if you think I'm wrong, you can't say it. I can't deal with that."

Okay, she's rolling her eyes.

"Fine." Letting her go, I stoop and grab the pink T-shirt she dropped and shove it back into her hands. "Just go ahead and do what you had planned for tonight. I can handle my mother all by myself." Oh, the self-pity. "Really, I'll be fine. You go and have a good time."

"Oh, please. That's your worst performance ever." She grins.

"Besides, I'd never leave you alone with your folks and Brian, so you're stuck with me. But you'd better have ordered egg drop soup."

A sense of well-being shoots from my head to my toes. It's good to have real friends.

Mom and Dad knock on the door promptly at 6:59 p.m. Laini sets her magazine aside and gives me a nod of support as I smooth my shirt over my jeans so that (God forbid) my midriff doesn't show. Gathering a deep breath, I open the door and wait for the inevitable.

"Hi, Mom and Dad," I say perkily. A little too perkily I suppose because Mom's eyebrow goes up—just the right one (how does she do that anyway?). "Good to see you." I'm distracted by Brian's absence and look past Mom's shoulder, but there's no sign of him. Something's up. I know Ma didn't go back on her invitation. "Here, let me take your coats."

"We're not wearing any," Mom says in *that* tone that sets my teeth on edge and makes me feel small—and not in a good way. "It's August."

Heat shoots up my neck and spreads around to my cheeks in a split second. "Oh yeah," I murmur. "Come in."

"Hello, Mr. and Mrs. Brockman." Good old Laini senses the need for a little rescue and jumps right in without even testing the water first. "So nice to see you again. How was the ride over?"

Dad opens his mouth to answer, but Mom butts in. "Traffic was terrible, of course. Frank here is getting blind as a bat, so we have to take cabs these days. And I abhor those foreign cab drivers. They all pretend they don't understand a word we say.

But you know darned well they're taking it all in and reporting back to their superiors."

I roll my eyes. No way I'm going there with her. Besides, I'm focused on what she said about my dad.

"Daddy? When did you stop driving?"

"Oh, you know your father, he can't see anything. He hasn't driven the car in months."

Mom's butting in and snappiness are starting to bug me. I've definitely decided I'm *not* going to allow an argument to arise between us though. I'll hold my tongue. But not without a lot of effort, let me tell you.

"Why not just get glasses, *Dad*?" I send Mom a pointed look and her expression darkens considerably. I might have crossed the line, but then, that's so easy to do with my mom. Her line is pretty thin.

"Oh, well, your mother thought they might not be able to—"

"For goodness' sake. The glasses he's wearing are about as thick as they go, and he can barely see through them anymore."

A sad kind of nostalgia creeps through me as I look at Dad. When did my hero start breaking down?

He smiles at me. "Your mother's right, honey bunny."

Uh, don't remind me of the bunny.

I know she's right in this case. I hate it that she is, but I know.

I loop my arm through his. "How's your blood pressure, Daddy?"

I see Mom's chest expand like she's going to answer for him, but then she just expels the breath and doesn't say a word.

"Fine, I suppose. I take my pills every day."

"That's real good."

"What time is that boyfriend of yours going to get here?" Dad just gets right to the point. "I'm hungry."

"Um. Actually, Daddy, Brian isn't my boyfriend. As a matter of fact, I'm not even dating him."

"Then how come you invited him to dinner?" Dad gives me a wink. "Trying to catch him with your cooking?"

Laini snorts but straightens up lickety-split when I send her the look.

My defenses go up a bit. "I didn't . . ."

"Now, Tabitha," Mom interrupts with a bit too much cheer in her voice—because she knows she's about to get busted and is doing her best to deflect blame.

I'd love to know what she was going to say to get out of this, but unfortunately, the buzzer goes off. Laini catches my gaze as if to ask whether or not she should buzz him up.

I give her a "might as well" wave and decide to take the fall for Brian's presence rather than cause a scene. Laini waits by the door for Brian, so I turn my attention back to the only man I love at the moment.

"So, what did my little girl fix her old man for supper? Your mother feeds me rabbit food and baked chicken." Dad grins and his chubby cheeks inch upward like a chipmunk. He's at least thirty pounds overweight (fifty—if you believe Mom about it) and has hypertension and type 2 diabetes. Suddenly, I'm not feeling so great about my dinner choice.

"Um—" I dart a guilty glance at my mom, "I called out for Chinese."

Mom's lips press together. She's going to blow a gasket soon. She's not in control of anything tonight, and I doubt she's going to put up with it much longer. As a matter of fact, I think she's . . .

But Dad cuts her off faster than she can pull her objections together. "I don't think a little decent food every now and then is going to kill me. Do you, Martha?"

"I surely hope not."

In those four little words I hear her saying to me, "If this Chinese food worsens his conditions, I will hold you personally responsible, young lady."

The weight of the world rests on my shoulders. Suddenly I'm responsible for global warming, the Middle East crisis, the imminent bird flu pandemic, overpopulation, and oh yeah, the astronomical cost of gasoline.

And to make matters worse, Brian saunters into the room with a cheap bouquet of supermarket wildflowers, winks, and moves in to kiss me on the cheek. In a move worthy of Charlie's Angels, I deflect the kiss, and he sort of stumbles. "Thank you for inviting me," he says, recovering from my rebuff as though he didn't even notice.

"You're welcome, but I—"

Enter Mom, once again. "Brian. It's so wonderful to see you again. I hope you're hungry. My daughter has made us a wonderful Asian feast."

Brian's eyebrows go up. "You cooked?"

"I ordered from Mr. Wang's," I mumble, not even attempting to carry out this ridiculously unfair ruse my mother somehow feels she's entitled to concoct at my expense. She has obviously convinced Brian I'm pining away for him. I'm humiliated, and it's going to be that much harder to break it to the guy that I'm honestly not interested.

I know there's not a thing I can do about it for now, so I lead Dad into the kitchen, pretending neither of us has a care in the world.

Mom starts in on me the second we sit and start passing around the Chinese cartons. "So, how do you like your gym membership?" Which means: You've gained weight, Tabby. How do you expect to keep a great man like Brian here interested?

"Five pounds doesn't matter that much," I mutter.

"You look great, Pumpkin." Good ol' Dad. Or wait. Does he mean I look good *for* a pumpkin?

Brian clears his throat—clearly planning to stay as far away from this topic as possible—and slides a chunk of sweet and sour chicken between his unbelievably white teeth—can you say caps?

"Of course she does." Laini's bright voice lifts across the table and for a second I think everything is going to be just fine.

Until my mother huffs. Then I know we're in danger of something hitting the fan. "Well, no one thinks she doesn't look good." Mom looks from Laini to Brian (who keeps his cowardly gaze averted) to Dad and finally back to me. "Did I say you don't look good?"

Must diffuse potentially volatile situation. Quick. I will revert to proven childhood tactic: agree with anything she says.

I can't look her in the eye when she's being indignant. "No, Mom."

"Of course I didn't. I merely asked if you've been using the gym membership I paid for."

"You mean the one I never asked for?" Oh bother. Did I say that out loud? I did, didn't I? What's wrong with me that I blurt things like that? Especially to my mom.

And now she looks hurt. Oh bother, again! I can handle Mom when she's sarcastic or angry, but when she's hurt . . . that's another story. Guilt slices through me like a samurai sword. "I'm sorry, Ma. I was just thinking today how much I need to start going to the gym. It's just that I don't have that much time."

Mom reaches across the table and pats my hand. "I understand."

Oh, the guilt! Just shoot me and put me out of my misery.

I glance at the clock. How much longer?

I actually kiss the closed door once my parents leave, Brian reluctantly tagging along behind them.

"Whew." And that's all Laini says. I know I owe her big for hanging around. Not that she said much. But when she did, it mattered.

A knock at the door a second later gives us both a start.

"Don't open without looking out the peephole." Oh yeah, rule number six. My heart gives a little leap when Brian's distorted face peers back at me.

I groan. "He's back."

Laini raises a palm. "I'm out of here."

I hesitate, about to beg her not to leave me alone with the guy, but I figure she's done her time. "Okay, go ahead. I can handle him."

I ease the door open, but only slightly. Just enough so that maybe he'll take the hint that I'm not inviting him back inside.

"Brian?" I say, like I didn't see him through the peephole. "Did you forget something?"

"Yeah." He pushes his way in. Not in a way that scares me, just like he figures I don't realize he needs more room to squeeze inside. His arms go around me before I can stop him, and he pulls me in for a brief, wet kiss. Grr-ross!

"Brian!" Flattening my palms against his chest, I give him a hard shove into the door.

"What the . . . ?" He frowns. "What was that for?"

"What do you think? Who said it was okay for you to kiss me?"

"Oh, come off it. Your mom filled me in on everything." He reaches out and fingers a strand of my hair, and I have to clench my fists tight in order to keep from slugging him.

"Look, I don't know what my mom told you . . ."

His chin goes up like a lightbulb just went off, and he suddenly gets it. "It's okay, sugar," he soothes. "I guess I moved a little too fast." Oh great. Whatever he got, it wasn't a clue.

"Ya think?"

"We can take things as fast or slow as you want."

Oh, dear Lord. Why am I being persecuted?

Thankfully, the doorknob rattles and Dancy enters. Her eyebrows go up at the sight of Brian. "What's going on?"

"Nothing," I say. "Brian was just leaving."

"Sure I am, sugar," he says with a wink. "I'll call ya later."

Oh gee, can't wait.

I close the door after him and Dancy frowns. "Since when are you Sugar?"

"Since my mother decided Brian is Mr. Right." I roll my eyes. "He thinks I'm sweet on him, I guess."

"Yikes."

"Did I hear the door?" Laini reenters the room.

"Yeah." I flop onto the couch and grab a throw pillow to hug. "He's gone."

"Whew."

"Tell me about it." I hug the pillow close and can't hold back a shudder. "He kissed me good-bye—thought I wanted it."

"Ew! What a creep," Dancy says, slipping her purse onto the hook next to the door. "I never understood why you went out with him in the first place."

"Blind date, remember?"

"Yeah, but you've been out with him several times over the last couple of years. Why do you do that when you don't even like him?"

"Chalk that up to Ma's guilt trips."

"Still, though."

"Dancy's right," Laini says, slipping a supportive arm around my shoulders. "Brian was nothing more than a rebound guy. You never would have looked twice at him if you hadn't been fired from the soap opera and down on your luck at the time."

Okay, this isn't helping.

Besides, Dancy hardly has room to talk. I'm about to mention Floyd Bartell when the stove timer buzzes and Laini hops up. "Cookies are done. You're going to love these."

"Sure," I say without even trying to drum up enthusiasm. My friend will understand. Besides, it's not like I'm going to turn down the cookies even if I don't display excitement.

Dancy shoves to her feet. "Want me to run you an aromatherapy bath? I brought home the new Cate Able book."

Dancy thinks soaking in aromatherapy and reading a book is a cure-all. The good thing about her position as an assistant editor at Lane Publishing is that she's always bringing home free books.

"That sounds good, Dan," I say pathetically.

"You should write a book based on your life, Tabs," she yells over the running water.

"Oh sure. *Loser Takes Manhattan.*"

She comes back into the living room. "Not about your life now."

She thinks I'm a loser? Sheesh. I was looking for a little support. "Thanks a lot."

Flopping next to me on the rust-colored sofa, she tucks a leg under the other and forces me to look her in the eye. "Seriously. A fictionalized tell-all about a daytime soap star. You could write about the sleazy head writer's husband who came on to you."

"Pul-ease, like anyone cares." Laini pads back into the room, carrying a plate of cookies. She's wearing faded flannel PJs she's had since college and a pair of yellow gripper socks she got the time she had her tonsils out two years ago. She gives me a look as soon as she realizes she's talking about the downfall of my very own career. "Of course *we* care since it happened to Tabby. But why would anyone buy a book like that?"

Dancy shrugs. "Sex sells."

I'm outraged. "Hey, there was no sex! Not even a measly, itty-bitty kiss. I was wronged and robbed." Have I mentioned I'm an actress? If I have a flare for the dramatic, is it really my fault?

"We know that. But this is fiction."

"Not very good fiction," Laini says.

Once again, two worlds collide. Dancy and Laini are great friends. We all are. But Laini is practical, and Dancy's head is stuck in the world of fiction. A meeting of minds is an unlikely concept when the subject involves budgeting and tax write-offs, or plot and characterization. And never the twain shall meet.

"I don't have time to write a book," I say glumly. "I have to find a job."

"Tabs!" Laini practically shouts. "Are you saying you lost the bookstore job?"

"How does someone lose a bookstore job?" Dancy asks. She sounds offended. Books and their stores are sacred.

"I was the rabbit again and . . ."

A deep groan escapes Dancy and she flings herself back on the couch. "They put you with kids?"

I nod, feeling tears burning my eyes. See? My friends understand that I am not kid-friendly. I've tried, truly I have. But kids hate me.

She grabs the box of Kleenex from the table next to the couch and tosses it to me. "Why does that old bat keep doing that to you? She knows you don't get along with kids."

"That's why," Laini explodes. Laini is not easy to rile, but when it happens, it's quite entertaining. She flaps her arms and paces the floor. Says crazy things that don't make any sense. Like I said, very entertaining. "She's been trying to get rid of Tabby ever since she realized Tabs was a soap star once upon a time. Jealous old cow."

There's comfort in having my friends convey the sentiments I'm no longer at liberty to express since embarking on my life as the new me. And she's not done.

"Putting Tabby with kids is like . . . asking a garbage man to cook without washing his hands."

"Hey!" Methinks there's a fine line between defending me and insulting me. Let's tread carefully here.

"You know what I mean. It's just not a good idea." She gasps. "We should sue that old biddy for entrapment."

Dancy and I exchange a glance, and I burst into laughter. Laini frowns and stops. I guess she realizes what a lunatic she's being because a quirky little grin tips the corners of her lips. Then a smile. Then she joins in the laughter.

When things settle into sanity once more, Laini looks at me evenly. "So what are you going to do?"

I glance from one friend to another, and I know exactly what I'll do. "I'm going to soak in the tub and read my new soap magazine."

"What about the new Cate Able book?"

"Cate Able." Laini laughs. "Does anyone else think that sounds like someone grasping to find a pen name?"

She's mentioned before how it sounds like Cain and Abel. Dancy and I give her a cursory chuckle.

"I want to read my soap magazine and see what's happening on the show."

My great friends nod. They understand. When I'm down I need to relive my glory days. Dream that the photos splashing over the center of the magazine contain my image as well.

A little while later, I sink into a tub of aromatic bubbles. I can't help but think how my life has changed in the past twenty-four hours.

Opening the magazine to a huge spread about *Legacy of Life*, I devour every word of the article, then close my eyes and relive my days as Felicia Fontaine. Tears are threatening when I have a thought: I have to forget the past. I'll never find a way to reboot my career while I'm wallowing in yesterday. Okay another goal. I will absolutely *stop* obsessing over my character, Felicia Fontaine, being killed off on the nation's number one soap opera and thus robbing me of my continued rise to fame and fortune.

But honestly, the entire situation smacks of injustice. It's not like I knew the guy I flirted with was the head writer's husband. Two words, people: *wedding bands*. Wear them. Otherwise it's just false advertisement.

Obviously, it's not going to be so easy to accomplish this goal. I close my eyes for a moment, still my soul.

Yoo-hoo, God? I hope you know what you're doing. Because when I was controlling my own life, I had a job. Now what do I have?

I sink down farther into the bubbles. Hey, at least I still have my health.

3

So much for having my health. Merely a week later, I'm writhing in pain, wishing God would just lift me home to heaven. The pain in my side is like a red-hot sword slicing through me. And I can no longer claim I simply have the flu or food poisoning from last week's Chinese food. By the time my friends convince me to hail a cab and go to the hospital, I'm close to tears. The bumpy, start-and-stop cab ride nearly kills me, and by the time we reach the hospital, pay the cabbie, and get inside, I'm mentally making out my will. Short and sweet though it may be.

An hour later, I am still waiting in the crowded room, with no relief in sight.

"Make them hurry, Dancy," I beg. "I think I'm dying."

Dancy's on her feet in a millisecond. I'm curled into a ball across three empty seats, oblivious to the fact that my head is in Laini's lap and I'm moaning and drawing attention to myself. Even in my fuzzy state of mind I can hear Dancy's authoritative sass. "Hey, lady, listen. I don't care if there are ten people ahead of her. My friend's suffering from appendicitis."

A murmur from the woman at the desk.

"No, that isn't my professional diagnosis, and no, I am not a doctor, but only an undereducated moron would just sit there and not consider the fact that a patient has been puking her guts up for twenty-four hours, so at the very least, she's severely dehydrated. She's also in massive pain—on the right side—and if her appendix bursts and she dies, *you* are the idiot that my lawyer and I are coming after." Her voice rises, and she addresses the crowded waiting area. "You're all witnesses. Anyone willing to give me a name and number?"

I hear rustling, and I'm assuming people are standing in line to get back at the hateful receptionist who has probably treated everyone equally badly.

Five minutes later I'm on a gurney in the ER, being attended by a slightly effeminate male nurse with soft, gentle hands who reminds me of Freddie, my friend who works as a physical trainer on the set of *Legacy of Life*. He shoots something in my IV, and I start to fly a little.

The next thing I know, I'm waking up. The searing pain is gone, replaced by a different kind of pain. Nagging, excruciating.

"That's it," a voice says somewhere above me. "Wake up now."

My eyelids flutter open, but they're too heavy to stay that way. I sigh, and the world once more goes dark.

"Come on now, wake up."

Leave me alone! I'm so sleepy.

"Kill me," I moan.

"You need to wake up, Tabby. You've just had surgery. We need to get you awake."

Surgery? "What do you mean?" I mumble, my voice hoarse and barely audible.

"Remember coming in here with all that pain in your side?" She doesn't wait for an answer, but boy do I ever remember. "Turns out you had appendicitis. From what I hear, your friend bullied the ER staff until they took you in and got a doctor to look at you. They yanked that sucker out just before it burst. Lucky for you."

Funny, I don't feel real lucky at the moment. I feel about

three steps away from death's door if you want to know the truth.

The nurse walks across my little curtained-off room and stands next to my bed, checking tubes and vitals. "How do you feel?"

"Not too bad." For having my guts ripped out.

She nods. "Good. If you decide you'd like something for pain, let me know."

My eyelids are so heavy. . . .

The next thing I know I'm having a nightmare that my mother is in the room.

"Stop hovering, Frank. She'll wake up when she's ready."

Or maybe it's not a nightmare. Now I could use that pain medicine. No, really. Not for the calming effects. Well, not just for the calming effects. I'm honestly in pain.

"Daddy?"

"There, see," Mom says, triumphant. "I told you she'd wake up on her own."

"How do you know it wasn't me talking to her?" Dad fires back in unusual defiance. Good for him. "Hey there, honey bunny. How ya feeling?"

"Could you ask the nurse to bring me something for the pain?"

"You be careful with that stuff, Tabby. You remember what happened to Rush."

Limbaugh. I swear. Mom is a crazed fan of Rush Limbaugh. I mean she lives by every word that proceeds from his mouth.

"Yeah, I should be so rich that I can afford enough drugs to get addicted," I mouth off, knowing she's not likely to get too mad when I'm lying here in pain, but I eke out a bit of a moan just to be on the safe side and foster some sympathy.

Dad comes to my rescue anyway. "Hush, Martha. You don't want our daughter in pain, do you?"

But true to her nature, Mom's not about to let a little something like me being in excruciating pain deter her from her principles. "Better a little pain now than rehab a year from now." The last of the great philosophers. "If it can happen to Rush it can happen to anyone."

Well, I suppose that's the truth. But Rush obviously didn't have a mother watching his every move. I send Daddy a silent plea. It's not lost on Mom, who huffs.

Dad squeezes my hand. "I'll buzz the nurse."

"All right," Mom says with that tone of hers. "But don't say I didn't warn you."

Fifteen minutes later, Mom asks me, "Have your friends contacted your employer to let them know you'll be out for a few days?"

I smirk. I'm blissfully feeling no pain—physically, emotionally, you name it. And that's probably why I let it slip. "No, Mom. No need."

Even Dad gives me a little frown. "What do you mean, bunny?"

Don't you just love it when dads use terms of endearment for grown daughters? It's like they can't quite let go. I hope he always wants to take care of me. Whoa, this stuff is making me . . . Where was I? Oh yeah.

"Daddy, my sweet Daddy." I smile and pat his round face. "I love you so much."

"My goodness, Frank. She's high as a kite."

"Shh, Martha. Leave the girl alone for once."

"Thank you, Daddy. Have I told you lately how much I love you?"

"You just told him three and a half seconds ago," Mom

shouts—or maybe not. Whoa, how much of that stuff did they shoot into my IV? I like it!

With that tender expression I know so well, Dad takes my hand, presses a kiss to my knuckles. "I love you too, baby girl. Now tell us what you mean about the job."

"Oh, Frank." I can hear a scowl in my mother's tone, and even the pain-numbing narcotics don't lessen the knot in my gut. Especially because I know Mom's not happy with me. But then, is she ever? "Obviously, our daughter has gotten herself fired again."

Dad's look is one of question and concern. Unlike Mom who just wants to harp. "Is that it, Tabs? Did you lose your job?"

"It was the rabbit. The kids. It's just not fair . . . know what I mean, Mom?"

"I have no earthly idea what you're talking about. And neither do you. Did you quit your job?" Mom takes a deep breath like she knows she's about to unload on me and wants to be sure she has enough air. Now! When I'm half dying from almost having my appendix explode like a grenade. "You have so much money all of a sudden that you can afford to lose a perfectly good job?"

"Gee whiz, Ma. I didn't exactly walk up to my boss and ask her to humiliate me in a rabbit suit and then fire me just to put icing on the cake." Okay, whoa, I'm flying a litt—lot.

The monitor next to me beeps a rising heart rate. This is what my mother does to me. Makes me nuts. My pulse goes through the roof. I swear, her presence is like an aerobic exercise, only without the muscle tone—and a lot more painful at times.

Mom's eyes dart to the monitor, and she gives me a startled look like she's just figured out that she makes me crazy.

"Martha. Go wait in the hallway."

You tell her, Dad. Send her out of the room. Be gone, bad cop!

"Perhaps you're right," Mom says. She clears her throat and steps to my other side. "I'm sorry I've upset you, Tabby. Get well soon and call if you need anything."

Bending, she kisses me on the forehead, straightens, looks down at me. I'm speechless. I honestly can't remember the last time my mother showed me any kind of physical affection. That was always Daddy's role in the family. I feel awful that I've thought "bad cop" about her. I'm just glad I didn't say it out loud. Can you imagine? The drugs must be throwing off my defenses because I grab her hand with both of mine and hug it to my cheek for a second. "Thank you, Mom. I promise I won't go into rehab like Rush. Unless I really, really need it."

She pauses, then brushes my hair from my face. "I'll be waiting in the hall for you, Frank."

My heart goes out to her. This is an uncommon feeling, but something about having my mother caress my head gives me a change of heart. I'm going to try hard to get along with my mom (and possibly live a lot longer if that verse in the Bible about honoring one's parents is to be taken literally). Maybe it's time to stop lying about my true financial state. Stop insisting that I'm this close to a Broadway play and maybe tell the truth about why I really got killed off on *Legacy of Life*.

But not right now because I'm getting the business from my dad. So much for good cop.

"She loves you a lot more than you give her credit for, bunny." Dad demands my gaze. "Now tell me about the job."

By the time he leaves, he's stuffed two one-hundred-dollar bills in my purse, despite my objections (very weak objections, I'm ashamed to say). I'm vaguely aware of his good-bye as the pain medicine finally gets the better of me and I can't keep my eyes open a second longer.

The next time I awaken it's to the sound of the phone chirping. "Hey," I hear Laini say in a whispered kind of voice. "Yeah, I'm at the hospital, but she's asleep. Oh, wait—she's moving. Tabby, you awake?"

I nod.

"Oh good." She comes to my bedside holding my cell phone. She sees my confusion and shrugs. "You left it at home the other night, and it was ringing like crazy all day. I think you're going to want to take this call."

"I think I read somewhere that you're not supposed to have a cell phone in the hospital. It can interfere with the machines."

"I'm going to go stand guard. Just make it quick. It's your friend Freddie from *Legacy of Life.*"

I take the phone. "Freddie! I was just thinking about you. You won't believe it, but there's this male nurse here that looks just like you. Well, he doesn't exactly look like you, but he acts like you and he has your smile. Do you have a brother you haven't told me about?"

"Girl, what are you talking about?"

It's so great to hear Freddie's voice!

"Sorry. You know I ramble when I get excited." I reach deep to take a full breath, and . . . Oh, ow. It hurts. I can't buzz for pain meds until I'm ready to hide the phone. And besides, maybe I'd better take it easy on that stuff. Because . . . well, you know—Rush.

"So how come you called after all this time, Fred? Is everything okay?"

"First of all, the phone works two ways, chickadee."

"You're right." We actually used to talk a lot, when I first left the show, but after I told him I became a Christian he backed off the friendship, hardly ever answers my calls, and never takes the initiative. But no sense in bringing that up. I know how it is.

"Tabby, girl." He loses a bit of the queen attitude. "Guess who's dying?"

A pain in my side alerts me that it's past time for more pain meds. Rush or no Rush. I groan. "Me."

"Stop being so dramatic. It's just a little appendicitis. People get it all the time. Focus, girlfriend. I have something important to tell you."

At the excitement in his voice, I'm instantly awake. Freddie has this perpetual buzz about him. He's always moving, always hyper. In the immortal words of Tom Hanks in *You've Got Mail*: Freddie makes coffee nervous.

And he doesn't even drink coffee. He's a purist. Freddie's the fitness trainer on location for the cast of *Legacy of Life*. We hit it off from the moment he said, "Honey, those thighs aren't going to stop jiggling on their own. Now I want to hear some grunting and see some sweat staining that three-hundred-dollar leotard or we're going to have issues."

"So who is dying, Freddie?"

"You have to guess."

"I can't. I'm in pain." I'm whining. But that's too bad.

He heaves a sigh. "Oh, all right. It's Lucy Marshall."

"Julie is killing off Lucy? Is she nuts?" Taylor Adams has been playing Lucy Marshall for the last fifteen years. She's another fan favorite and is part of a super couple. I don't see the fans standing for this one. I'm envisioning boycotts and mail bombs. You just don't mess around with soap fans—they'll eat you alive. And I have a feeling Julie Foster is about to be toast with a capital T.

"Julie's fit to be tied along with everyone else. Taylor got a part in the next Brad Pitt film." He snickered. "She thinks she's going to be the next Angelina. They threatened to sue, but her contract is up in another month anyway."

"What are they going to do?" Or the better question might be, why do I give a flip? I mean they put me out to pasture, sent me on a one-way mission to the planet unemployment, burned me in a fiery inferno of which I still feel the heat. But I can't stand it. "Freddie! Spill it!"

"They're bringing back an old favorite. Someone they killed off."

"Who?"

"Guess." Good grief, not this again. Fine I'll play his little game.

"Anthony Drake."

Villainous male character Anthony Drake has died at least three times and manages to come back each time they settle the contract disagreement. But Freddie cackles into the phone, and I know I've guessed wrong.

"Please. Drake? Not this time. After he asked for a two hundred percent raise during last contract negotiations? Who does he think he is, Deidre Hall? He's dead and buried this time, baby. And good riddance."

How does Freddie get all this juicy info?

"Who, then?"

"Du-uh! Who do you think?"

And suddenly, my heart starts racing. Because I think I know where he's going. "Me? Freddie, are they planning to bring back Felicia Fontaine?"

"You got it, honey. And high time. Do you know ratings have

been dropping like the Cubs' chance to make the World Series since you got the ax?"

Yay! Yippee and hallelujah. "Freddie, are you sure?" Trying not to sound too excited here. And trying to keep my voice down so the nurses don't confiscate my phone before I get the details.

"Honey, have you ever known me to be wrong?"

Nope, not one time. Freddie is a very responsible gossip. He always checks his facts before spreading rumors.

Still, I've been through a lot of disappointment lately and, out of habit, a horrible thought shocks through me. What if they want Felicia back, but don't necessarily plan to hire me to play her again? "Are you sure they don't plan to recast the role?"

"They wouldn't dare." His assurance is immediate and forceful. "They need ratings with Taylor jumping ship. Bringing in another woman who is supposed to be you will backfire and they know it. After all, there is only one Tabitha Brockman."

"They could say Felicia had plastic surgery."

"Oh, please. Do you really think they're going to resort to that old standby? Squeeze, honey. That butt's not going to tighten itself."

"What?" How does he know about those extra twenty pounds?

"I'm having a session with Julie." He drops his volume. "She's put on at least ten pounds since she married Trey. I swear I'm going to have to start hiding the morning Krispy Kremes."

I feel the blood drain from my face. "Hold on, hot dog. What do you mean? Julie and Trey are married?" Trey O'Dell—the guy who plays my on-screen husband, Rudolph.

"Oh, sure. You didn't know that?"

Obviously not.

"What about Trey's *wife*?"

"He left her for Julie."

And she had the audacity to call me a home wrecker (only she didn't use such a nice word to describe me). "Holy cannoli."

"You got that right, baby." He chuckles into the phone. "Julie has her issues, but you have to admit she's a great writer."

Nod. Nod. Grudging agreement. Still . . .

"How is she going to feel about me coming back and working with her husband after what went on before?"

"I don't know, but it was Trey's idea to bring Felicia back. Julie had to get the story line approved, so obviously she's convinced Jerry she'll be okay with it."

Trey's idea, huh? Then maybe he's forgiven me for punching him in the jaw and throwing a full glass of red wine in his face. And for ruining his new silk button-down shirt. Which he had tackily confided cost him four hundred dollars. The guy is a great actor, but he's all hands.

"Between you and me," Freddie says, bringing me back to the present. "I think Trey knows you're the only way to save his job."

"Me?"

"Fans love you. They love the sizzling romance between you and Rudolph. It's a love that will forever be true. And not even a fiery inferno could separate you."

Freddie sounds absolutely swoony, so I feel the need to put a little reality on the topic. "Rudolph has been in at least three relationships since Felicia was killed," I point out, a little miffed actually at my TV husband's fickle heart.

"But none of those imposters were his true love. The fans haven't tuned in for a story line between him and another woman. So it's either spice up his character again by bringing you back or write him out of the show. Anyway, I heard Jerry telling his assistant to find your contact information. Anita Madison canned you, didn't she?"

"No. *Legacy of Life* canned me," I say, a little offended. "Anita merely dropped me from her client list after Jerry let me go."

"Oh, I see the difference. Not." Some sensitive guy Freddie is! "Anyway, you know, Julie is her best friend and you had that affair with Julie's husband . . ."

"I did not!"

"Sure, whatever. Anyway."

"What do you mean, Julie and Anita are best friends?" That's news to me.

"How else do you think that you, an unknown, got that walk-on role in the first place? Julie talked Jerry into it as a favor to Anita."

Jerry Gardner is the executive producer of the show and the only decent one of the white-collar set if you ask me.

"Anyway, Freddie. The fact is that Anita doesn't represent me anymore, so how are they going to contact me without finding out I already know they're looking? I can't call them, it'll ruin negotiations."

"Don't panic, honey," Freddie says. "I've got that all worked out for you. Kyle Preston is expecting your call."

"Kyle Preston." My heart flutters. Everyone's dream agent. A hotshot negotiator with a face that makes Brad Pitt look like the elephant man. "How do you know him?"

"I train him, and it just so happens that today was his upper body day. I somehow let the rumor slip about Jerry wanting to bring Felicia back to the show. And how Anita dumped you like day-old coffee grounds after they killed you off."

"Gee, thanks."

"And he said he'd be interested in hearing from you." By the lilt in his voice, it's pretty obvious Freddie knows he's done a good thing. No. Not just a good thing. A great thing.

"Thank you so much. Give me the number."

"What are you going to do for me if I give you the number?"

"Now, Freddie!" Freddie always likes to play this game. Usually, I just laugh it off, but this time . . . hey, I have a lot at stake. "Or I'm writing your number on the ladies' room wall at the nearest truck stop."

"Sheesh! Looks like you lost your sense of humor when you lost your job. Or did that happen when you went all Christian on me?"

For some reason my face goes hot. It's not that I'm ashamed of my relationship with Christ. It's really not. It's just that Freddie makes fun of all the Christians on the set. I used to laugh at his antics, but now . . . "Freddie! Give me the number or I'll find another trainer to help me lose these twenty pounds."

"Twenty! Oh brother. Girl, what have you been eating?"

"Never mind about that."

He gives me the number and lets out a long-suffering sigh. "Meet me at the old Bally's on Fiftieth tomorrow at one."

"Are you trying to kill me? I just had my appendix out."

"Good grief. What a baby. Fine. Call me when you're ready."

"I will."

"So, you still on that Christian kick?"

"Yeah."

"Hmm. I guess I'll have to deal with it."

I can't help but smile. Who knows? Maybe God will use me in Freddie's life.

Just then Laini gives me the slash across the throat motion and points toward the hall.

"Gotta go, Freddie. The nurse is coming."

I disconnect and bury my phone under the covers just as the nurse steps into the room.

It rings almost immediately. I look up, guilt-ridden, but keeping my eyes widely innocent. "Hello, nurse. How are you today? I don't think we've met. My name is Tabby." I stretch out my hand, then grimace at the pull in my abdomen. "Ouch."

"Take it easy," the nurse says. "And you might want to answer your phone."

"Phone?" I lay my hand over the hard lump beneath the paper-thin blanket. "Why would I have a phone when it's clearly against the rules?"

She slips the blood pressure cuff around my arm. "Which rules would those be?"

I stare. Am I imagining things due to the pain? "The ones about not using cell phones on planes or in hospitals."

She smiles. "Planes, no. Hospitals, yes. Shh. Let me listen."

I hush until she gives me the nod and takes the stethoscope out of her ears.

"You mean I can use my cell phone?"

"Sure. As long as it's not back in radiology."

Now I feel pretty darn stupid.

"Well," she says, smiling brightly. "I can tell by your face that you must be feeling better."

"Yes, I am." Not so much physically, but definitely emotionally.

She has no idea just how much better I'm feeling.

Tabby Brockman is back in action!

4

ack in action is a bit of a stretch, I'm afraid. It's been a week since I got out of the hospital, and I still feel like I've been hit by a Mack truck flying down the highway at a few hundred miles per hour. And that's putting it mildly.

To make matters worse, I still haven't heard a word from Kyle Preston, the agent who is supposedly hot to trot for a chance to represent me. Methinks my dear friend Freddie may have overstated the man's interest a bit. I've left three messages on Kyle's voice mail and guess what? Not a peep out of the megacute agent. I'm about to get desperate and call Anita Madison to take me back. I mean if Julie Foster is willing to write for my character again, who is Anita to stand on principle?

Still, in the spirit of fair play and my own aversion to crawling back to the woman who dumped me, I've decided I'm going to try Kyle's number one more time and let him know this is his last chance. If he doesn't call me back this time, it's his loss. I pick up my cell phone just as the little sucker rings and scares the blazes out of me. Well it isn't so much a ring as it is the theme song from *Friends*. Yes, I'm still hoping for a reunion show. And no, I'm not obsessed. Much. Anyway, so the phone blares out, "So no one told you life was gonna be this way . . ." and I jump, which hurts my stitches. "Hello!" I growl because who has the audacity to call me and scare me half to death when I'm just about to use my phone?

"Tabitha Brockman, please."

Okay, I'm not one hundred percent sure, but he sounds suspiciously like the bill collector from Visa. I'm ashamed to say I racked up about eight thousand dollars while I was still employed by the soap—I mean a girl has to have her Prada and Jimmy Choos right? It's all about image. I can't walk into the Emmy awards wearing a Gap shirt and Payless shoes. Who do you think I am—Sharon Stone?

Paying the minimum every month is definitely a trap, but what's a girl to do? Unfortunately, I missed the last payment, minimum or otherwise, due to my loss of job and recent medical malady. I'm just about to slather on the appeal for sympathy when I realize . . . he's still going to want to know when he can expect payment.

Making a split-second decision that I'm totally not proud of, I deepen my voice. "Tabitha? Why—um—no. Tabitha just stepped out, I'm afraid. May I take a message?"

Oh, the guilt. But faced with the necessity of begging a bill collector to wait a few weeks until I can get back to work and subsequently receive a paycheck, what was I to do? The impending demand for payment is more than I can stomach today—literally. And do you *know* the minimum payment on an eight *thousand* dollar credit card?

"Oh, she isn't there?" The voice sounds rather amused. "Well, tell her Kyle Preston called, will you?"

"Oh, Kyle is that you?" A better liar would have at least said good-bye and called him back as "Tabitha." But I've never been able to pull off deception. It just doesn't work for me. Which is a good thing, I guess. For the most part.

A chuckle reaches my ear, and I feel my cheeks warm. "You'll have to do a better acting job than this if I'm going to get you a good deal from *Legacy of Life*."

"I wasn't acting. I was lying," I defend, feeling as though my reputation has been besmirched.

"Is there a difference?"

"Yes, and I'm not good at lying. I am, however, very good at acting." I'm about to make the spiel to convince this man that I am his dream actress, when it suddenly dawns. "Wait, did you say you're going to take me on as a client?"

"Well, of course. Why else would I have called?"

How am I supposed to know? I don't really know this guy, do I? But that's okay by me. As long as he gets me back where I belong—on the number one daytime drama in the country.

"Now, Tabitha, I know you've just had surgery, but we need to get the ball rolling on this. I'll fax over a copy of my agent agreement. Sign it and fax it back to me. That will get things started."

We talk for another few minutes and he asks me questions like, "What was your salary per year before you were killed off?", "What size was your dressing room?", "Boxers or briefs?" He laughs, "Just kidding."

Very funny. Whatever. The guy might be cute, but he's definitely not my type. Well, except for the drop-dead gorgeous thing. But I like more depth. Less oily-car-salesmanship. So I agree with myself that this will be a business-only relationship. Even though he didn't ask for more anyway. Better to be prepared, I always say. Or at least, my mom always says that.

I got a new agent; I got a new agent." I sing as Dancy pops in at noon to bring me egg drop soup.

"He finally called?" She gives me a thumbs-up and hurries past. "Be right back."

"Yep," I holler after her retreating form as she heads into the kitchen. "I just faxed back my contract with his agency, and Freddie is passing along my contact information to Jerry, the producer, as we speak."

Dancy returns carrying a tray with my soup, transferred from the plastic container to a decent bowl (not that I mind plastic, but Dancy was raised on fine china so we humor her), and a soupspoon and a glass of iced tea, transferred from Styrofoam.

"Thank you," I say. I'm truly grateful for the way the girls are taking care of me. The alternative was going to my parents' house while I recover. And that would have been, you know, detrimental to my recovery.

Perched on the arm of the couch, Dancy gives a little frown.

"What?" I say, because I know that look.

"Oh, it's nothing, really."

"Oh, sure. Out with it." Anyone who brings me egg drop soup can say anything she wants without fear of my anger.

"Are you sure you want to go back to that show?"

I laugh. Surely she jests. She deadpans back at me. Okay, maybe she's serious. "Are you kidding?" Not only will I be paying my bills—going back to *Legacy of Life* means I return to the show that fired me. I am no longer a reject. I'm a commodity. A hot one, if I do say so myself.

A shrug lifts those perfectly shaped shoulders that Laini and I both envy. "You weren't all that happy when you were working there, Tabs. I don't know. Do whatever you want, but I think you'd be happier trying the stage or maybe some prime-time acting."

"Good idea! Why didn't I think of that? I'll just hop on over to the set of *CSI* and see if they're looking for any help. Or wait, I know. I'll put in a call to Spielberg. I've been meaning to get back to him anyway."

"Mock me if you will," she says. "But we both know you haven't tried that hard to get another regular acting job."

"Hey, a lot you . . ."

I was going to say "know about it," but she holds up her hand to shut me up. "I know working at the bookstore didn't leave you much time to go on auditions, so don't get mad. But now that you have a new agent, maybe he can help you land a gig you'd be happier with."

This woman works in publishing, which isn't too much different than showbiz. She knows the way things are. Why is she busting my chops? "Dance, the reason Kyle Preston even looked twice at my résumé is because *Legacy of Life* wants me back. If I tell him I don't want to do it, he'll drop me like a bad habit."

A grin tips the corners of her baby doll lips. "Bad habits are hard to drop. That's why people have so many of them."

Okay, that was sort of funny. But I'm not even close to being in the mood for her quips. "Yeah, well. That was a bad example." She's only looking out for my happiness, I get that, but the girl needs to understand that not everyone thinks I'm as wonderful as she does. "Trust me. Kyle Preston won't be interested in another has-been soap actress looking to trade up."

"So you do see being on a soap as the bottom of the barrel."

"No. I see dressing in rabbit suits and hopping around the kiddie room as the bottom of the barrel. I see soap acting as a way to pay my bills and gain a little bit of fame."

"Fame . . ." She gives a snort

"Okay, fine. I'm not going to be insulted. Ever heard of Kelly Ripa?" I give her that look that clearly says, "Try to deny it, babe."

"Not until she joined Regis." Oh, she's giving me the look right back. Dancy hates all soaps. Or really anything having to do with romance. Which I happen to think is a conflict of interest since she spends most of her days proofreading romance manuscripts.

"Okay. What about Meg Ryan, huh? She started on soaps and look at her now."

"Yes, and she got famous *after* she left the show. Because of that movie *Innerspace*."

"No. She met Dennis Quaid because of that movie. She got famous because of that scene in *When Harry Met Sally*." And I can't believe my so-called friend brought that up. She knows how upset I still am about that particular Hollywood split.

"Oh yeah." She stands. "Look, it's not that I don't support your decision to reprise the role of Felicia Fontaine. It's just that you sort of changed after you started on that show last time. And it took a while after you left to get back to the Tabby we knew and loved in college tent theater."

Is that all? How cute is she? Filled with tenderness, I give my friend an affectionate smile. "Honey, I'm much older and more mature now than I was right out of college when I got that part. I'm not so easily swayed anymore." Is it my imagination, or is that my mom's patronizing tone coming out of my mouth?

"I'm sure you're right." Still, she doesn't look all that convinced.

"Okay, out with it. What's bothering you the most?" Better to just get everything into the open up front. I'm not one to avoid confrontation (unless it's with Mom) and neither is

Dancy (except with her mom and dad), so if anyone can have a heart-to-heart with me, it's her.

"Here's the thing, Tabs. You were a Christian last time you worked there, but you didn't stay strong. I highly doubt there's been much of a spiritual reformation on the set since you left. How are you going to handle the temptations without compromising?"

"Such lack of confidence," I say, trying to lighten her up with a grin.

"No. I have complete confidence in you. But we both know how easy it is to get sucked into compromising. You sure you're ready for this?"

I give a shaky little breath. Because, you know, I'm not one hundred percent positive I can stay the course. Carry my cross, hold to the rock, and all that other Christianese designed to keep us steady. I *think* I can, but can I really? "God'll keep me strong, Dancy. I have to believe He's the one who called me back to the show."

You know, maybe like Lazarus. Back from the dead.

"Okay, I have to get back to work," Dancy says, popping up from the couch. "I'm sure you're going to do great. Maybe you're right, and this is God giving you a second chance at being a light in that place." She gives me a little smile. "Besides, Laini and I are right here to knock some sense into you if it seems like you are being influenced by bad . . . influences."

"I'll definitely count on you to be my watchdogs. I do not want to backslide or turn out to be a big jerk like Rachel Savage—like that's really her real name anyway. Who has a name like 'Savage'?"

"Fred from *The Wonder Years*. And his brother Ben from *Boy Meets World*."

A couple of good points. Still I'm just stubborn enough to

maintain my opinion. "Well, they don't have a sister named Rachel." I'm almost positive of that fact—er—theory.

Rachel plays in a rival soap and was up for the same Emmy I was that year. Neither of us won, but she went on to beat me out of the Soap Opera Award for Best Actress that year. She gloated in the bathroom later. Which I thought showed her utter lack of class. Laini and Dancy, who were there as my guests, saw the whole exchange and totally agreed with me. No class. None whatsoever. But since she's such a fabulous actress, not many people see through that fakey sweet façade of hers—and those of us who do know better than to bring attention to it. That would just make us look jealous, which we sooo aren't.

Dancy gives me a smart little nod. "All right. Then that's our code word. *Savage.*"

"Huh?"

"You know. If you do something diva-ish or just not like you, I'll say something like, 'Stop acting so Savage.' And you'll know what I mean but no one else will, except Laini, so you won't be embarrassed."

Reluctantly, I give her a nod. I mean it's not going to happen. I've grown a lot since then. But whatever will give her peace of mind. "Well, I guess that would work."

"Okay, good. I'll let Laini know the code."

I can already tell Miss Code Word is expecting to be using the "Savage" decoy a lot. Sheesh. She must really have faith in me.

During the next four weeks while I'm recovering, industry buzz starts to circulate about the impending return of Felicia Fontaine. I've been featured in *Soap Opera Digest* and *Soap*

Opera Weekly and have been scheduled to appear on *The View*. I wonder which of the ladies will still be around to do the interview. They must really think Felicia's return will be a splash.

I haven't started filming my scenes yet since it'll take another month to finish wrapping up my on-screen husband Rudolph's current relationship. I don't think they're killing her off. I've heard through the grapevine (i.e., Freddie) that she will be sailing away on a yacht—despite the fact that *Legacy* is supposedly set in a Midwestern town, not a seaport—but whatever floats their boat (pun intended) works for me. Just get her out of there so I can come back.

The really great news is that I've lost about ten of my twenty extra pounds. The bad news is that I've been starving myself to do it, so I don't have much energy. And because of this weight loss, Mom's not at all happy with my two roommates. Go figure. She doesn't hesitate to share her displeasure as she stands in our living room glaring at us like she's the principal and we just ran the science teacher's underwear up the flagpole. Don't ask me why he didn't have them on—this is only an example of how scowly Mom is right now.

"Just look at her," she says, giving them a dressing-down that I know so well. "You promised to take care of her and just look. She's too skinny, if you ask me."

"Six weeks ago you said I was fat, Mother."

Mom's lungs pull in all the extra air from the room as she gasps. "I most certainly did not say you were fat."

"Oh, you so did too." I shoot my eyes over to Laini. "Didn't she? That night they came for dinner?"

Laini looks sick. Like a deer hypnotized by headlights. Her

eyes are wide with fright. She shakes her head as if to say, "If you love me, leave me out of this."

Fine, I say back with my eyes. *Be a big fat chicken!*

"I never, ever said you were fat," Mom reiterates, obviously bolstered by Benedict Arnold's silence. "I only asked about that gym membership you weren't using."

I know, I know. I'm an ungrateful wretch of a daughter. But need I remind her that I never asked for the stupid membership?

"Is this how it's going to be now that you're on that show again?" she asks.

"How what's going to be?" I try to stay calm, cool, and collected. Just like the *Mona Lisa.* Unshakable. I even give a little smile, but that backfires.

"You think this is funny?" Mom's voice shakes a little. "Honestly, Tabitha. I don't like this side of you at all. Maybe it's not a good idea for you to go back on television if it's already affecting your personality for the worse. You'll be missing church soon and going to those wild parties."

Okay, that "wild party" comment elicits a genuine smirk from me, and my mother's chest puffs out like she's about to blow venom. "Mom, I'm sorry. Seriously, I don't think anything is funny." Well, *Monty Python and the Holy Grail*—that's funny. Oh, and of course all the episodes of *Friends*, especially the one where Phoebe first sings "Smelly Cat." And the jellyfish episode. Oh! And that last scene in *A Christmas Story.* Where the Chinese staff tries to sing "Deck the Halls."

Fa ra ra ra ra . . .

Anyway, I digress. The main point I'm trying to make is that I don't think this is a laughing matter. "I'm sorry, Mother. I wasn't laughing." How do I tell her I was shooting for serene but it didn't work so well? Note to self: practice facial expressions in mirror. Especially the expression of serenity as it apparently makes me look like I'm smirking.

"Mom, honestly. I'm sorry if I was rude, but I'm not at all too skinny. According to my scales I need to lose another ten pounds at least."

Mom gives me a once-over. "What size?"

"Huh?"

"What size are those jeans?"

This is outrageous. Why should I have to put up with this interference into my private life? I'm a grown woman for crying out loud. Almost thirty years old. I don't have to tell her what size I wear. But when she looks at me like that, I just—

"Eight."

She gives another scowl and shakes her head. "And you want to lose another ten pounds?"

"I need to be at least a size six, preferably a four—since there's no way my body is going to shrink to a two or a zero—but I think the last ten pounds will get me to a four, and I can tone up the rest with Pilates." And I'll still be the fattest female under fifty on the show.

"Listen to yourself. You'll be downright sickly if you try to lose another pound. Be proud of those curves. Look at Marilyn Monroe."

"You mean the dead one?"

She scowls. "What about that one brunette? Kirstie Alley? She's curvy—downright fat."

I grin—can't help it. "Not anymore. 'One eight hundred call Jenny.'"

"What are you talking about? Oh!" Mom's eyes go big. "That was her?"

"Um-hum."

"She looks good, doesn't she?"

Case in point.

I'm not arguing with her anymore. "Look, Ma, I'm an adult. If I think I should lose a few pounds, I have the right to do it without you yelling at my friends or me." I say that with all the respect I can muster. I don't want to hurt my mom, but come on . . . I'm an adult.

Her eyes narrow like she's going to send me to my room, then she gives a huff. "Just don't come crying to me when you're all skin and bones and the tabloids are having a field day."

O-kay, how about I change the subject? "So, how are Dad and the twins?"

The twins being Michelle (whom we call Shelly) and Michael, my twenty-five-year-old siblings. Both live at home with our parents and neither has a decent job.

Mom seems as willing as I am to let the subject of my independence drop. She gives a wave. "Michael just moved into an apartment close to his college with two other students."

"He did? No one told me he was moving out."

Mom rubs her forehead the way she does when she's stressed. "We didn't want to believe it until we saw it materialize. You know we've been through that song and dance before. But last night he moved his things."

"Even that old record player with the eight track?"

Her face clouds. "Well, no. Not that. Or the eight track collection. But I told him if he doesn't come get it in two weeks, I'm putting it on the curb for the garbage truck to pick up."

Sure she will. But I smile and nod. What's it going to hurt to let her think I'm giving her the benefit of the doubt?

"Good for him for finally growing up. How's Shelly? Did she get that job in Doctor Payne's"—don't go there, it's been done over and over and isn't funny anymore—"office?"

"She did get the job. Right after he told her she's pregnant."

"*What?*"

A heavy sigh blasts from her chest. "Yep. I always thought if one of my daughters got pregnant out of wedlock it would be . . ."

Okay, she stops herself, but was it really soon enough? I mean gee whiz already.

"Thanks a lot, Mom."

"I'm sorry. It's just that you were always the rebellious one—still are. Shelly's always done exactly what we've expected of her."

"Obviously not *everything*," I sass because I'm feeling a little bit raw over my character assassination. She thinks just because I'm independent and don't want my parents running my life at twenty-nine years old that I go around saying yes to anyone who wants to get me in the sack? Well, I don't.

"Yes, well, that's obvious, isn't it? At least with you I always knew what to expect."

"You did?"

She gives me a rueful smile. "Yes, exactly the opposite of what we told you to do."

Ouch. Let it go, Tabby. Just let it go. "How far along is Shelly?"

"Two months."

"How did this happen?"

Mom gives me the look, and my face goes hot. "You know what I mean."

She heaves a sigh. "We hardly know anything about this Drew fellow. Apparently, he's some sort of actor or model or something unstable like that."

Because actor must equate with unstable. I'm slightly offended.

I mean, isn't it enough that she insults me to my face on a regular basis? Must she also do it subconsciously? I'm this close to speaking up in my defense and the defense of all responsible working actors, but then I decide, why even bother? Why waste my mojo on an attitude that is never going to change? "Is Shelly getting married to this guy?"

Mom's frown deepens. "Turns out her boyfriend already has another girlfriend. And he's chosen to run off with the one he didn't get pregnant."

I feel a gasp coming on, and I'm too shocked to suppress it. "Is Shelly ever going to get it together and stop screwing up her life?"

Mom gives me a stern look, and I know I've crossed a line at the mere hint of disapproval of my sister.

"Be careful of the beam in your own eye, young lady."

Sigh. I guess out-of-wedlock babies must be a splinter in my sister's eye while my obvious need to drop a few pounds is a beam.

"Okay, Ma. Didn't mean to criticize." By pointing out the obvious. "How's Daddy?"

"He isn't feeling well. The doctor insists he needs to lose weight, but he's having a terrible time sticking to a diet." Her face twists with worry. "I find food wrappers all over the house. The man is hiding food from me. Isn't that odd?"

"It's an addiction, Mom. You have to help him. Not harp on him."

As soon as the words leave my mouth, I regret it. Mom's face crumples. "So now I shouldn't worry about fat around his heart? I don't do anything right, do I?"

I know how she feels. And yes, she might be a little melodramatic at the moment, but apparently she's having a bit of a hard day. My heart goes out to her. You know, everyone has a right to be comforted on days like this.

I walk across the room and put my arms around her slim body. She melts into me, this strong woman I've pulled against my whole life. I feel terrible that I've popped off with my opinion and hurt her deeply. "I'm sorry, Mom. Of course you should be concerned about Dad. Make him do whatever the doctor says."

I should just tape my mouth shut. Then it can't do any damage.

5

can't believe this!"

I totally can't believe what I'm reading.

"What's up?" Laini's tiny feet pad into the living room at the sound of my outburst. Once again the apartment smells of great baking. Tonight, Laini is trying her hand at apple turnovers, and I'm so glad because I really need something carb-laden to take the edge off after reading the drivel in front of me.

"This script Julie had couriered over," I say smacking the pages with the back of my hand. "It's total garbage."

"What do you mean? I thought Julie was a great writer."

"She is!" Personality notwithstanding. "She's got to be doing this on purpose."

Laini hands me a small plate with a warm turnover. "Here, I'll trade you. Let me read that while you try the recipe."

"Deal. I'd rather eat anyway."

I hand her the script and dive into the warm, fruity sweetness surrounded by baked dough. Laini should really be a baker.

When I look up from the turnover, Laini's flipping through the pages, a frown creasing her brow. "Okay, where are your lines?"

"I don't have any," I say glumly and shove another bite in my mouth.

"You have a week's worth of script and not one line?" She turns her incredulous gaze to mine. "That stinks."

"Tell me about it." I point to the script with my fork. "Look at page six."

She turns a couple of pages and reads aloud. "Felicia's eyes roll beneath her closed lids at the sound of her sister's voice."

"That's all the acting I do all week. Otherwise, I just lay there and try not to laugh at the bad dialogue between the nurses."

"So Felicia's just been wrapped up in Legacy, Illinois, in the hospital where her sister works for three years?"

"I know . . ."

"It just seems like when they change the bandages, someone would have recognized her. Or what about her wedding ring?"

"Page ten," I say around sugary apple filling.

Pages flip and she starts to read. "'The unknown hospital nurse takes Felicia's ring from her finger and slips it into her pocket.' I don't get it," Laini says.

"Okay, they created a flashback scene where I am brought into the hospital burned beyond recognition. The assumption is that the no-name nurse pulls my ring off because it's so big and valuable. She thinks I'm going to die anyway, and we'll never find out who I am."

"Haven't these writers ever heard of DNA testing and fingerprinting?"

"Well, there's no one to test her DNA against and unless she's a felon, those tests wouldn't help figure out her identity anyway."

Laini shrugs. "I guess. It just seems a little over the top. Don't you think so?"

"That's just the way soaps are. Anything can be written to explain anything. They're not highly based in reality." I grin.

"That's why they're so popular. Housewives want that hour of escape."

Laini hands me the script. "Well, maybe the next week will be better for you."

"I hope so." It's just so disappointing. I mean I've been waiting and waiting for them to send me my first scripts. And today I get next week's script, and I don't say one darn word all week.

"So how's the apple turnover?" Laini asks.

Ah, something happy to talk about. "This is fantastic. Did you make this from scratch?"

"Of course!"

"Laini, I swear you should have your own bakery."

I see interest flicker in Laini's eyes. "Wouldn't that be fun? But bakeries don't make enough. I'd go broke in three months."

"With food like this? Are you crazy? You'd be a millionaire in three months."

Laini reaches for my plate and stands up. "Thanks for the vote of confidence, but I think I'd better stick with what works."

"You'll never get anywhere if you don't step out in faith, Laini."

She gives me a grin. "Okay, but right now I have a job that pays my bills. As long as I can bake for my grateful friends, I'm happy."

"You can bake for me anytime." If I weren't so scared of Freddie's militant torture, I'd ask for another turnover.

Laini turns suddenly and gives me a wide-eyed smile as though she's had a brilliant thought. "Hey, when I come back, want me to help you run lines like the old days?"

I give the pages in front of me a once-over and stare at the back of her head as she retreats into the kitchen without waiting for my answer. Run lines? Is she kidding me? What lines?

I'm not sure, but I honestly don't think my mouth is supposed to be covered here. My whole face is wound up in gauze, except my eyes. And staring at myself in the mirror, I'd just as soon they were covered too so I couldn't see how hideous I look. I know that horrible Julie Foster wrote me into the script this way just to keep me anonymous a little while longer. She's so vindictive. And if you want to know the truth, I think she's sort of nervous about me kissing her husband once Rudolph discovers to his surprise and joy that Felicia wasn't killed, but merely maimed (another fact I'm not so happy about) and suffering from severe amnesia.

And lest anyone forget, let me just insert a little history: Julie divorced the slug husband who made a pass at me three years ago at the Christmas party—right before she killed off my character in a fiery inferno. Then she started dating a sitcom actor from a poorly rated, cancelled-after-six-episodes show that taped in the same building as *Legacy of Life*. After they broke up, I'm not sure what happened, but apparently, Trey caught her eye, left his wife, and married Julie. So she is now at least three men out from the one who supposedly broke her heart by attempting (but never succeeding) to kiss me.

Now that we're up to speed, let me just reiterate how unfair it is to bring me back and keep me wrapped up and then scarred up. If I know Julie, she'll prolong my hideousness as long as she can. So unprofessional. And so not fair. Who wants to kiss a guy with chronic coffee breath anyway? Not to mention the fact that he smokes, and last time we played a romantic scene together, he tried to slip me the tongue and I had to stomp on his foot.

Okay, it's getting awfully hard to breathe here. I *know* my mouth isn't supposed to be covered. I *do* have some lines as I go in and out of an anesthesia-induced sleep on this first day of shooting since my return to the übersoap. Uh. Makeup ditz, hello? I raise my hand to Tonya, the twenty-year-old makeup "artist."

"Everything okay?" she asks, looking at me in the mirror.

I point to my mouth and widen my eyes. I'm seriously losing the battle against my fight for air and my head is feeling woozy, then I realize my passive nature isn't going to help me here. I yank at the wrappings myself just as the girl realizes maybe I'm this close to death. "Oh! Miss Brockman. I'm so sorry." She makes a leap for my wrappings and relief is forthcoming. I take in a few gulps of air.

"Please don't tell anyone," she begs. "I'll for sure lose my job this time."

Has she killed anyone? Because I was almost done for. "This time?"

She nods miserably. "Last week I used superglue on Joseph Toreno's fake mustache. I didn't know it was superglue. But it took a few days for the stuff to loosen enough for him to pull it off. He refuses to allow me to work on him anymore."

Who can blame him? I give her a nod of sympathy. "Have you considered a different career? You're pretty enough to be on TV."

"Thanks, but I'd die if anyone paid that kind of attention to me. Besides, hair and makeup have been my dream all my life. I went to cosmetology school just so I could get this job." She ducks her head. "I'm not really supposed to tell people this, but Sharon Blankenship is my mom. She pulled strings to get me hired. She'll kill me if I'm fired."

Sharon Blankenship. The matriarch of *Legacy of Life* and diva to put all other divas to shame.

"I'll let you in on a little secret," I say.

She leans over my shoulder, and I lower my voice to a conspiratorial whisper. "If Sharon's your mom, I don't think you have to worry about getting fired." Her face immediately perks up. I smile. Now that I can breathe again, I'm feeling more generous.

A stage guy shows up just as Tonya puts the last of the gauze in place. I look like a crazed mummy, with fabulous violet eyes. Contacts for the part. But they really are gorgeous. The stagehand ogles the pretty makeup girl and barely notices Mummy-girl. "They're ready for Miss Brockman."

"She's ready to go." Tonya flashes me a bright smile and I'm charmed. I think I might have found a new friend.

Okay, so what do I have to do all day? Lie in a very uncomfortable hospital bed while "nurses" bustle on and off set, messing with my IV and talking around me.

Old Nurse says to New Nurse, who is unfamiliar with Felicia's situation. "Oh, isn't it just a shame? Imagine being so disfigured and in a coma for three years." (Oh, masterful writing, Julie. I'm awed. Really. *Not.*)

New Nurse: "Isn't there any way we can find out who she is?"

Old Nurse: "We've exhausted every avenue at our disposal. Until she wakes up . . . if she ever does, we'll just have to wait and pray for the best."

Nurses bow their heads for a moment of silent prayer. *Pu-lease.*

Oh, oh, my big moment. Time to put all that acting experience into motion. I move my right index finger. The camera is zooming in, but the praying nurses don't notice that their patient is obviously coming out of her three-year coma.

And cut.

And there we have it. Acting at its most brilliant.

"Squeeze those muscles, Tabby. You're as flabby as old lady Blankenship."

If I weren't going ten miles per hour on the elliptical machine and dripping with sweat, I'd take the time to tell Freddie-the-horrible to keep those remarks about our show's matriarch to himself if he knows what's good for him.

"I. Am. Squeezing. You jerk." I can't breathe, and I know that's not good.

"Your butt is that squishy even *while* squeezing? Oh this is so much worse than I expected."

Okay, the guy has been training me for more than a month, so he knows exactly what my glutes look and feel like. He's just being mean and trying the tough love approach to get me to work harder.

"Okay, Freddie, who told you to get me to lose more weight?"

Mr. Innocent gives me those eyes. "I don't know what you're talking about, Cupcake Abs, and what are you doing slowing down? Get back up to speed, and for that little 'break' I'm adding five more minutes."

Totally unintimidated, I come to a complete stop. Freddie

looks like he's going to go through the roof. "What do you think you're doing? Step it up, girlfriend."

"Not until you tell me."

"Okay, fine. Jerry."

"Bull. Jerry couldn't care less. Have you seen his wife?" Two hundred pounds if she's an ounce, and Jerry adores the Missus.

"Okay. It was Julie Foster."

"Julie?"

He gives a nod. "The cow says she's not writing for an overweight heroine. It's too hard for audiences to believe the hunky guys like Trey are in love with fat women when there are so many hot women running around."

"Hunky?" I can't help but laugh. "If they had to kiss his coffee breath, they wouldn't think he's so hot."

"I just do what I'm told." He has that eye of the tiger, and I know I'm about to get yelled at so I move my legs and go back to the torture. But I'm definitely having a talk with the powers that be about this.

Jerry, I can't physically get below a size six, and even a six is pushing it. I'm genetically predisposed to a size eight or above."

A snort from Julie raises my hackles. I whip around in Jerry's plush office and face her. "Why can't you write me in as curvy, not fat?"

She ignores me and stays focused on Jerry. "Jerry, sweetheart, no one is going to believe a man like Rudolph will fall in love with someone with a large behind."

Oh, she is begging to be tossed out of that chair onto her own boney backside.

"What are you talking about?" He frowns and eyes me up and down. "She looks like she hasn't had a meal in a week."

Hello? Remember me? Still in the room here.

Julie turns to me and gives me a once-over without making eye contact. "She's at least a full size bigger than the last time she was on the show. Trey would never be attracted to . . . that."

Jerry scowls and I can see he's growing impatient with her. "Well, this isn't about what Trey would be attracted to. It's about what Rudolph is attracted to, and his love for Felicia has nothing to do with the size of her derrière."

Oh yeah! My new hero. Jerry Gardner. Who would have ever thought? As much as I hated to be a tattletale, I can't help but feel a sense of satisfaction. Maybe there are just times when a girl needs to go to the powers that be.

Jerry swings around and shoves his finger toward me. "Next time you have a problem with Julie, go through Zoe. What do I have an associate producer for if people are going to just go over her head?"

Humiliation burns my cheeks, and I can feel Julie's mocking gaze on me.

I stand and give my ex-hero Jerry a two-fingered salute. "Will do. Thank you for not making me lose more weight than is healthy for me."

"You're welcome. Now get out of here. Both of you."

Julie jerks to her feet and slides around me, avoiding any physical contact. I guess she's afraid some of my chub might wear off on her and make Trey lose interest. I mean really, given her track record with cheating husbands, who can blame her?

I follow her out and she spins on her stilettos, glaring at me like she needs an exorcist. "Don't get too comfortable, chickee. You won't be here long."

I stand there gaping at her as she sashays away, leaving me

slack-jawed and speechless, wishing I had a quippy comeback.
But then, I never really do.

So, how are things going now that you've been back to work
for a while?" Through an uncommon series of events, Dancy,
Laini, and I are all three home tonight for dinner, and Laini has
cooked us a fabulous shrimp scampi (from a box, but still),
a lovely Caesar salad, and she's baked a cake with the words
Break a Leg written on it. Triple-layer chocolate cake with
chocolate frosting. I'm in heaven.

We are sitting at our small, neglected kitchen table catching
up for the first time in weeks. I relay my day of stardom.

Dancy spears a juicy shrimp and pops it into her mouth.
"Do you have any lines yet?" she says around the bite. Her
mother would be mortified with her lack of table manners, but
Laini and I couldn't care less. Dancy's come a long way out of
all that snootiness of Fifth Avenue old money.

"Oh yes. Want to hear them?"

They give me an enthusiastic response, so I mold my face
into something truly pathetic, I'm sure. "Rudy," I whisper in
a barely audible tone. I open my eyes and look at my friends.
"And then the Old Nurse says, 'Did you hear that? I think she
said something. Honey, what did you say?'"

Mold my face back to pathetic. "Wh-where's Rudy?"

Eyes open. "And New Nurse says, 'Who's Rudy?'"

Back to pathetic face. "'My husband.' Eyes closed, my head
goes to the side as I pass out, camera fades to black, and that's
the way the show will end for the day. Tune in tomorrow for
more of *Legacy of Life*."

"Brava, brava!" My friends clap and whistle, and I feel like
I've just won an Emmy.

"Thank you, thank you." I grin and raise my wineglass filled with Diet Pepsi. "To fulfilling our dreams."

"Hear, hear," Dancy responds by lifting her own glass of diet something or other. But . . . Laini isn't lifting anything, least of all her head.

Dancy and I give each other a look and set our glasses down. Clearly one of us isn't in a toasting mood.

"Everything okay, Laini?" I ask, feeling a sudden knot in my stomach.

Her face clouds and sudden tears well up in her eyes.

"What is it?" Dancy's voice echoes my concern.

But ever self-sacrificing, Laini shakes her head. "Forget it. I don't want to dampen the evening. This is your night, Tabs."

Reaching out, I take my friend's hand. "Are you okay, Laini? You don't have cancer or anything do you?" I'll just die if my friend has cancer. Cancer runs in Laini's family. Or is it lazy eye?

"For crying out loud, she doesn't have cancer." Dancy gives me that "shut up and listen" look of hers. So I do.

We both turn our silent attention to Laini who finally caves under our scrutiny.

"Well, it's just that . . . ACE Accounting is going out of business."

"What? That's absurd." I'm shocked. How can the accounting firm with the all-time best accountant ever go under? Especially right before tax season. I voice the questions. Laini smiles. "Thanks for the vote of confidence. But it's not about me not being good enough. Thomas Ace, the older brother, has been embezzling. He's been brought up on charges, but the other brothers have to declare bankruptcy."

"So essentially," Dancy says, a frown creasing her brow—another thing her Botox-addicted mother would be appalled to witness, "you and the rest of the underling accountants are out on your rears?"

A miserable nod barely moves my friend's head. It's like she's too depressed to even respond. I can't believe it! That just stinks for my pal. And I know how she feels, believe me. If anyone can sympathize, it's me. "Laini, that's so rotten. What are you planning to do?"

"Well," Dancy says. "Obviously Laini is going to have to stay rent and all other bills free until she finds another job." Dancy meets my gaze. "Right?"

"No, you guys," Laini protests. "I couldn't. Really. I'll just," she gives a huge gulp like she can hardly force out the next words, "move home with my parents for a while."

"That's a terrible thing to even think, Laini." Tragic really. "Of course you'll stay rent free. You guys saved me from the streets—or worse—moving back in with *my* mom. Why would you even hesitate to tell us about this? Am I a jerk and don't know it?"

"Well, you've been talking about saving for your own place," Laini reminds me.

"That was before I knew my friend needed me. And you know darned well I'm way too needy and dependent to wander around all by myself in a condo. I'd rather just stay right here."

Laini laughs and swipes tears from her cheeks. "You're a terrible liar." She squeezes my hand and reaches for Dancy with the other one. "But thank you. Both."

I smile at my bosom buddies and raise my glass again. "All for one and one for all."

We let go of each other's hands and this time, we all raise our glasses.

Apartments are a dime a dozen. Friends are forever.

It's been about three weeks since I attended church. I'm ashamed to admit that, but my focus has been a bit off since I went back to work. We film about three weeks in advance, so this past Friday was the first episode with my hospital scene where I'm calling for Rudy. Of course once I'm fully awake, viewers will realize that calling for Rudy was subconscious on Felicia's part and she doesn't really have any memories of her beloved husband.

So anyway, I feel a bit out of the loop as I step back into the four-hundred-member church. People look at me and give me that "long time no see" look. Some are obviously thrilled to see me. Some seem resentful that I've been gone and others ignore me like they couldn't care less if I'm there or not.

Between Sunday school and church there's a fellowship time that includes baked goods and coffee. I head to the fellowship hall. And yes, I have ulterior motives. I want to know if anyone saw *Legacy of Life* on Friday. If they did, will they know I'm the actress in the gauze?

Of course, the problem with looking for validation among church folks is that those who do watch soaps won't admit it. So even though I have had a few women and one man give me the thumbs-up, I can tell no one wants to talk about it and take a chance on being overheard. So I figure I'd better just let it go.

But, I mean, what's so taboo about it anyway? I don't do nude scenes, my character doesn't cuss, any love scenes are going to be between me and my "husband." So lighten up, people. I have to believe that God is the one directing my life. After all, we make a deal, and right afterward I get fired from my job and whammo—*Legacy* decides the answer to their falling ratings is none other than little ol' me. How can anyone *not* see how much of a God-thing that is?

I see the worship leader cram a last bite of muffin into her mouth, take a swig of coffee to wash it down, and head out of the fellowship hall so I assume it's about time for the main service to begin.

I spot my parents and Shelly when I enter the sanctuary. We've been sitting in the same pew for fifteen years. And Mom's been wearing the same outfit for the same amount of time. I mean, sure, she buys new ones when the old ones wear out, but I've never seen her wear anything but a black skirt with a black jacket, a white shirt and a pair of black pumps— one-inch heels. I swear I think we're in a rut. I hesitate, about to duck into a backseat somewhere and escape the Brockman pew, when Mom turns and spots me. How does she always know? I give a tentative half-smile and with resignation striking a sharp chord in my chest, I drag my feet up the aisle and slide past Dad (who sits on the end) and Mom (who of course sits next to Dad) and take my seat (as the first child) by Mom. Shelly barely looks at me. Which is fine with me. What am I supposed to say? "So, Shell, when is the blessed event?"

I'm spared the necessity anyway, because no sooner do I sit, than she springs up, shoves past my knees, Mom's knees, and Daddy's knees, then sprints up the aisle.

"Should I go after her?" I ask Mom.

Mom scowls. "What are you going to do about morning sickness?"

Oh . . .

My mother looks downright ready to throw up herself. She has a sick kind of "why is this happening to me?" expression on her face. Like when one of us brought home less than an A on our report card. Or a tattle note from the teacher.

"Michael didn't show up?" I say, more to change the subject than anything . . . get Mom's mind off my sister who we are probably both envisioning hugging the toilet.

I guess mentioning Michael's absence wasn't a good thing either. Her face clouds, and I swear if she doesn't stop frowning so much, no amount of Botox will ever be able to smooth out those lines between her eyes. Not that Mom would ever stoop that low anyway. I'm just saying . . .

She ignores the question and stares stoically ahead.

Shelly returns a minute later, pale, shaky, and looking as though she might need to bolt again any second. And lo and behold Michael stumbles in ten minutes into praise and worship. It's obvious he just rolled out of bed. I feel Mom heave a sigh of relief and relax a little.

I wonder what people see when they look at our family . . . a decent set of parents saddled with one daughter pregnant out of wedlock, a twenty-five-year-old career college student for a son, and me, an actress on a soap opera—something many people consider evil or at the very least immoral.

I'm so caught up in my thoughts that I scarcely notice I'm panning the congregation. That is until my gaze comes to rest on a guy who has special written all over him. And he's looking back at me. He smiles in a knowing way, like we've met or something. But I'm sure I would remember if I'd seen him somewhere before. I don't know, maybe he's a fan of the soap. Or—and wouldn't this just be my luck?—what if his wife is a fan of the show?

I try to catch a glimpse of his left hand, but he's too far away. Darn it. Just as I'm about to smile back, someone nudges into the row. I look up and there's Brian staring down at me like he owns me. He stands there making a total spectacle of himself and our family until Shelly scoots over and lets him sit by me. I'm horrified. Truly. And as much as I'm dying to see Mr. McDreamy's reaction, I'm too humiliated to glance over there again. But then it gets worse. Brian grabs my hand and laces our fingers before I realize what's happening. Mom smiles and pats my knee.

Okay, this is the last straw. Mom has got to stop trying to get me to marry this guy. Really.

Freddie's really kicking my butt here. Sweat pours from my head like a cloud burst over me. I'm totally soaked, head to toe. "Give me a break, Freddie!" I gasp as he turns the treadmill up to 6.5 mph.

"You used to run an eight-minute mile, girlfriend," he says without mercy. "You're out of shape and flabby as Rosie O'Donnell. I know you've been gone for a while, so you have an excuse for being as big as an elephant. But do you want to stay that way?"

"Hey, don't be mean. In what universe is a size six big as an elephant?"

"In this one, baby girl." He kicks the treadmill up another notch to 6.6. "It's brutal. I hear Rachel Savage just made 'Best Bod' in *Soap Mag.*"

"Like I give a flip."

"She's gone from a size six to a size two. I mean her 'before' photo is the same size as your everyday photo. What do you think of that?"

Oh, it's on! "Crank it up to seven-point-zero, Freddie."

Rachel Savage is going down.

No fat, carbs, or chocolate will touch these lips from here

on out. I will not be tempted by delicacies and fetching sweets no matter what yummy smells pour out of my own kitchen. If I'm going to compete in this business, I will have to make some sacrifices. There's too much at stake. Even if I have to be a skeleton, I'm hitting a size four.

6

can't believe it. I just can't believe it." Dancy and I are standing in line at the grocery store, and all I can do is stare in horror at the cover of *Soap Mag*. I can't believe it. I won't.

But there it is. A cover story exclusive: *Rachel Savage to join the cast of* Legacy of Life *in the role of Lucy Marshall.*

Mindless of the little checkout girl who is staring me down, I grab the magazine from the rack and thumb through it until I find the story.

Executive producer Jerry Gardner has confirmed that Rachel Savage will take the role of Lucy Marshall. The role was vacated by Taylor Adams last month. Adams will star opposite Brad Pitt in his new action/romance movie set to start filming next month in Morocco.

Rumor has it Savage chose not to renew her expiring contract with *As the World Turns* after being offered the role of Lucy.

"After six years on *ATWT*," Savage says, "I felt my story line had run its course many times over. The writers were not interested in pursuing challenging new paths for my character. I look forward to working with so many talented actors on *Legacy*, especially Tabitha Brockman."

"'Chose not to renew her expiring contract'? 'Especially Tabitha Brockman'?—you know that was nothing more than a challenge!" I shake the magazine at Dancy who is starting to look uncomfortable. "Of course she chose not to renew her contract. She lives to torment me. She's coming to my show to torment me. I'm looking forward to working with Tabitha Brockman, my eye!"

"Oh sure. It's all about you, isn't it?" Dancy grabs the magazine and tosses it onto the conveyer belt.

"What are you doing? I'm not buying that garbage."

"You wrinkled it. You have to buy it, sunshine."

I did? Yeah, the paper is definitely crumpled. The checker gives me a bewildered frown and rings it up.

"Sorry," I say meekly. "I didn't mean to."

She shrugs. "Doesn't matter to me, it's your money."

I slap my palm against my forehead. "I'm going to kill Freddie!"

"What did he do?" Dancy's been tossing groceries and diet soda onto the conveyer belt. I help a little, but for crying out loud—I'm in the middle of a crisis. The last thing I need is to break a nail to top it all off.

"He told me they were going to kill Lucy off. I was counting on it! Now they're recasting her? With Rachel Savage?"

"You're warped. You know that?" Dancy nudges me. "Look, just because Rachel's coming to *Legacy of Life* doesn't mean she's doing it to yank your chain. Maybe it's a career booster for her. *Legacy* is a higher rated show, as you've always loved to point out."

I give a very unpleasant snort, and I don't particularly care if I sound like I have sour grapes over the whole "Soap Opera Awards" incident. "I can't work with her. I mean it. I'm not doing it. It's either her or me." What if they pick her?

"Look." Dancy lifts a bag into the waiting cart as the checker stares at us, eavesdropping on our conversation. "So what if she's on the show? Isn't Lucy Marshall Felicia's nemesis anyway?"

"Yeah, what's your point?"

"Well, it fits. You won't even have to work at any scenes the two of you share."

The checker lets out a little *eep* as the man in line behind us sets a box of tampons on the belt and scowls. The man probably just wants to buy his wife's feminine products and get the heck out of there before any of his buddies catch him being a nice guy. But the grocery store employee just figured it out, and she can't take her eyes off me. "Oh my gosh. It is you, isn't it?" Oh great. The girl's shrieking a little and drawing attention. "I can't believe Felicia Fontaine is in my line buying . . . olives."

"Down, girl," Dancy says. "My friend isn't herself tonight. No autographs please."

The girl acts as though Dancy's not even there, let alone speaking. She stares straight at me, leaning across her register to get a closer look. "So you really don't get along with Rachel Savage? And she's going to play Lucy?" Her eyes are sparkling with intrigue. "Are you going to cut up all of Rachel's costumes and set fire to her trailer?"

I can't help but consider the possibilities. "Hey, now that's an—"

Dancy reaches around and covers my mouth. "No. She isn't going to do anything vindictive or illegal. And if any of this ends up in any magazine, we'll sue your behind for defamation. Got it?"

The girl rolls her eyes. "Yeah. Got it."

The guy behind us is not impressed to be in the presence of a soap actress. "Hey, can I get some service please?" Thank goodness for Mr. Tampons. His outburst gives us the opening we need to get away from the curious stares of the checker and the other onlookers who are trying to figure out if I'm someone they should recognize.

We walk out with our groceries. "So what do you think?" I ask. "Am I toast?"

"Oh, she's going to tell everyone who'll listen. And she'll have the store cameras to back up her claim that you were in her line, so they'll believe her."

"Then we'll sue her behind like you said."

"Oh please. What's the point? She's a checker who makes minimum wage at most. What are you going to take from her? A ten-year-old car with a hundred thousand miles on the odometer?"

"Yes, I'll give it to my sister. She needs a car now that she's going to be a mother."

"Then buy her one. It's not that girl's fault you had to go and open your big mouth in public. What did you expect?"

Oh, I hate it when she's right. So I do the only thing I can do. I pass the buck. "I blame you for this. Why didn't you stop me? Friends don't let friends say dumb things." My arms are about to fall off from carrying two full bags of groceries while Dancy hails a cab.

"Yeah sure. And what happens in Vegas stays in Vegas. And for your information, I *did* stop you. From incriminating yourself."

Oh yeah, she did do that, didn't she? I give her a grudging nod. "Thanks."

"That's what friends are for." She opens the door of the yellow cab as it screeches to a stop.

Oh well. Tomorrow is Thanksgiving, and I'm going to try hard not to think about bad things and just be thankful that God gave me back my job. I'll enjoy a worry-free day with my slightly weird family.

I'm miserably full as I walk into the apartment after Thanksgiving Day with the family. One thing I can say for Mom: the woman cooks like a pro. I mean really, Rachael Ray has nothing on my mom—except maybe a sweet smile and a great sense of humor. But, you know. That's all.

Laini is watching a marathon of all the Thanksgiving episodes of *The Waltons* on TV Land as I waddle through the living room to the kitchen and slip plastic containers of leftover turkey, stuffing, gravy, and pie—glorious chocolate, pumpkin, and apple pie—into the fridge. So much for no fat, carbs, or chocolate. In one day I've fallen completely off the wagon.

Back in the living room, I drop to the couch.

She looks over at me. "So, how's the family?"

"Dad announced he's starting Weight Watchers on Monday."

"Good for him!"

"Yeah, except he's eating like he's storing up for the winter. I swear he ate half of everything Mom cooked—including a twenty-pound turkey."

I toe off my shoes. "Let's see, what else. Oh, Shelly can't stand the smell of turkey so she stayed in her room all day with the ionic breeze blowing on her. And Michael brought a girl without telling Mom." I grin because really, the expression on Mom's face was the best part of the whole day. "She has a tattoo on the back of her hand that says 'bite me.'"

Laini's eyes go wide. "Wow. I can't believe your brother had the guts to bring her home."

"Me neither. I think he really likes her. Her name is Joy."

"What's going on?" Dancy enters carrying a huge bowl of popcorn. "Who likes whom?"

I repeat the evening's announcements.

"Well, you know what this means, don't you?"

"What?" If anyone can find light at the end of the tunnel, it's Dancy.

She grins and passes me the popcorn. Which I take because after all, I've already blown my diet today, so what's a couple hundred more calories and a few more carbs? And fat from the butter. I grab a handful of the yummy stuff and wait for my friend to reveal her words of wisdom. She doesn't disappoint.

"With Mike dating a bad girl, Shelly pregnant, and your dad eating diet food that presumably she's going to have to cook, your mom is going to be too preoccupied to concentrate on you."

The light flashes on. My brilliant friend is absolutely right. Finally, for the first time ever, the heat is off me. Hallelujah!

7

This heat is really getting to me. Golly. I never realized how stifling gauze can be under all those lights. What is it, anyway? Nothing but transparent strips of cloth, but here I am sweating like a pig beneath the layers.

When the director, Blythe Cannon, yells "Cut," I wade through all the wires and tubes that make the scene "authentic" and practically make a dive for the water table. I grab a paper cup and position it quickly under the spout, my dry mouth yearning as the clear liquid spills into my cup. I raise it toward my face. At the same time I see something orange flying toward me. There's not even a second to duck or jump back.

Crash! Splash!

What the . . . ? Oh, it feels kind of refreshing, having water poured all over my face and down my hospital gown. A nice cooling off, if you want to know the truth. Almost as good as the anticipated drink.

A child's scream of terror fills the set, and I nearly jump out of my skin. Since when do they let kids in here? And what's the deal with the screaming? A rolling blob of orange captures my attention. I look down and there's a Nerf football on the floor.

Outrageous! Apparently I've been the victim of a poorly aimed game of catch. Irritated, but willing to let it go, I'm about to turn back to refill my water when pain slices through my shin bone. I look down, and *shock* is a mild word for how I'm feeling as I stare at a scowling little boy of no more than six or eight. And it really doesn't matter because the little twerp kicks me. It's highly doubtful he'll make it to whatever his next birthday is supposed to be if I get my hands on him. "What do you think you're doing?" I ask.

"You can't eat my sister, mummy!" He yanks up the Nerf and spirals it at me. "Hey!" I duck. "Would someone get this kid away from me?"

"Sorry about that. Jeffy, leave Miss Brockman alone. She's not a mummy. That's her costume for her hospital scenes."

I turn at the sound of authority and look right into the most amazing blue eyes I've ever seen. Such a deep, deep blue they are practically navy. His appearance is understated, which I find myself unbelievably attracted to—501 Levis, a black T-shirt, and a long-sleeved, button-down shirt to even out the look. I wonder who he plays and how can I convince Julie to let me dump Rudolph and start up a romance with this man. I can just imagine the chemistry. As a matter of fact, I'm already feeling it. There's something so familiar about him. As though we've met in another lifetime. . . . Oh, wait. I don't believe in reincarnation, so that's not it.

He gives me a sheepish grin. "Sorry about the kids. They, um, apparently thought you were a mummy."

"A mummy?"

He lifts his hand and points to my face. Darn it! I forgot I was wrapped up. I look hideous. No wonder he doesn't seem all that interested.

I catch a whiff of his amazing aftershave, and I'm at a total loss for words. My stomach is dipping and diving, and I desperately need that drink of water. "Yes, well," I hear myself saying. "Children should be better supervised, you know?" I glance down at his left hand. *Score.* No ring.

He takes a clean cup from the dispenser, fills it with water, and hands it to me in the most charming, gentlemanly manner. "I'll be sure to remember that from now on," he says, his face suddenly without expression. "Sorry again."

Remember? What's he going to remember? My phone number? No. I didn't give it to him yet. Oh yes, that children should be better supervised. But why would he need to remember that?

"Let's go, kids," he calls. "Your day is over."

I'm left holding my glass of water as the two hoodlums, a boy and a girl, take their places, each on one side of the beautiful man and slip their chubby little hands into his.

What just happened?

"Wouldn't you love to do a romantic scene with him?" Tonya says. I was so focused on the hot guy walking away from me, I didn't even see her walk up, to be honest.

"What character does he play?"

"Who, him? Don't you know who that is?"

Sounds like someone important. And he just handed me a cup of water. Obviously attracted to me, despite my mummified appearance. Oh my goodness. Now I remember where I've seen him. That's the guy I was staring at when Brian showed up at church and completely humiliated me a couple of weeks ago.

So not only is this man gorgeous. He's a gorgeous Christian. Do you know how rare that is? And look, he's good with kids. He can be the part of us who makes us the favorite aunt and uncle. We most likely won't have children of our own for at least ten years.

I'm immersed in my fantasy life with Mr. Whatever-his-name-is, when Tonya totally pops my balloon.

"He's a stage dad."

"P-pardon me?" It sounded almost like she said he was a stage dad. Which is ridiculous because that would mean— "Those kids are his?" I shriek.

"Yeah, I think he does other work too, like computer something or other, maybe, but mostly he takes care of those two monsters."

"He wasn't wearing a ring." What is it with people not wearing their wedding rings? I think I'm going to start a movement to make it illegal. Leave your ring off once—get a warning. Twice—pay a hefty fine. Three strikes, you're out—off to jail for at least a year with marriage classes mandatory for rehabilitation. Four times—the chair. No, that's too harsh. Still, four-time offenders should at the very least be locked up and the key totally thrown away. Forever. I don't think it's at all unreasonable to make people pay for breaking marriage vows. I mean, if you break any other kind of legal contract you can at the very least be sued. I don't know. Maybe it's just me, but if there were consequences for breaking up marriages, maybe people would stop doing it.

Tonya reaches for my wet gauze, which I admit is starting to irritate. "He isn't married."

"What? Don't tell me he adopted those two?" Why would a gorgeous, single, Christian fellow like that adopt not one, but two kids? He'll never find a decent woman with those two hanging on to him like a couple of spider monkeys.

Tonya gives me a look that doesn't say a lot for my brainpower—which is especially insulting coming from a girl like her. "His wife died a year ago. She was a piece of work, let me tell you. Always coming to the set in slinky outfits that showed her 'girls' off—if you know what I mean. I don't know what David ever saw in her. I think they were separated for a long time before she died though. I never saw him until afterward."

"David—so his name is—"

She gives a nod. "David Gray. And believe me, they've tried to get him to audition, but he's not interested. He's an independent consultant for some software company. Works flexible hours from an office at his house. As near as I can tell, he hates days on the set. As a matter of fact, he says when the kids' contracts are up, they'll have to recast Felicia and Rudy's twins because his will be gone."

"Felicia's twins?" I laugh. "I'm Felicia. You must mean someone else." I toss her a patronizing smile as David and his children walk through the stage door and out of my life.

Tonya's silky eyebrows go up. "Hello? They were two when you were killed. Don't you even remember you had twins?" She grins. "Some mother you are. Of course, these twins are not the same ones that played the newborns. These two came right after you left the show."

Okay, I vaguely remember babies on the set from time to time. But it's not like we really dwelt on it. And weren't they kidnapped for the first year of their life? So we didn't exactly have much interaction.

It all comes rushing back now. I *did* have twins. How could I have forgotten that scene? It was a very touching elevator scene during a power outage whereby Rudy was forced to deliver his own babies. I was performer of the week in *Soap Opera Mag* for the very real way I portrayed a woman in labor—which I admit was rather ingenious, particularly since I've never actually been *in* labor.

But there's no time to relive that glory moment. I have to think. To wrap my mind around this new happening. Let me figure this out. If those two kids who just threw a Nerf at my head and kicked my shin—which still hurts by the way—are supposedly Felicia and Rudy's kids, that means . . . oh, Lord. They're going to be *my* kids, which means a lot of interaction.

I think I'm going to be sick.

I might as well borrow the bunny suit from my former employer and start hopping.

I can do this," I say confidently. Laini, Dancy, and I are having dinner at the Waldorf-Astoria in an elegant restaurant called Peacock Alley—my treat because it's my turn a hundred times over.

"Okay." Dancy sips her glass of peach tea and nods like she knows what she's talking about. "Here's what we're going to do. We're going to go to a day care and ask the workers to teach you how to get along with kids."

"What?" I practically choke on a bite of salad. "No one in their right mind is going to let me anywhere near their kids."

"She has a point, Dance." Laini chomps a breadstick. "Maybe you should just ask for another kidnapping story line. That should buy you a good six months at least, as long as it takes things to wrap up on soaps."

"Oh sure. Like the fans are going to stand for Felicia being gone for three years, finally coming back, and then the kids are stolen?" Dancy forks her salad. "No way. We want to see happily ever after. The perfect little family of four. At least for a while. You can't toss the kids to the wolves just because our friend here is scared to death of anyone under the age of eighteen."

Laini and I stare at Dancy.

"What?" she asks.

"You hate romance. You hate soaps."

She shrugs. "I watch *Legacy*. So sue me. Sheesh."

I can't believe it. "Why didn't you ever just say so?"

"I didn't want to hurt your feelings after the way they

dropped you. But you're the one who got me hooked on the show in the first place."

"Dan, I never asked anyone to stop watching it. Good grief. I never stopped watching it myself."

I turn to Laini with an is-there-something-you'd-like-to-tell-me look. She stares back with total innocence. "Oh, not me. The only thing I know about that show is what you've told me. As far as I'm concerned, soaps just cause college freshmen to look for unrealistic romance and dowdy housewives to fantasize about a life they'll never have with men that are way out of their league in the first place."

I dip a fat shrimp into cocktail sauce and allow the taste to explode across my tongue. "Hey! How would you feel if I talked that way about accountants? All those budgets making people fantasize about how they might actually get out of debt. Utter garbage!" I toss a napkin at her.

She laughs and catches it easily. "Touché."

"How's the job search going?" Dancy asks offhandedly as she takes another sip of peach tea.

Laini pauses a second then looks from Dancy to me. "Actually, I've decided to get out of accounting. I'm going to go back to school for interior design."

"What do you mean?" I ask. How can Laini just change careers like that? Presto change-o. Two weeks ago, Laini was talking about starting her own company. Now she's decided to get out of accounting altogether?

"I never really liked numbers, you know. I was just good at math. Dad was a hotshot accountant and after he died, I don't know, I just felt like I should follow in his footsteps. It seemed to mean a lot to Mom."

"Oh," Dancy and I say in unison. It's terrible to be at a loss for words when your best friend is baring her soul. But to be honest, I don't know what to say and knowing me, if I tried to make her feel better I'd end up making it a lot worse. Dancy's the one who usually comes through in these situations. But she seems preoccupied with her chicken marsala. I give her a little kick under the table.

She frowns and shrugs. Looks like it's up to me. "Okay, where did this whole idea of interior design come from?"

"I've always loved decorating. You know that."

It's true. Hers is really the only style in our little apartment that has any class to it. I'm hopelessly color-blind, and Dancy always has her nose in a book. She'd be fine with white, bare walls.

"Remember during college theater—I made the sets?"

Dancy gives a little laugh. "I remember you always had paint on your hands or in your hair. And Robert Candor was always yelling at you for using the wrong colors."

Laini jerks her chin. "Robert. What did he know about designing anything? Besides I read somewhere recently that all men are at least partially color-blind."

"So based on your job in college tent theater, you're going to give up accounting?" Dancy asks.

In my mind's eye, I see our red-haired friend covered in paint and carrying plates of cookies and pastries to practices. "Hey, you were really great. Wasn't she, Dan?"

"Yep. Very talented." She slips another bite into her mouth and keeps her gaze on her plate.

I scowl at Dancy. What's her deal tonight?

"Laini, I think you have a real shot at it, if you're sure you really want to give up accounting. I support you one hundred percent."

"Thanks." Laini beams. "I always wanted to be an interior designer, but my parents weren't too keen on the idea. I took some classes when I could slip them in without Mom and Dad realizing they were paying for extra classes."

"Sneaky," Dancy says and reaches for another slice of bread—so far she's eaten an entire basket by herself. If anyone recognizes emotional eating when she sees it, it's me.

"Dancy, are you okay?" I ask.

"Of course. Why wouldn't I be?"

Laini and I exchange a look. Dancy's voice trembles and her lower lip is quivering. "Okay, fine. I didn't get the promotion."

It takes a second for her words to sink in. Then I realize what she's saying. "They didn't make you a full-fledged editor?" This is outrageous. "They're nuts!"

Laini frowns. "Who got it? Not Fran?"

"No, thank God. You wouldn't be Tabby's only unemployed friend if they'd given it to Fran."

"If not Fran, then who? I thought she was the only other person in the office going for it."

"She was."

"Well then?" This is starting to feel like Who's on First.

Dancy shrugs. "Some jerk coming over from the London office. Jack Quinn."

"Do you know him?"

She shakes her head. "No. But I will since I'll be his assistant." Tears travel down her cheeks.

"What? Dancy?" I grab her arm because she looks like she might croak.

She points. I turn and my stomach rolls. Brian is sitting at a nearby table with an older couple. I'm about to duck when he notices me and grins widely. I swear, I should have known better than to bring my friends to Brian's favorite restaurant. But who knew he'd be coming here tonight? He has to save for three months to afford a meal at such an expensive restaurant.

I'm just about to excuse myself and head to the bathroom when the smartly dressed woman he's with slides out of her seat, motions him to follow, and makes a beeline for me. I slide my gaze over her and realize this must be Brian's mom. She owns her own little vintage boutique on Horatio Street, near Eighth Avenue. Brian says she actually serves champagne to her customers while they browse.

I paste on a smile as she approaches, with Brian following at her heels like a lapdog.

"You're Felicia," she says, completely ignoring my two friends. "I mean Tabitha Brockman." Her eyes are bright, voice breathless, and I have to wonder if she's been drinking a bit too much wine. "I can't believe my little boy is dating Tabitha Brockman." She turns abruptly to Brian. "Aren't you going to introduce us?" Oh brother. Before he has a chance to introduce me as his girlfriend, I reach out my hand. She latches on and pumps my arm like she's trying to make me fly. "It's just wonderful to meet you. Can I have your autograph?"

"Mother," Brian says, protesting but obviously pleased with himself. "I'm sure Tabby and her friends want to be left alone."

"Oh, well, what's it going to hurt for her to scratch her name across a napkin?"

Or more to the point, why would anyone ask me to? Still, this is my first instance of intrusion since I've been back on the show, and the woman is obviously a huge fan.

"It's all right. I don't mind." I take the napkin and pen, spirits momentarily lifted.

"I'm so glad they brought Felicia back." Now I recognize the brightness of her eyes for what it is. This woman's actually about to cry.

"Rudolph has been so unhappy. He's just never found anyone else who completes him the way you do."

Oh boy. Security? Is it just me, or is my stalker's mother now acting suspiciously like a stalker herself? What if this is a family of crazies? And my mother wants me to marry Brian and raise a bunch of little stalker kids?

"Well, thank you for your support. I'll be sure to pass along your comments to our producer."

"You will?" She takes the proffered pen and signed napkin and clutches them to her ample bosom.

"Sure she will," Dancy pipes in. "Well, are we about finished here?" She looks up at Brian's mom, who can't seem to tear herself away. "Tabitha needs her beauty rest. She has an early call in the morning."

"Oh, of course. I'm sorry." The woman's face turns bright red and she backs away like I'm the queen or something. "I'd love to see you come into my boutique," she says. "I'll give you half off anything in the store, if you'll mention the shop in one of your interviews."

"That's very generous of you. I'll speak to my publicist about it." I stand and turn and my gaze falls on Brian. "Well, you two enjoy the rest of your meal."

"I didn't know you had a publicist," Laini whispers as we walk away.

I send her a wink. "I don't."

We laugh together, but inside I'm fighting a knot in the pit of my stomach. Today must be my day for disappointments in the man department. First the gorgeous guy with two kids. Then the guy I'd love to get away from, not only won't he leave me alone, but now I've apparently passed muster with his mom. Aren't I lucky?

8

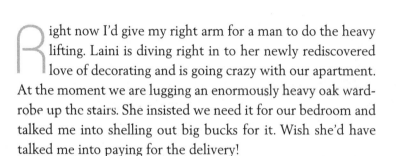

Right now I'd give my right arm for a man to do the heavy lifting. Laini is diving right in to her newly rediscovered love of decorating and is going crazy with our apartment. At the moment we are lugging an enormously heavy oak wardrobe up the stairs. She insisted we need it for our bedroom and talked me into shelling out big bucks for it. Wish she'd have talked me into paying for the delivery!

But I have to admit she has a good eye for furniture. I just wish she had bigger muscles.

Dancy groans under the weight of the huge box. "Please, can't we just set it down for a second?"

"Okay," I say. "Good idea. On three. One, two, three."

We all breathe audible sighs once we're relieved of the weight. "Note to you, Laini," Dancy says, still huffing. "Next time you want to bring home a couch or appliance or anything over fifty pounds, bring home a sexy, muscly man to go with it."

Laini grins. "Believe me. I wish I knew one."

"Don't we all."

"I know some," I say in a nongloating way. "But none of them want me."

"Brian does," Laini says with a laugh.

"Oh please. Don't give me a nervous breakdown."

"We're pathetic," Dancy says. "We're going to be living together when we're eighty."

"Well, I can think of worse company," I say entirely from my heart. "But I'm not giving up. Let's have a party."

Dancy gasps. Something Dancy rarely does, so Laini and I are immediately intrigued. "Let's have an unveiling Felicia Fontaine party."

"What? That's not what I meant." Although the idea does have merit. Actually . . .

Laini adds an enthusiastic, "That's a great idea! When's the unveiling, Tabs?"

"Um. I'm still wearing gauze, and we tape about three weeks in advance, so it'll be at least a month. Is that too far away?"

"That's perfect," Laini says. "We'll have plenty of time to prepare the guest list and decide on a menu. It can be a New Year's Eve–slash–Felicia unveiling party! What do you say?"

We're all very into the idea of killing two birds with one stone.

"In the meantime, let's get this thing up the stairs so I can soak in an aromatherapy bath," Dancy groans. "I'm going to need it."

We're close enough to our apartment at the top of the stairs that when the door buzzes, we can hear it.

We all look down and can see through the glass door that . . . Brian is standing there, nose to the glass looking in.

I can't believe it.

"Weasel boy," Dancy says, bitterness edging her voice. "Do you want to buzz him in?"

"Of course she doesn't," Laini says.

"Hey, wait a minute, guys. If we let him in, he can help us carry the wardrobe inside."

"Oh no, you don't." Dancy reaches for me and misses. "Grab her, Laini!"

"Tabby! If you let him in, he's going to think you want to

date him." Those words from Laini are enough to accomplish what a full body block failed to do. I stop and stare down at him. He's just standing there like a puppy in a window, waiting to be noticed. My heart sort of goes out to him. And he *does* have man muscles that we desperately need. So, in a moment of weakness, I do what I know I shouldn't do. I step inside the apartment and buzz the guy in.

I mean, maybe it's a sign that he's supposed to help, since he showed up right when we needed some muscle power.

A sign, my foot," Dancy nearly explodes later that night after Brian helps us get the wardrobe settled, eats us out of house and home, and finally takes the hint we'd like him to leave when Dancy gives a great big yawn and says, "Brian, you must be exhausted after all that moving. I know I'm ready to hit the sack." I let Brian out, deflect a lip-lock, and kiss his cheek in farewell. A harmless "thank you."

But Dancy doesn't see it that way. She's livid. "I can't believe you kissed that guy!"

"It was more of a peck on the cheek than a kiss. You make it sound like we made out."

"When you don't even like a guy, you shouldn't lead him on just to save you the trouble of moving furniture."

Okay, her high and mighty attitude is beginning to tick me off a little. I mean, come on. I fed him, let him watch my TV, and gave him a kiss on the cheek. I don't think I promised forever.

"Why do you care anyway? Do you have a thing for Brian now? Because I'd be happy to have you take him off my hands."

She scowls at me. "Do whatever you want. But don't come crying to me when you can't get rid of him."

She stomps off and slams her bedroom door. I press my palm against my aching forehead. I hate fighting with my friends. It just feels wrong. I mean, it's inevitable when three women share an apartment. There will be tension no matter how close we are, how much we care for each other. Sometimes, we have to each go to our corners and catch our breath, tend the wounds, and come back, ready to tap gloves and make it about friendship once again.

In my corner, I switch on the TV and flip through the channels. The sound of "Did you ever know that you're my hero?" stops the surfing. *Beaches*? How can I stay mad at my friend when Barbara Hershey is dying of heart disease and her best friend Bette Midler is nursing her? Sort of. Darn it. I can't let Dancy go to bed mad. What if she wakes up in the night with heart disease or is abducted by aliens (and who has proof there *aren't* any)?

Shoving up from the couch, I pad down the hall to Dancy's room and tap on the door. "Dan?"

"Just a minute."

But it's too late; I've already opened the door. She's wiping her eyes. "Oh, Dancy. I'm sorry."

She straightens her shoulders. "No. I should mind my own business. You have a right to kiss anyone you want to."

Okay, I was not kissing! But that little reminder wouldn't bode well for this particular situation whereby we are making up. So I let it go. "You're just being a good friend and looking out for me."

She hesitates. And we start to laugh. "Okay, so that's that. Fight number eight million, six hundred nine thousand and two is officially over. Right?"

I smile. "Right." I flop down at the foot of her bed. "So, how was work today?" See how we do that? Just clear the air and pick right up. The key to really great friendship is never holding a grudge. That and lots of chocolate. And the fact that we both—along with Laini—love Billie Holiday and Karen Carpenter.

"Horrible. Jack came in. 'Just to get a bit of a peek at the office.'" She does air quotes and gives a really bad Hugh Grant imitation. She rolls her eyes. "Which means I had to do the whole song and dance while he was there and pretend I'm honored to be working for him."

"Maybe he won't be any good and they'll fire him," I offer, hoping it helps.

She throws me a patronizing smile. "Sure, maybe. An award-winning editor isn't going to be any good at his job."

"It was a thought."

"I know. Too bad it's not true. They could fire him and hire me."

"Which they should have done in the first place."

"I guess."

I can tell Dancy's not in the mood to talk. She's not usually a deep talker anyway. And now, she keeps glancing at her laptop, which has booted up as we've been chatting.

"Going to do some work?"

She nods. "The new Tad Goodman mystery. I swear I don't know how he ever got published. His manuscripts come in so cluttered. He's wordy, uses poor grammar, bad sentence structure, predictable plots. This one is going to take a complete rewrite and he's going to throw a fit and we'll probably have to hire a ghostwriter to do it because my boss is such a wuss he refuses to let Tad go but he knows we can't publish the books the way they come to us."

Her long face is my cue. "Well, I'll leave you alone so you can work."

Dancy gives me a nod and turns to her laptop. "Thanks for coming in here. I don't like it when we fight."

"Me either."

She smiles. I smile back. And that's that.

Good grief, Tabitha. Play off the other actors. You're acting like you're the only person in the scene."

Blythe has been hollering at me all day. I know my head isn't in the scene. I keep wondering where David is today. But why does this director have to be so uptight? She's great, but such a sergeant major.

"Sorry, Blythe. I'm trying." A very humble response. I'm proud of myself.

"Well, try harder," she snaps back. "Stop being such a diva."

Diva? Okay, if she's going to be insulting.

"Places, please. And . . . action."

Felicia: "You're my sister?"

Concentrate, Tabby. The woman has just revealed she's your sister. Show some emotion. I force myself to tear up. No easy feat.

Nurse: "Yes. And I can't believe you've been here the whole time, and I never knew it was you under the wrappings." (*Gag me now!*) "Mother will be so happy."

Felicia (I lay my hand on the nurse's arm in an attempt to play off the other actress, as directed): "But I can't remember any of you. Maybe it would be better to wait for me to meet her. I don't want to disappoint her."

Nurse (Covers my hand with hers. Oh, that's good! This girl is great—a totally different sister than I had before. The last one was fired after showing up drunk three days in a row, I understand, per Freddie's gossip chain): "Sweetie, you'll soon find out that our family sticks together through thick and thin. Mom will want to baby you and take care of you while you recover, whether you regain your memory or not." (She gives a slight laugh.) "Trust me. You'll be in good hands."

Felicia: "I just . . . but what about my face? The doctor said I'll have at least six months of surgeries before I look like myself again. I-I don't know if I want anyone to see how hideous I am." (Julie wrote "what a monster I am" but I changed it.)

Nurse: "You're hardly a monster, Felicia."

"*Cut!* For crying out loud will you two please play the scene together?" Blythe glares at me. "Say the right line so you don't throw anyone off."

"Fine," I mumble. I guess "monster" it is so that Miss I-can't-improvise doesn't get thrown for a loop.

"*Action!*"

Yada yada.

Monster . . .

Nurse: "You're hardly a monster, Felicia. Although you are a little heavier than you used to be."

What? I never saw that in the script. I'll kill Julie Foster. . . .

"Cut!" Oh. Did I just say that?

"Excuse me; did someone hire you to take my job without telling me?" Blythe glares at me and walks to the set. "What's your problem?"

"Did you hear what she just said about me being heavier than I used to be?"

"Yeah, so?"

"What sister is going to say that to a woman who feels like a monster with all of her scars?"

Blythe takes a breath like she's going to blow a gasket at

me, then a reflective frown creases her brow. She turns to June Wright, the actress playing my nurse/sister. "She's right. Lose the line."

"Not until you take it up with Julie," June says, giving her a haughty sneer.

Blythe's eyes narrow, and she steps all five feet of her pudgy body into Miss Nurse's personal space. "You're going to do as you're told."

June backs down as quickly as she attempted to stand up to the little director. "Fine."

"Good." I swear Blythe is part bear. She literally growls on the way back to her spot. "Don't make me do another take, you two."

"Action!"

Yada, yada—no weight gain line.

Nurse: "Besides, we don't love you for your outward beauty. We love you for the good person you are inside. That goodness shines from your beautiful eyes, and no one will even notice your scars."

I allow tears to well up once more and press a kiss to the back of her hand. (Incredible acting, I must say.)

Felicia: "Thank you for that." (My voice is barely a whisper.)

Nurse: "You'll let Mom come see you, then?"

I nod.

Felicia: "But only her."

Rudolph enters.

Rudolph: "What about me? Don't you want to see your husband?"

"And, cut! That's a wrap. Go home everyone," Blythe hollers. "Way to go, ladies."

I smile at June. "You're really good."

She looks down at me with haughty disdain. "Warn me next time you plan to kiss me. Got it?"

"Uh. Sure. Sorry." Talk about a diva!

A stagehand comes to my aid, helping me remove the tubing and wires from my body.

"Wait, Tabitha and Trey. Stay here. I want to go ahead and film the next scene between you two. You have your pages memorized, right?"

"Right," I say. Mostly.

With a weary sigh I lie back in the bed and the stagehand reconnects all my wires. My face is unwrapped and full of fake scars. It's quite humbling to see myself like this. I've been totally dreading this coming scene with Rudolph. He has to kiss me before he realizes I have no memory of him. Apparently, none of his friends have bothered to disclose Felicia's unfortunate case of amnesia.

Laini and Dancy are both on the set today. They've come to watch the first scene where Rudolph sees Felicia. Looks like they're not going to be disappointed. I send them both an apologetic shrug. Dancy grins. She's in pure heaven being on the set of her favorite soap. Just wait until I tell her what June Wright, Felicia's so-called sister, said to me. Hateful broad!

"Quiet," Blythe calls, and the set immediately hushes.

Trey is at my bedside, ready to lay it on thick.

"Action!"

Rudolph: "Darling, my beauty. I can't believe it's really you."

He moves in for a kiss. Ugh. Coffee breath. And unless I miss my guess, he ate seafood and garlic for lunch. Someone get this guy a tube of Mentos. *Please.* Thankfully, the kiss is short and he pulls me into his chest, and I feel . . . oh my gosh I feel nauseated. Because yes, on top of the bad breath, Trey has a case of B.O. How can a semi-hot soap star be so hygienically challenged?

He caresses the back of my head as he smothers me to him, then pulls away, keeping his hands on my upper arms.

Rudolph: "I can't believe it's really you." (Uh, didn't he already say that?) "You're as beautiful as the day we met." (Okay, even on a good day, that's a bad line. And not the greatest acting.)

Felicia (Oh no! I feel a laugh coming on): "I-I'm sorry. I don't know who you are."

"Cut! Tabitha. Can we please do the scene without you laughing?"

"I'm sorry, Blythe. I'm okay now. The—um—wire was tickling me."

"Well, move the wire so that it doesn't tickle you and let's get this scene wrapped up."

"Okay. Will do." I fiddle with a bit of tubing. "Ready."

"Action."

Rudolph: "Darling . . ." yada yada.

Kiss kiss. Big whiff of sweaty male. *Ew.*

Felicia (Oh, Jesus, help me. Trey has a toupee. I had no idea!): "I don't know you."

I'm cracking up and so are the spectators on the set.

"Cut! Tabby! For the love of Pete. What is wrong with you? Now, listen here. Stop that laughing. When you look at Trey, I want to see love in your eyes this time. Capiche?"

"But I don't even remember him," I fire back. "No one's going to believe it if I look at him with love in my eyes." If only they had to inhale what I'm enduring over here. Dare I ask for some strong air freshener? A Yankee candle maybe?

"Your *soul* remembers him. Rudolph is the one and only for

Felicia. Her memory is gone, but her heart knows him. And I want to see that heart in her eyes. Is that clear?"

"Yes, Blythe. I'm sure I'll get it right this time."

"What's a matter, Tabby?" Trey asks in a slightly taunting tone for my ears only. "Did you forget how to act?"

"Did you ever know how?" I hiss back. Not nice. And completely immature. But he's always gotten on my nerves, and even more so now that he's married to the head writer.

"Action!" Blythe yells in a tone that says, "You'd better not make me say 'action' again for this scene."

Rudolph: Yada yada.

Felicia: "But I don't remember you."

I see movement and for some reason I lift my eyes straight ahead to the set—and I take a sharp breath. I can't help myself. I haven't seen David Gray since the day his rug rats assaulted me. He's standing there watching me. Oh, he smiled. It's all I can do not to smile back.

"Cut." Oh shoot. "Tabby. That's perfect. That's the look."

Oh. My. Gosh. I'm still staring at David, except his smile is gone—replaced by a sort of questioning frown.

"Okay, we're going to do it again," Blythe calls out. "Only look at Trey this time when you give that look. Here we go. Action."

I don't know how I make it through the scene, but Blythe seems happy with it.

Laini and Dancy rush me the second I step out of the dressing room looking like me again. "That was fabulous, Tabs," Laini gushes. "I had no idea you're such a great actress."

I won't even state the obvious that if she watched the show, she'd be aware of my brilliance on a daily basis.

"Okay, I want to talk about that look you gave the stage dad." Dancy, of course.

"How do you know who he is?"

"So you aren't denying it?"

Darn. She got me.

Laini pipes up. "We saw the kids. Besides, he introduced himself. So, what's with the look?"

So they're both going to hound me for answers.

"I don't even know the man. He distracted me, that's all." I scan the remaining faces. My stomach drops as a high-pitched squeal breaks the sound barrier inside the studio. "David!" My jaw goes slack and my gut clenches as a skinny blond flies into his arms.

"Is that who I think it is?" Dancy asks.

"Yeah," I reply, not entirely able to mask the disappointment running through me. I mean, what gives Rachel Savage the right to waltz in here just when I'm making a connection with a guy and jump him like she's married to him or something?

Just as I'm about to turn away and slip outside, I catch a glimpse of the twins running toward their dad and Rachel. "Kids!" she says, stooping with her arms wide as they both dive in for an embrace, nearly knocking her off her four-inch stilettos.

"That would have been priceless," Laini whispers.

I grin and nod, envisioning Rachel landing flat on her behind. But you know, some people just don't end up a laughing-stock and some do. And that's the difference between Rachel and me. I'd be picking myself up off the floor right now, while she, on the other hand, is beautiful and confident, exuding maternal warmth and looking very much like the completion of David's little family.

"Let's get out of here," I say, unable to spend one more second watching the scene playing out in front of me.

But we don't even get two feet before Rachel calls from across the room. "Aren't you going to say hello, Tabby?"

I stop. Feel the challenge, baby.

"Don't let her get to you," Dancy says under her breath, and I'm gratified to know I'm not the only person who caught that tone.

I paste a smile on and raise my eyebrows at Laini to ask if it's good enough.

"Perfect," she says. "No one would ever guess you want to deck her."

I turn and face Rachel, who is flanked on either side by my TV children.

"Hi, Rachel," I say with forced gaiety. "Welcome aboard. I hope you'll feel right at home."

Rachel's smile broadens, and she hugs each twin against her. "I already do."

"Good." I smile down at the kids, who have kept their distance from me ever since the mummy incident. "I guess I'll be seeing you two soon in our scenes."

They duck into Rachel's hips. Kids. Why? That's all I can think of. Why?

David steps up, and I feel the heat scorch my cheeks at the memory of "the look of love."

"Well, we'd better go," I say before he can even open his mouth.

"We're just leaving too," he says in a sexy, husky voice that I swear I'd think was put on if he was an actor instead of a computer geek.

"Why don't we all walk out together?" Rachel suggests, her smile wide, but her eyes narrow. Oh, is the size two best bod winner feeling a little threatened?

"Great idea." I give her a semi-sweet smile. "I always feel a little odd waiting for a cab after dark."

"Want a lift home?" David asks.

"Oh no. That's not necessary." Dancy jabs me in the ribs with her elbow. But I'm not backing down. I have no intention of letting him think I was hinting. Or more to the point, letting Rachel suspect it.

"Well, we'll at least wait until you can get a cab."

See, he's very thoughtful. Perfect boyfriend material. Unlike Brian, who is just annoying—especially since I let him come in and help me with the wardrobe. (Which is big and not exactly right for the apartment.)

We walk outside and a camera flashes.

Rachel huffs. "Goodness, I can't go anywhere these days without photographers hounding me."

"You could always wear a wig and dark glasses," Laini drawls, and Dancy snickers, leaving me to keep my composure.

"Give us a smile, Tabby!" the photographers call out. I could kiss every single lens-stuffed face for making this about me instead of Rachel.

I wave and smile, giving my sexy, one hip forward, skinny pose.

"Thanks, Tabby!"

"Anytime."

"Miss Savage, can you give us a smile?"

"Why, sure, fellas." The words are like smooth butter gliding from her lips. She's going to make the most of this moment.

My heart is just sinking when I feel a shove from behind, knocking me into Rachel.

"Oops," Dancy says. "Sorry. I stumbled." Oh! She so did not!

The photographers chuckle, and I can only imagine the kind of shot they got.

"All right, guys," I call out. "Play nice. You know what that's going to look like. I got shoved into Rachel."

"Sorry," James Iams (like the dog food) says, putting away his camera. "That photo is going to sell for a lot."

Jerk. I can't believe I gave that guy my sexy pose.

Rachel gives a half laugh and waves. "It's all right, boys. Just make sure it's clear I was the one assaulted by Tabitha and not the other way around."

"Hey!" I speak up in a knee-jerk reaction. "You know I didn't do that on purpose."

"It's true," Dancy says. "I bumped her."

"And I bumped Rachel after my friend bumped me."

Rachel gives an exaggerated wave. "We believe them, don't we, boys?" Her giggle puts the last nail in my proverbial coffin. I can just see tomorrow's soap mag headline . . . it'll be Lindsay Lohan and Hillary Duff all over again.

God, will you cover your ears just for a second?

I hate her, hate her, hate her!

Okay, God. You can uncover them now.

God bless Rachel Savage.

9

With Dad on a diet, Mom has suddenly become Nurse Martha and is making sure he sticks to things. Therefore, Christmas dinner was a meager affair with turkey breast, no ham . . . potatoes mashed with chicken broth (who came *up* with that idea?) and sugar-free pie—which wasn't too bad, but definitely not what I was expecting. All in all, a disappointing day as far as food goes, but Shelly is feeling better and is starting to glow a little. Mike brought his weird girlfriend again. Funny thing is, I think she's starting to grow on Mom a little. At least she helped with dishes. And those are always points in anyone's favor. If one needs the points. And Joy does.

I make it home by ten Christmas night. I don't really expect Laini or Dancy to be there—I figure they'll stay the night in their childhood bedrooms. Which is where I would have stayed if my stomach hadn't been growling so loudly. But to my surprise and delight, they've both beaten me back to the apartment.

They're debriefing in the kitchen around leftovers they brought from their respective mothers. I find it difficult to hide my enthusiasm. "Glory be, turkey and ham!" I two-finger grab a slice of baked ham. I don't care which of my friends brought it home. All I know is that I'm starving and this is heaven.

"Hey," Dancy says, "where's your leftovers?" Traditionally we eat for a week on the food we bring home from holidays. And my mom sends the most and the best. Since we are going to be a few containers short this year, it looks like we'll be eating for only a day or two. Possibly less. Oh man, that's good ham. Yes, I'll definitely be eating for a while here.

"Sorry," I say with my mouth full, but too hungry to care about my appalling lack of table manners. "Dad's on a diet. Mom didn't make much, and what she did make tasted diet—trust me, you wouldn't have wanted it."

"Oh my goodness. You poor thing." Laini springs into action and starts piling up my plate. Keep it coming, girlfriend. A fat homemade yeast dinner roll finds its way to my plate. Real mashed potatoes and giblet gravy. Rice dressing, regular dressing, green beans (okay, I'll eat a few, but who wants to waste precious stomach room on vegetables when there's four different kinds of pie for dessert?). Yams, which I actually don't like all that well, but always eat a little since it's tradition. And to top it all off, a wonderful seven-layer salad with real bacon bits and sugar.

I eat and eat as the girls talk around me. Laini chickened out about coming clean with her mom about learning interior design because three of her aunts were there asking financial questions and gushing over her wonderful accounting abilities. Grandma obviously has a thing for *Legacy of Life* because she kept grilling Laini about me. Her mom was weepy all day as she has been for the last three Christmases since Laini's dad passed on. I think it's an attention getter, personally, but I wouldn't say that to my friend. Anyway, the aunts are why Laini didn't stick around. Two of them are sharing her old room, and she would have had to either sleep on the floor in the living room or with her mom, and neither seemed like a good choice.

Laini sighs and grabs a fork and dives into a slice of pecan pie.

"He was a jerk when we were kids," Dancy is saying of the guy her mom is perpetually trying to fix her up with. "And he's an even bigger jerk now. When is my mother going to get it through her head that I am not Bridget Jones, and that Floyd Bartell is definitely no Colin Firth? There is no possibility of a love connection. The man is an absolute troll every day of the week."

"Even on Christmas?" I quip. "Seems like he could take a day off once a year."

Laini giggles.

Dancy isn't amused. "No. On Christmas he turns into an evil elf—the kind that smashes all the doll heads after he puts them on the doll bodies. Do you know I once caught him looking in my window trying to catch a peek?"

In my mind's eye, I picture a sixteen-year-old pervert. Suddenly I see her point. "Ew. How old were you?"

"We were both eleven. Isn't that revolting?"

I snicker. Laini snickers. And then the two of us are laughing so hard, tears are streaming down our cheeks.

"Oh sure. Laugh. But you wouldn't think it was funny if you were the victim of some peeping Tom."

"Oh, oh my gosh. Stop," I say, begging for mercy. "You're killing me here. I ate too much."

"Serves you right," Dancy grouches. "Glutton."

"Okay, we're sorry we laughed, Dan. I'm sorry you had such a rotten day."

Dancy scowls. "You know the Peeker was bad enough, but guess who else was there?"

"Um. Who?" I decide no more making fun. Not when there is more turkey on my plate.

"Jack Quinn. Of all people."

"Who's that?" I say with my mouth full.

Dancy frowns. "Would you swallow?"

"Sorry." Oops, still full.

"Swallow!"

I do and take a gulp of Diet Pepsi. This is great.

"Jack Quinn is my new boss. Remember?"

"What's he doing?" Laini asks. "Stalking you?"

"No. Apparently, he's a friend of Kale's."

Laini frowns. "I thought you said he was from London."

Dancy nods glumly. "He went to NYU. He and Kale were college buddies or something stupid like that. So now my boss and my brother are golfing pals."

"This might be a good thing, Dan," I say. "What guy is going to be mean to his best friend's sister? It's just not done."

"Trust me, Jack Quinn couldn't care less about friendship when it comes to making my life miserable."

I'm suddenly over the food and focused on my friend—well, maybe one last bite. "What did he say to you?"

"It wasn't so much what he said as his attitude." She drops her tone and mimics: "I'm God's gift to women, but you can't unwrap the package because you're not good enough."

"Dancy! Did you make a pass at the guy?"

"He wishes!" She sends me a look of total outrage. "I'm going to take a bath. Mom got me the new Jodi Picoult book for Christmas."

Dancy cracks me up. She gets electronics and diamonds and five-hundred-dollar Jimmy Choos for Christmas, and what does she get excited about? A new book. The girl works for a publisher and gets all the reading material she can handle. It's just not normal. She stuffs her new book under her arm as she grabs another Diet Pepsi and heads toward the bathroom.

An hour later, I've eaten all I can hold, said good night to Laini, and am lying in bed, seriously considering a run to the twenty-four-hour pharmacy on the corner for a bottle of Tums. My stomach is absolutely telling me about my gluttonous rampage after a month of forcing tofu and salad with no dressing down the pipes on a regular basis. I run my hand across my tummy and discover a belly bump. I'm slightly mortified at my lack of self-control. I mean, Shelly having a belly bump is one thing, the girl is four months pregnant. Me? I'm a compulsive over-eater. In a few years I'll be signing up for Weight Watchers if I don't take care of myself.

Sometimes overeating makes you sleepy. Sometimes it just makes you so miserable you can't sleep, and the last option is my problem. It's been two hours since I put away the food and cleaned up the kitchen, and I'm wide awake.

When the buzzer buzzes, it nearly sends me through the roof.

Laini mutters something unintelligible and tosses a pillow over her head. I hop out of bed and head to the living room.

"Who is it?" I hiss.

"Brian."

"Brian? What are you doing? It's almost two in the morning."

"You didn't call."

"What?" Oh, my gosh. Was I supposed to? I honestly can't remember. "I'm sorry, Brian. Can I call you tomorrow?"

"Well, I have this gift for you. Can I come in just for a few minutes?"

"Don't you dare let him in this apartment, Tabby," Dancy growls at me from the doorway to her bedroom. "Go away, Brian!" she calls.

"Uh, Brian. That was Dancy. I'm sorry. I can't let you in this late. It's against the apartment rules."

"Oh. Well, how about coming down for a few minutes?"

"Don't do it," Dancy warns. "You know what it's going to look like to him if you go running down the steps in the middle of the night."

"He has a present for me."

She sighs. "Fine. Do whatever you want. But don't make any more noise."

I press the button. "Hey, Bri. I'm sorry I forgot to call you. Honestly. But this will have to wait until tomorrow."

"But . . ."

"Good night, Brian!"

I wait. No more buzzing. Thank goodness he got the message.

The phone rings, and I make a leap for the crazy thing before anyone hears it. I knock my toe against the coffee table leg in the darkened living room. Wincing in pain, I snatch up the receiver midway through the second ring. "Brian! Look. You can't call or come over here this late. It's just . . . impolite."

"Tabitha?"

A voice that definitely isn't Brian's.

"Ma? What's wrong?" Immediately my mind goes to my sister. Miscarriage?

"Honey, it's your dad. He's in the hospital ER. They think he might have had a heart attack."

10

So they wouldn't let you in to see your dad?" Laini's voice over the phone is filled with sympathy.

Emergency triple bypass. And it could have been worse. Dad was carrying our old baby crib in from the garage and had a heart attack. I've been at the hospital for the past eight hours and haven't so much as caught a glimpse of him.

"Only Mom for now. They'll let us in once they're sure his vitals are stable and he's fully awake. I just wanted to let you guys know I won't be home tonight. I'm going to stay with my mom to make sure she gets some rest."

"Okay." She pauses a minute. "Dancy says to tell you we need your okay on the final guest list for New Year's Eve. Do you feel like dealing with it?"

"New Year's Eve?"

"The party."

"Oh yeah. Don't worry about it. Whoever you guys want is fine with me."

"I thought we'd invite your brother and sister."

I hesitate. Typically I prefer to keep my family away from my friends unless I need my friends as a buffer—like that dinner fiasco a few months ago. It's just easier that way. But I think about Shelly and her total lack of a social life these days. I mean, when you devote all your attention for two years to a

guy and blow off your friends, guess what? You end up alone.
But she can't help that she's one of those all-or-nothing types.

Mike has plans with "bite me" girl, I already know that. "I'll
ask Shelly if she wants to come," I say.

"Call tomorrow and let us know how your dad is, okay?"

"Will do."

I hang up and walk back to ICU. Shelly is curled up on one
of the love seats. I stare a moment at my beautiful little sister.
Her long lashes brush her cheeks, her tousled hair giving her a
childish appearance that takes me back twenty years to when
she followed me around mercilessly. All I wanted to do was get
away from this girl. But in this moment, watching her in such
a vulnerable state, all I want to do is draw her close and make
everything okay.

I sit cautiously across from her so the movement in the room
doesn't disturb her. But my efforts fail. She comes instantly
awake and slowly rises to a sitting position. She smiles when
she sees me and her cheeks go up. I hadn't noticed before how
round her face is becoming. She's adorable.

"How are you feeling?" I ask.

"So tired. They say you're supposed to start getting some
energy in the second trimester. Figures I'd be the one woman
in history to break the mold."

"Just give it some time. You haven't been in your second
trimester long."

"I guess," she says, stretching her back and yawning incredibly widely.

"Hey," I toss out, "we're throwing a New Year's Eve party.
You want to come?"

Her eyes go wide. "Seriously?"

"Yep. You're already on the guest list. You can, um, bring a
date if you want."

"Oh, good. I hear Drew left his other girlfriend and is back in town."

"Hey, no. That's not what I—" I toss a three-month-old copy of *Highlights* at her. She catches it easily and laughs. I'm feeling all warm and cozy when the door opens. When I look up, my jaw drops. It's David Gray.

"H-how did you know I was going to be here?"

"I didn't." He gives me a wry smile.

"O-oh." My face warms.

"My sister's an ICU nurse. I brought her some lunch. I saw you through the glass—that's why I opened the door. Everything okay?" He raises his eyebrows, and I can't help but think how sweet he is to be concerned.

Isn't that sweet?

"Huh? Oh, my dad had surgery this morning."

He sits next to me on the love seat. "Heart surgery?"

I nod.

His chin lifts in a nod. "How is he?"

"They won't let anyone but my mom into his room until he's more stable."

"I see. Well, sometimes that's the way it is. I'll pray for him."

My attention grabs onto the word "pray."

"Thank you, David. I—" I wave toward Shelly. "We appreciate it."

"Yes, we do." Shelly steps forward and extends her pudgy hand. "I'm Shelly, Tabby's sister."

His gaze wanders to her slightly protruding stomach and tenderness washes over his expression. "It's nice to meet you, Shelly."

"How do you two know each other?" Shelly asks. The girl is as obvious as a pair of candy apple red stilettos.

"David's twins play Felicia's kids on the set."

Her face goes all know-it-all. "I see." She glances around. "Is your wife with you, David?"

Oh, Lord. I'm going to kill her. But David seems to be taking it all in good-natured stride.

"I'm afraid my wife passed away more than a year ago."

Shelly's eyes go wide. Serves her right. "I-I . . ."

David spares her the embarrassment. "We were separated for several years before her death."

The question looms in the air, but I know better than to ask, and Shelly seems to have learned her lesson.

He smiles softly, as though anticipating the fact that I'm dying to ask. "She wouldn't divorce me. I'm not sure if it was my money or my charm. But I'll give her the benefit of the doubt."

"Oh."

He glances at his watch, and believe me, I don't blame him. "It's about time to pick up the kids from a birthday party, so I'd better go."

"Nice to meet you, David," Shelly says, smiling in her award-winning, Julia Roberts kind of way.

He winks at her and grins. "Nice to meet you too." Then he turns his attention toward me. "Tell your friends thanks for the invitation, and I'll see you New Year's Eve."

"What do you mean you'll see me New Year's Eve?"

"What do you mean, what do I mean? They didn't tell you they'd invited me?"

"I, um, haven't had time to check the guest list because of," I wave toward to door, "you know, Christmas and then the surgery and all. It's been pretty hectic, and I haven't been home a lot."

Which of my traitor friends is trying to steal this guy out

from under my nose? Hmm? I want to ask him which one invited him, but my pride won't allow it, besides I see . . . *Brian*? Staring through the glass window on the door. Horror of horrors. Why is Brian here?

David turns as the door opens. "Hi, sugar," Brian says, eyeing David as he enters the waiting area. "Sorry I couldn't make it this morning." He kisses me full on the lips. Okay, I'm going to slug this freak. I have to fight not to wipe off his lousy kiss with the back of my hand.

"How did you know I was here, Brian?"

I feel David's gaze on me, and it's taking every ounce of willpower not to flat-out say, "This creep is not my boyfriend." But of course that wouldn't be nice, and I'm nothing if not nice.

"I talked to your mom earlier."

Figures.

"Are you going to introduce us?" Brian asks, putting his arm around my shoulders and pulling me tight against him. The show of testosterone is truly annoying, and . . . ouch! Ease up on the grip, buddy.

"Brian, David." The total lack of enthusiasm in my tone is truly uninspired. "David, Brian."

They shake hands in that macho squeeze-the-blood-out-of-my-hand kind of way.

"Excuse me," Shelly says in a way that eases the tension a little. "I'll be back in a few minutes."

Poor Shelly. The baby must be sitting right on top of her bladder.

"Oh! Hon," Brian says.

Hon? Since when? I thought I was "sugar."

"Yeah?"

"Can you spot me a ten for the cab? I was in such a hurry to get here, I forgot to grab my wallet."

Okay, this is getting old. Brian must be delusional. Still, I can't very well shoot him down right here in front of another guy. That would be mean. But just as soon as we're alone . . .

I head for my purse. "Um, all I have is a twenty."

He snatches it out of my hand and kisses my cheek. "Thanks, hon. Be right back."

"That was . . . He's not . . ." I can't even say it. Because I know it will sound lame.

David's eyes shine down with kindness that reminds me of Dad. For some unexplained reason, tears well up and my nose starts to burn.

"Hey, are you okay?"

David reaches out and thumbs away a tear from my cheek. Just like Rudolph did for Felicia when she was crying because she wanted so badly to remember the love they once shared. How can the motion be the same, but the emotions welling up inside of me be so different? "What's wrong?" David asks.

"I just really want to see my dad."

"Hang on. I'll be right back."

"What are you going to do?"

"You'll see."

A grin tips his mouth, and he sends me a wink before disappearing through the door. A minute later, he's back with the pretty redheaded nurse I remember seeing earlier.

"Vanessa, this is—"

"I know, Davy," the young woman cuts in. She stretches out her hand, and the smile definitely reaches her eyes. "The mother of your children."

I suck in a cool, quick breath. Is she clairvoyant? Prophetic? Does she know something I don't know? Has David talked about me? Reality check. Duh, Tabby. She means—Felicia. Just in time, I save myself a year's worth of embarrassment. Two reality checks actually. The first one is of course the reference to the fictional family of Felicia, Rudy, and their twins. The second one is not quite as easy to forget. David Gray is the real father to those two. Might as well put all these butterflies in the stomach behind me. Because it is not going to happen between David and me. Never, ever.

"That's me. Mother of twins." I accept her handshake. "It's nice to meet you, Vanessa."

"Same here! All the nurses have been dying to come in and ask if you're Tabitha Brockman, but we didn't want to bother you."

Ah, so David's sister is a fan. How sweet is that, that he wants to make her happy? Although from my perspective, he could be considered a little insensitive with my dad, you know . . . still unconscious and all. To be honest, I'm kind of relieved to discover David's not as perfect as he seems. It makes the fact that he's off-limits to me much easier to take.

Still, that's not Vanessa's fault. "You can call me Tabby."

Her face lights up like I just told her she's the next contestant on *The Price Is Right*.

"Call me Nessie!"

I can't help but respond to this display of genuine friendliness. "Nice to meet you, Nessie."

"We're all so glad *Legacy of Life* brought Felicia back."

"So am I." She has no idea. Believe me.

"Well, come with me, Tabby. I'm going to take you in to see your dad."

I whip my gaze to David. "Oh!"

He gives me a puzzled look. "You thought I was bringing my sister in here as a fan?"

I realize my mistake as soon as his eyes meet mine. "Nuh, uh."

"Yes you did."

"Of course I didn't think you brought your sister in here for an autograph when you know how worried I am about my dad. That would make you a big jerk."

His brow goes up. But I change the subject quickly. "So, Nessie. How's Dad doing?"

Nessie clears her throat. "He's been awake for a while now. I think maybe your mom could use a little break. And I'm sure you could use the reassurance that he's doing well."

"Is that okay? I don't want to get you into trouble."

She turns and laughs. "I asked the head nurse if Tabitha Brockman could please go see her dad, and she practically swallowed her dentures. I could tell she wanted to pull rank and come tell you herself, but I mentioned that you're personal friends with my brother and she backed off."

"Yes, that's the way it is," I say. "Best buds. That's David and me."

I glance at David, and I can't quite decipher his expression. He walks behind me, and I hear him whisper over my shoulder, "I can't believe you thought I was bringing my sister for an autograph."

Before I can form a retort, my eyes land on Brian as he turns down another hall that will lead him back to the waiting room we've just come from. Okay, I do not need him to see me and bother me again. I stop short to give him a few steps' leeway. My body jars from behind as David runs into me and grabs me around the waist to steady us both.

I turn my gaze away and resume my trek down the hall after Vanessa before Brian catches sight of me.

"You okay?" David asks.

"Yeah, you didn't hurt me," I murmur. "Sorry I stopped in the middle of the hall."

"It's all right. So . . . your boyfriend . . . Why are you ducking him?"

Okay, this would be the perfect time to fess up. To get myself off the hook. But I'm conscious of David's sister within earshot, not to mention the stares and whispers coming from the nurses.

"Here we are," Nessie announces outside a curtained room. She glances at David. "You can't go in."

"I know. I have to get back to the kids anyway."

I reach out and touch his arm and immediately regret my impulsive action. Why do I always have to be so touchy-feely?

He doesn't seem to mind, and for an instant I think I see something flash in those movie-star eyes. My stomach trips over itself. "I just want to thank you for this."

He gives the hint of a smile. "Anytime."

And somehow, I believe he means exactly what he says.

Tubes and wires poke out of my dad, and I swallow hard to keep from crying out when I walk in. He looks so frail and helpless. Mom gives me a small, tired smile.

"How is he?" I whisper.

"Doing well, according to the doctor."

Dad's eyes open. "You don't have to whisper. I'm awake."

"How are you feeling?" I ask, taking his hand.

He raises my hand to his lips and presses a dry kiss to my fingers. "Better, now that I see your face."

"I've been praying," I say because I can't think of anything else.

"I know. I could feel those prayers."

Vanessa enters. "We're going to take him upstairs to a room now."

"Are you sure he's well enough to leave ICU?" Mom asks. "He looks pretty weak to me."

Nessie's smile is both firm and kind. "Yes, ma'am. The doctor has released him to go upstairs, so we'll be moving him. He's stronger than you think. As a matter of fact, he'll be up walking and taking an assisted shower tomorrow."

Mom opens her mouth like she's going to argue again so I pop forward and put my hand on her arm. "We'll leave and let you get him ready to move. Where should we wait?"

"I think your mother could use something to eat and maybe a cup of coffee," Nessie suggests. "By the time you're done, he should be all settled into his new room."

How adorable is she?

"I am not leaving my husband's side," Mom says. "Now you can just—"

Who knows what she was going to say? Dad breaks in weakly. "Martha, honey. Let the nurses do their job. It would make me feel a lot better knowing you're getting some strength up. I'll need you later."

Mom hesitates and, not for the first time, I marvel at the way Dad handles her so deftly. Sure, Mom's the dominant one of the two, but when it matters, Dad can hold his own.

"Come on, Ma. Shelly could probably use some food too. She wasn't feeling that well earlier."

Mom immediately perks up. "All right. Frank, honey, I need to go tend to our girl. I'll be up to check on you after I make sure she's taking care of herself."

Good ol' Mom. Give her someone to hover over and she's happy as a clam.

I kiss my dad on the cheek. "I'll be around too, Dad. Get some rest."

"Make sure your mother doesn't wear herself out. You know how she is."

"Yeah, I know."

Brian's hopeful face greets us as soon as we step out of the room. How did I forget he was here? Shelly's standing next to him scowling at me like I've done something wrong. I mean, so I didn't wait around for them when I had the chance to see Dad. Big deal. Get over it.

"Well, hello, Brian," Mom says and my defenses shoot up like a force field around the starship *Enterprise*. "How nice of you to come support Tabitha during this time."

"I couldn't stay away," he beams, keeping his gaze on my face. "My girl needed me."

He often can't stay away. If only he *could*. And . . . his girl? Since when? What is this guy's deal?

"Brian . . ."

I'm about to tell him to take a hike when Mom places her hand on my arm. I turn to her, and her eyes glow with warning. I know, I know. There's never any excuse for rudeness. But gee whiz. I'd like to push this guy off a bridge. Of course, knowing him, he'd swim to shore and thank me for the cooling off.

I figure I can put up with him for a little while longer, but as soon as we're alone, I'm definitely ending it once and for all.

"Brian and I were just talking about the New Year's Eve party," Shelly says, giving me a pointed glare. "But I guess you haven't gotten around to telling the guy you're dating about it."

Uh, maybe there's a reason for that, the little brat. She hasn't changed one bit since childhood. I mean . . . except for being pregnant.

"Don't worry," Brian says, and I can hear a little bit of hesitance in his voice. My heart lifts. Maybe . . . just maybe this is finally the moment he gets the picture that I do not want to go out with him.

But then Mom pipes in. "Of course it must have slipped Tabitha's mind. She's been so busy lately with that soap opera of hers." Without another word she starts down the hall toward the cafeteria.

Shelly waddles forward to follow Mom as I stand helplessly by with Brian's arm weighing a ton on my shoulders. My sister gives him her million-dollar smile. "Great. I'll see you there, Brian."

I stare slack-jawed at Shelly because I cannot believe she's just invited Brian to *my* New Year's Eve party.

Brian's beaming in my direction. "Sounds like a blast, hon."

Okay, enough with the "hon" already. And why aren't you looking at my sister? She's the one that invited you, dipstick.

And then I get it. As I take in Shelly's expression, I realize the girl has a crush on Brian. And I'm thinking this might actually be a good thing. I just need to shift Brian's attention from me to Shelly. I mean, he's an okay guy—just not for me. And Shelly's never been all that picky where guys are concerned anyway. Maybe this is God's solution to my problem.

Well, I doubt he'd give my pregnant sister a crush just to bail me out of a case of unwanted attention. But all things work together . . . right?

11

Eight o'clock on New Year's Eve rolls around much faster than I'm prepared for, considering I just got back from helping Mom get Dad settled into his bed at home. To top it off, I just heard from Brian. His assistant manager called in sick with a 102-degree fever, and Brian has to work tonight. My little plan to make him look twice at Shelly will have to wait. And after I snagged a great little black "maternity" dress from the wardrobe room at work for her to wear.

I can tell Shelly's disappointed, but she's covering it well and is being sweet and charming to my roommates, who both think she's a lot of fun. I deck out in my own new little black dress, which I'm still calling "little," even though so far I can't force my body below a six. Could be the late-night fridge raids, but I'm not admitting to anything until I hit a size eight and need an intervention. Freddie is certain I'm cheating on the food program he's put me on anyway. And really, I'm not sure the amount of calories I'm on can be considered a "food" program at all. More like a deprivation program. I think the terrorists actually use his program when they're trying to get military secrets out of their prisoners.

And okay, I do cheat. I don't wimp out on the exercise, but come on—I need to eat. Especially with all those workouts. What am I supposed to eat? Four calories a day after working out for two hours? That's just wrong. Mean, really. And Freddie can just lump it. My fans loved me at size six three years ago, and they'll love me again at the same size. I've just decided it's not worth the ache in the pit of my stomach to lose another ten pounds that by all the charts I don't even need to lose. Hollywood can go suck an egg. (Only of course they won't do that because there are too many calories and five whole grams of fat per serving.)

By eight fifteen, the place is buzzing with our guests, but David Gray hasn't shown up. I figure he won't. But then, why do I care? I am *not* planning to make sure I'm near David at midnight. I wouldn't kiss him if my life depended on it.

Okay, that's not exactly true. I might be tempted to give David the mildest of pecks on the cheek. But even if it were on the lips, it would be brief. Well, unless he grabs me and deepens the kiss while I'm too surprised to resist. By then it will be too late. Thank goodness for the distraction of needing more Ritz crackers and canned cheese from the kitchen.

I stand in the doorway between the kitchen and living room watching my friends rally around my life-of-the-party sister and celebrate the upcoming new year, and I feel an incredible emptiness. I think I'll just go to my room and read a book. Or maybe study my lines for next week when I go back to work.

I'm headed that way when the doorbell rings, stopping me in my tracks. Laini sends me a wink and opens the door. David's eyes fall on me. I see the slow rise and fall of his chest as he breathes in and out. What was I planning to do? Well, whatever it was, seeing David standing in my doorway put a stop to that. I look at my watch. Not even nine yet. Three more hours before the ball drops. And you can bet I'll be standing right next to Dreamy David when the clock strikes twelve.

Okay, I have to get away from David right now! Someone get me out of here. After a really great couple of hours—laughing, talking, playing *Scene It?*—we're now to the part of the evening I'd forgotten all about. The unwrapping-of-Felicia part of the party. We're going to watch my episode where Felicia's face is unwrapped and Rudy sees her again for the first time. This is horrible. Blythe told me during editing that they decided to go with the original take—"That one's more believable than the ones where you're looking at Trey."

Oh, Lord, here it is.

"Wow, Tabs," Shelly breathes. "That look on your face . . ."

"It's acting," I say quickly. "That's what I get paid for."

Dancy and Laini exchange glances and smirk. I'll kill them later, thank you very much. I've always wanted my own apartment. If I can dodge the authorities after I commit the murder, I'll be on easy street.

"I don't know," Shelly is saying. "It's almost like—oh, I know. Remember that scene in *Somewhere in Time?*"

Oh please, Lord. If you love me, don't let her bring up *Somewhere in Time.*

Too late. Laini jumps on the bandwagon. "You mean when Christopher Reeve falls in love with the photograph of Jane Seymour in the past and then when he goes back to the future, that look of adoration on her face is because he walked by?"

"Yes!" Shelly says. "That's it." She grabs the remote and rewinds. "See, she's not even looking at Rudolph. She's looking past him like she's remembering their love." She sighs and turns to me. I'd love to wring her scrawny little neck, but she's just being too sweet. "Tabs, you are truly a masterful actress. I completely forgot it was you in that scene." Okay, I forgive her.

"Thank you." I smile. "How perceptive of you to pick up on the fact that I was looking past Rudy into a memory."

And how convenient for me.

Dancy pops up from the couch. "Yeah, right," she mutters.

David snickers. I turn my glare on him, and he has the audacity to smile. Really big.

"Jerk." I start to get up, but he grabs my arm.

"Hey, don't be mad," he whispers against my ear, his breath fluffing up the loose strands of hair and tickling my neck. I shiver. He tightens his grasp on my upper arm and I lean back against him. "I'm flattered to be your inspiration."

"Okay, folks," Laini announces. "It's almost time. Get ready!"

"Ten . . ." David's index finger touches my face, turning me toward him. "Nine." He's looking deep into my eyes. I can't breathe. "Eight." Can I wait seven more seconds? "Seven." His sensuous mouth softens. "Six." I run my tongue across my lips. "Five." What did I eat? Surely no garlic or onion. "Four." David's head dips toward me. "Three." I lean closer. "Two."

"Hey, thanks for holding my spot, man." Someone grabs my arm and hauls me up from the couch.

"One." I'm standing, staring into Brian's face. "Sorry I'm late, babe." And just like that his cool lips are on mine. Brian, still in his black pants and white shirt that he wears to work, smelling of grease and steak.

I feel like hitting someone—namely my sister for spilling the beans about the party in the first place. I don't mean to be a spoilsport or anything, but gee whiz, I was this close to kissing the man of my dreams. How come all of a sudden I'm kissing

Brian instead while all around us the room is starting to fill up with the sound of "Auld Lang Syne"? I mean, can an old acquaintance really be forgotten and never brought to mind? Brian, for instance.

Is that such a bad thing to wish for?

12

arenting isn't on my list of accomplishments, I'm afraid. And no matter how hard I try, I can't seem to get it right.

"Come on, Tabby, get into the scene. You're seeing your children for the first time in three years."

"I don't remember them, Blythe," I remind the pushy director. "How can I be emotionally connected to children I don't recognize?"

"Your heart. Remember? Your heart always remembers. So there is going to be a place in Felicia's soul that reaches out to her poor motherless children. She longs to embrace them, to hear them call her mommy."

Good grief. Is she crying?

"You're an actress," she snaps. "Act like it. Everyone take five."

Oh good. A few minutes to center myself. Okay. I close my eyes and try hard to focus. Somehow I have to get into this scene.

"You don't have kids, do you?" I know it's Jennifer, one of the twins. I recognize the voice.

Centering, here. I keep my eyes closed and try to ignore my little three-and-a-half-foot intruder.

She tugs on my sleeve. "Miss Brockman?"

My eyes pop open. "What, Jenn?"

"You don't have any kids, do you?"

Okay, let's twist the knife a couple of times. I give a fake smile. "No. I don't."

"My mommy died, so I don't have a mom either."

Something squeezes my heart as I look into innocent blue eyes. I kneel down until I'm eye-to-eye with her. "I know. I'm really sorry about that."

"Only she's not going to come back like you did."

"That's very true."

"Know what I do, since I don't really remember having a mom?"

"What?" How cute is she?

"I imagine you're my real mommy. Jeffy does too. And that way we can pretend we really are yours."

A lump tightens my throat, and I swallow hard to relieve the ache. "That's so smart of you and Jeffy."

"Do you think you could pretend you have kids? Then maybe you could get the scene right." She gives me a frank stare. "Daddy said if we got done early we could go ice skating."

Okay, talk about your ruined moments. Here I was feeling all sorry for her. Humiliation burns through me. I'm being coached by a five-year-old. "Sure, Jenn. I'll work on it so you kids can get out of here."

She nods. "Good. Let's try to get it right this time."

My jaw is hanging open as I watch her sashay across the set like she owns the place and grab a donut from the table.

"Smart little thing, isn't she?"

I turn to find Sharon Blankenship watching the little girl with an amused expression on her normally harsh features. Smart wasn't the word I was rolling around, but yeah, I guess she is.

Sharon is one of those women who always have just a bit of an edge to them. Intimidating as heck—not the type you'd associate with the warm fuzzies. Next to Sharon, my mom is mother of the year.

"Yeah," I say. "She's—something—all right."

"You're scared to death of those two." She's not asking. My defenses go up.

"Scared? Don't be ridiculous."

"Listen," she says, commanding my focus. I turn and look her square in her pinched face. "I'm going to give you some advice because you've been nice to my daughter."

"I like Tonya. She does a good job with my makeup." But that doesn't mean I need coaching from not only the youngest member of the cast, but now the oldest as well.

I see just a flicker of softening. Ah, the way to her heart is through her daughter. Information that might come in handy if I had any desire to get to her heart—which I wasn't positive she possessed until this moment.

"So what's your advice to handle these scenes with the kids?"

"All right. It's obvious you're not a motherly woman."

I open my mouth to protest, but she raises her hand and I zip it.

"That wasn't an insult. I'm not known as the motherly type either. You have no personal experiences to draw from where children are concerned. So you'll have to work twice as hard in the beginning to convince your fans that you are a mother to these two children."

I feel all the fight go out of me, and I slump down on the green print sofa. "Tell me what to do."

"Isn't it obvious? You'll have to act, my dear."

How sage. "That's your advice?"

She chuckles. "Did you think there was a magic formula?

How do you think writers sit in a corner and write about romantic places and undying love?"

I give a pathetic shrug. "How should I know?"

"Don't be surly or I won't help. I can't abide ingrates."

"Sorry."

"All right. Writers draw from their imagination and become their characters. You have to do the same thing."

Isn't this the same advice little Cindy Lou Who just gave me?

"You are also going to have to do some research. Spend a few days with a family. Watch all the old reruns of *7th Heaven*. Do something to get your head in the game. You're going to blow this otherwise. And Jerry won't hesitate to kill you off again if the fans express too much discontent."

"What do they want to see?"

"A family reunited."

"This is a soap, for crying out loud. Why do people have to have kids on a soap? This isn't *7th Heaven*, for the love of Pete."

She chuckles. "You have two demographics that represent our viewers. College students who want to see young, hot bodies . . ." She waves toward the bikini set—the fresh-faced group who have all the nightclub and beach scenes. Okay, I see her point.

"What's the other?"

"Moms who sit in front of the soaps and fold their laundry. Or take a few minutes to rest and put up their feet while the babies are down for a nap. Whatever they're doing . . . they're watching you while they do it."

"Don't they watch to escape?"

"They want to escape their own lives for an hour. But soap moms don't look dowdy or fat or frazzled. Their kids don't get too dirty or bite the other kids at day care. It's the ideal family life. And you have to make these moms believe that you love your kids as much as they love theirs."

Now that sinks into my PMSing brain.

"Places!" Blythe returns with her coffee and megaphone.

"Wait. Blythe, can I speak with you?" I turn to Sharon. "Thank you. You've helped a lot. Will you excuse me?"

Sharon sends me a self-satisfied smile. "Of course."

Blythe's face is twisted in irritation. "What can I do for you, Tabby?"

"Listen. I know I'm having trouble getting into the scene with the kids."

"Yeah, you're going to have to get your head in the game," she says. "We need to film this."

"I know. I understand, really. But I need you to give me an extra day to do some research."

Her face mottles and I think she might burst a blood vessel in her brain. I'm truly concerned for her. "What do you mean? Mess up the schedule? Do you know what Jerry will do to me if I mess up the shooting schedule?"

I'm guessing not a thing. Blythe is his golden girl. She's won more daytime Emmys for directing than any daytime director in the last decade. I think he'll forgive her.

"Can you please film another scene today and let me take the twins on a sort of field trip?"

"You want to . . . ?" I think she's about to tell me to get my fanny back to the set when her expression shifts from ticked off to reflective. "You know. That might not be a bad idea." She looks across the room. "Mr. Gray. Can you come here a sec?"

My heart thrums in my chest as David strides confidently toward us. He gives me only a cursory glance and looks away. My stomach dips with disappointment. He left immediately after midnight on New Year's Eve, without even saying good-bye, and I haven't seen him in the week since. I want so much to tell him that his was the kiss I was looking forward to. But I'm pretty sure he wouldn't be too receptive to my explanation so I figure it's best to leave it alone.

"Tabby here wants to take your kids out for a play day. Is that okay with you?"

His gaze flickers to me with a puzzled frown. "Why do you want to do that?"

I'm about to open my mouth, but Blythe answers for me. "Research. She needs to wrap her head around the idea of being part of these kids' lives. She's the worst mother I've ever seen."

And she's seen every mother in the world? I couldn't possibly be the worst. Still, my cheeks go hot beneath David's scrutiny. "Yeah, I, um, need to wrap my head around being a mom. Do you mind?"

His eyes cloud over, and I think I see disappointment there. He doesn't want me to hang out with his kids? Doesn't he think I can handle it? "We're going ice skating today," he says with a nonchalant shrug. "I guess she can come with us if she wants."

I'm about to say, "Hey, don't do me any favors, bud. I'll go find another set of twins to conduct my experimental research." But Blythe pipes up like I have no say in the matter.

"Okay, great." Blythe moves her attention back to me. "Here's what we're going to do. We'll shoot the scene today. And if we need to reshoot some of your dialogue, we can do that and plug it in."

"Fine."

I spend the next two hours listening to Blythe yell at me and watching a couple of kids look at me like I'm a total moron.

I'm not in the best mood—and neither are they—by the time Blythe calls a wrap.

"Sorry, everyone," I say and head to makeup to get the scars taken off my face. Tonya's eyes are filled with compassion.

I slump into the makeup chair, afraid I'll be fired any second. "You saw that, huh?"

"Yeah. You'll get it. You're a fabulous actress."

"I'm not so sure about that." As a matter of fact, my confidence has completely fled. "The kids are more convincing than I am."

"Well, they've had a mom. You've never had kids. And you're not crazy about them, are you?"

It's not that I don't like kids. Honestly. I like kids. I just don't "get" them. I don't know how to talk baby talk. I'm pretty much a total failure when it comes to trying to relate to them. I don't know why I have such a hard time. I just do.

"All done," Tonya announces.

Freddie breezes into the room just as I'm about to beg for help for my splotchy face.

"Guess what I just heard," he says, flopping into the chair next to mine. "Good grief, Tonya—do something about her face. It looks horrible."

"Gee thanks, Freddie." I give Tonya my best pout in the mirror. "I've got plans with David and the twins. Do you think you could . . ."

She grins. "Say no more. We'll have you fixed up in a jiff."

"Okay, Freddie. What did you hear this time?" I'm amazed that I'm too weary and disheartened to be turned on by the latest juicy gossip.

"Rachel Savage caught her husband, Seth, with another woman and that's why she didn't renew her contract with *As the World Turns*. She refuses to work with him."

Ever since he missed the memo about Lucy being recast, I'm not completely convinced of Freddie's ability to head up the rumor mill with integrity and reliability anymore. But I'm willing to give him a grudging benefit of the doubt. For now.

I find it difficult to drum up enthusiasm for anyone catching a cheating husband. Seriously. The only emotion the news evokes is compassion.

Obviously, my lack of response offends Freddie to the core. "Don't tell me you're going soft on me, girlfriend. After I walked all the way over here to cheer you up."

"Sorry, Freddie. I just don't think it's ever happy news when a marriage breaks up."

He rolls his eyes and pushes to his feet with dramatic flair. "I forgot you have a new set of *morals*." The air quotes do not make him look manlier. But of course that's not what he's going for. He winks, though, and I know he forgives me. "Make sure you don't miss our workout session tomorrow." His eyes pan me. "A little too much Christmas candy?"

I stick out my tongue.

"Oh, one more thing," he says, pausing at the door. "Julie's the one who talked Jerry into recasting Rachel in the role of Lucy instead of killing her off."

"Why would she do that?"

"Why do you think?" he asks caustically. "This rivalry between you and Rachel isn't exactly a secret."

"Rivalry?" I say in an airy, and completely unbelievable, lilting tone. "That was a hundred years ago."

"That long?" He snickers. "Well, not everyone is as forgiving as you are. Julie wants to see you squirm."

"Don't be silly." But given the writing she's been doing for me, I'm not convinced of my own words. Freddie might be right.

"I think that's really nice of you not to laugh about Rachel's husband cheating on her." Tonya's voice is so quiet, I almost don't hear her.

I look up, but she's keeping her gaze firmly on my makeup. "Thank you," I say, for lack of anything better.

She goes on like I didn't speak anyway. "You know, when a woman isn't very nice, there's usually a reason. And beneath it all, she usually has a good heart."

I have a feeling she's talking about her mother. The woman's been through five marriages and has definitely not been known as the sweetest of women during her decades-long career. "I agree with you," I say softly.

"The only real friend Rachel has around here is David Gray, you know?"

"What about Julie?"

Tonya shrugs. "I don't know. Something's not right, but I can't quite put my finger on it. I used to see Rachel and her husband meet Trey and Julie on set and the four of them would go off for an evening together. But it's kind of . . . different. Julie never seemed real happy about the arrangement."

"Well, Julie's never happy with anything. Is she?" I say cattily. I know I'm being a jerk, but Julie's so mean to me I feel slightly justified.

"Maybe not. But I think she might have a good reason."

Suddenly, Tonya's generosity breaks through my cynicism. Shame nudges me. "Do you go to church, Tonya?" I ask out of the blue.

She smiles and nods. "Don't tell my mom, though. She's a die-hard agnostic. She'd kill me if she found out I'm a Christian. Mr. Gray and the twins go to my church."

"You belong to Eighth Avenue Community?"

She shakes her head. "New Wine Fellowship. Just down the road."

"I've seen it on the way to work. David goes there? But I saw him at my church a few months ago."

She nods. "They haven't gone long. He was church hunting for a while I think."

"Hmm." I guess that's all there is to say about that. But sheesh. What's wrong with my church?

"All done." Tonya's voice takes on a chipper tone, so I figure she's not in the mood to delve into her mom's issues. Which is probably just as well since I have issues of my own right now. I look at my reflection and breathe a sigh of relief. "You're a miracle worker."

A flush of pleasure creeps across her face, and she gives me a tentative smile. "Thank you."

"Well, I suppose I'd better face the children." Is it my imagination, or do I sound shaky? I'm such a coward. I walk out of the makeup room feeling a little more confident. Until I see the three of them huddled together, waiting with obvious impatience.

"Finally!" Jeffy says crossly. "Can we go now?"

My cheeks burn, and I look at the floor.

"All set?" David's soft voice commands my gaze, and my eyes meet his.

"Sure. Sorry it took so long."

He smiles. "They're kids. They haven't learned the fine art of patience. All right, then," David says. "Let's go."

"Okay. Looking forward to it." I smile my best Felicia Fontaine, and he smiles back. Ha, don't tell me I'm not an actress.

"You're dreading every second of this." He laughs, the mirth rising all the way to his incredible eyes.

"What? Don't be ridiculous."

He pats my shoulder like I'm one of his kids. "You'll be fine. I'll make sure they take it easy on you."

"That sort of defeats the purpose of trying to get the full effect."

A smirk twists his lips. "Trust me. You can't handle the full effect." He leans in closer and whispers, "Not yet, anyway."

Now what was that supposed to mean?

The kids beeline to the door and wait for David to get there. See, they're well behaved. But I'm looking forward to my solo car ride over to the skating rink. Fifteen blissful minutes all to myself to regroup and organize my thoughts. In the parking lot, I smile at David. "Okay, I'll see you over there."

In a flash, he takes my arm and steers me in the opposite direction.

"What are you doing? I have my friend's car today." I thumb point over my shoulder.

"I can't let you drive separately."

"Look, seriously. Dancy's car . . ."

He stops and takes my shoulders in his hands, meeting me eye to eye. "There's nothing more real about parenting than sharing a car ride with two hungry, tired five-year-olds."

Ominous premonition slithers through me. I think this is going to be one long night.

13

I almost feel sorry for anyone who isn't from New York. Rockefeller Center is the most magnificent place on earth. Well, except maybe Paris, or Rome. And then there's the Taj Mahal. Oh, well, you know what I mean. It's amazing and I love it.

David and the twins carry their own skates inside. "Where are yours?" Jenn asks with a haughty tone that sets my teeth on edge.

This is a test. I can tell by the way she's staring and waiting for an answer. If I say I don't have a pair of my own, she'll have no respect for me. So I say what comes to the tip of my tongue. "I, um, didn't have time to go home and get them. I'll have to rent a pair, I suppose."

"That's yucky." She wrinkles her deceptively adorable nose. And I can't really fault her, can I? Because renting skates other feet have sweat in really isn't all that appealing to me either.

Oh, here's my out. "I think you're right, Jenn. That isn't very sanitary. I suppose I'd better sit out and watch the rest of you this time." I glance at David and feign a look of regret. Now, that expression I have down pat. But why is he giving me that skeptical raised brow like he doesn't believe I'm on the level?

"What?" I say.

"Nothing." Okay, how come his look of innocence looks so real? Has he been taking acting lessons?

"I mean it. I'd skate if I'd brought my own skates." And I do have some, buried away in Mom's garage somewhere. "But I'm not going to wear rentals. Do you know how much bacteria collects in those things?"

His eyes go big. "No. How much?"

I smack him lightly on the arm. "Jerk."

He tosses back his head and laughs. It's the first time I've heard full-blown laughter from this man, and I must say, I'm charmed to my bones. "Come on," he says, motioning toward an empty bench. "The kids and I will get our skates on, and you can watch our shoes."

I make a face. "I knew I'd come in handy for something."

It takes a full fifteen minutes for David to lace up Jenn's skates, then Jeffy's, and then get his own skates on. I'm amazed at his patience while faced with the children's impatience. I watch his gentle hands as he lifts their feet and pats their thighs to let his children know when one skate is secure and he's ready for the next. I'm mesmerized by this display of tender loving care. It's so natural, as though he's acting on instinct and doesn't even have to try.

He looks up and catches me staring. I feel my cheeks warm, and he gives me a puzzled frown. I need to say something to break the tension. "I, um, you're a great dad."

Gentleness spreads over his face, and I catch my breath as his eyes trail downward to my mouth. He wants to kiss me! For saying he's a good dad. David reaches out and squeezes my hand. In the second it takes me to recover from his touch, he leans across the bench and presses warm lips to my cheek. "Thank you," he says. "That means a lot."

We look deeply into each other's eyes and something electric passes between us. Something real. A beginning, I think.

"Well, what a coincidence!"

What? Who dares to interrupt my moment with Dreamy Dad? I barely refrain from uttering a groan as Rachel Savage, accompanied by Julie Foster and Trey O'Dell and two little kids, barges right in and stands in front of me. Freddie was right! They are pals. And probably conspiring together at this moment how they might make my life at work even more miserable than it already is. I have to admit—albeit grudgingly—that Rachel is radiant in tight white pants and a white suede jacket, lined with faux fur. Her black hair is twisted into two braids falling adorably on either side of her head, giving her the appearance of a beautiful Indian princess. She turns a gorgeous, intimate smile on David. I feel sick as he bends forward and kisses her cheek in greeting—didn't he just do the same thing to me? What is this—par for the course for this guy? Does he kiss anyone who smiles at him? Suddenly I'm not feeling all that warm and fuzzy.

I clear my throat and haul myself to my feet, giving the too-beautiful-to-be-real woman a nod and trying on my best "genuine" smile. "Rachel, congratulations for landing the role of Lucy. I'm sure you'll bring a unique energy to the character."

Disbelief flashes in her dark eyes. If I didn't know better, I'd think she was about to ream me. But then she wouldn't make a scene in public. You never know who's watching.

"Thank you, dear," she gushes. "Let me introduce you to my nieces, Katie and Nellie." The girls are miniatures of their aunt and carry the same haughty expressions that don't seem to go with their angelic faces any more than it goes with Rachel's. Besides, they can't be more than eight and ten, and high and mighty attitudes on little girls are never becoming.

"Nice to meet you, girls." I give them each a smile. They don't smile back. What a surprise. "This is Jenn and that's her brother, Jeffy. They play on our show."

"We know that," Katie, the older of the two girls, says like I'm some kind of moron—which is exactly how I feel. Sheesh. I should have let David introduce his own kids.

"Girls, you remember Mr. Gray," Rachel says to her nieces. (I suppose she's speaking to them, anyway, even though her eyes are roving over David shamelessly.) "This is a pleasant surprise, running into you, David." Her voice is low and husky. What a Jezebel! I cut my gaze to David's face, but I can't tell what he's thinking. There's no way he could not be affected by her beauty and that new size two bod she's flashing around like she's God's gift to men or something. I hate to say it, but she's not acting very broken up over the end of her marriage.

Julie steps forward. "I hear you had a little trouble with today's scene, Tabby."

I see satisfaction, even challenge in her beady little eyes. Why does she have to be so mean and scary?

"That's what we're doing here," David says. "Tabby is trying to get used to being around the twins."

"Oh, it's too bad you're having such a hard time, Tabby." Rachel *sounds* and *looks* like she really means that. But come on. She's not a bit sympathetic to my plight. As a matter of fact, if I had to guess, I'd say she's gloating.

Trey snorts and speaks up in an apparent need to insert himself into a situation where he's been ignored so far. "My wife is hanging out with the father of my children."

What an idiot.

David presses his lips together in a grim line while Julie and Rachel give Trey a cursory chuckle. Julie slips her hand through his arm possessively. "Just remember who your real wife is, darling," she says, looking straight at me as though to warn me away. Good grief. Why can't she just believe that I never went after her former husband, and I'd definitely never go after this one. Even if I weren't a Christian—he gives me the creeps.

"Come on, Daddy. Let's go skate!" Jenn is tugging on David's jacket sleeve.

"Oh, good idea." Rachel turns to her nieces. "Girls, lace up and let's get going."

"We're going to take off," Trey says. He kisses Rachel on the cheek like they're all the best and oldest of friends. Julie bends and hugs her. "We'll see you on the set tomorrow."

"Tomorrow?" I can't believe she's starting so soon. "But Taylor's going away party is tomorrow."

Julie's eyes flash dislike for me. "Yes, we don't plan to have a break between days. Rachel's character is in the middle of the Felicia story line so Rachel will have to jump right into the role of Lucy." She gives me a knowing look. "But she won't have a problem with anything I've written for her. She's a real pro."

I squirm beneath the little dig. She's definitely making reference to the trouble I'm having with the twin scenes.

"Good to hear," I say, tight-lipped.

Julie's face shapes into an expression of smug satisfaction at my discomfort. "Well, we'll be seeing you, Rachel. Bye, Tabitha."

"Bye, bye." Rachel wiggles her fingers in a wave, then sits with a sexy pose. She lifts her own skates from her bag. Figures she's going to show me up in front of David and the kids. "I just love skating." She smiles up at him. David averts his gaze as she leans a little too far in her low-cut collar. "Remember when Kylie, you, and me used to skate on the river back home?"

"Yes, Kylie was a great skater." David really doesn't want to talk about this. I can tell.

But Rachel seems to need to take a little trip down memory lane. She looks up at me. "Kylie, David, and I are all from the same town in Wisconsin. They were childhood sweethearts. David the captain of the debate team, and Kylie head cheerleader. They were always an unlikely pair."

David's lips quirk up with a bit of amusement. "Kylie was always just a little out of my league."

Rachel's cheeks darken a bit. "I didn't mean . . ."

"It's okay, Rach. Our differences were the things that kept us from making a successful marriage."

"I know she loved you."

"I'm sure she did." David clears his throat and abruptly changes the subject. "Well, I'm going to take the kids out to the rink." His eyes rest on me. "You going to be okay sitting here?"

"Oh, you aren't going to skate, Tabby?" Rachel's eyes are innocently wide and shine with just a touch of delight. "But you'll miss all the fun."

This chick is clearly challenging me. I suck in a breath. There's only one thing I can do. Take her down.

And really, how hard can it be to remember how to skate? Granted I wasn't that great at it when I was a kid. But even if I'd been a young Michelle Kwan, it's been more than ten years, closer to fifteen since I had on a pair of skates. I'll be polishing the ice with my behind. I have a choice to make. Let her show me up while I sit on the sidelines or go down fighting.

Let no one say that Tabby Brockman is a coward. Swallowing hard, I stand and head to the rental booth.

"Where are you going?" David catches up to me and falls into step.

"To rent my skates, of course."

"Tabby, you don't have to prove anything," he says wryly.

"I don't know what you mean."

"Come on. Just sit and observe. There's no shame in that. We'll call it research. Which it is, remember." He stops in his tracks, as though I'm going to agree to what he's just said, but I know if I don't keep moving, I just might take the easy way out. "All right," David calls after me. "Have it your way."

"I intend to," I fling over my shoulder.

I have to stand in line five whole minutes. And five minutes in a line when Miss Rachel is doing spins around the man I . . . well, I mean the father of the children who are playing my children. I can't let her get by with it, can I?

"Size seven and a half," I tell the guy at the counter. I want to add "stat," but restrain myself.

"Fresh out."

I stare at him for a second, thinking I must have heard wrong. "What? How can you be out of size seven and a half?"

"You'd think it wouldn't be possible," he says with a shrug and a mocking grin. "But here we are, all out of that size. What are the odds?"

Smart aleck. I give him a snarly glare, and he gives me attitude. Punk. O-kay. "Do you have a seven?"

"Yeah, but I suggest going with the eight if you're determined to skate in the wrong size."

Oh, sure. My feet are going to slide all over the eights. There's no way I'd be able to stand up, let alone skate. I toss him a condescending smile. "Yeah, thanks. The seven please, *kiddo*."

He shrugs. "Suit yourself."

"Thanks, I will." Ten minutes later, I regret that decision. My feet kill me the second I lace into the foot corsets, and again, I'm faced with a choice. Go back to the arrogant rental kid and admit I've made a mistake or once again go down fighting. And so I choose B. Go down fighting. And I do. Go down that is. The second I hit the ice, I—well—hit the ice.

I try to stand up, but even hanging on to the wall, I can't seem to get a foothold. "Need some help?" Rachel's mocking tone shoots through me like a stream of acid. She comes to a graceful stop and crosses one foot over the other. Show-off.

"No thanks. Just getting my sea legs."

"Okay. Don't say I didn't offer."

"I won't." I wave her on and down I go again. She laughs and skates away. Note to self: keep two hands on the wall at all times. Also, set fire to Rachel Savage's dressing room at first possible opportunity.

"May I?" My heart skips a beat as David slides to a stop and holds out his hand. Funny how my reaction to his offer is so much different than when Rachel did it.

"Thanks. It's starting to come back to me." I take his hand, and he helps me stand, then slips his arm around my waist to steady me.

"Like riding a bike. Stay with me until you get your footing."

Be happy to, Romeo.

I think this experiment in family life is sort of a failure. Here I am, hanging onto David for dear life while Rachel buzzes by me, laughing and chatting with Jenn and Jeffy as well as her two nieces. What is she? Aunt of the year? As much as I hate to admit it, she does have a way with the younger set. I should probably keep my eye on how she relates to them and then emulate it during my scenes.

I'm starting to freak myself out.

"You okay?" David's voice breaks through my introspection.

"Sure. Why wouldn't I be?"

He clears his throat, as though weighing whether he should state the obvious, which is that Rachel is stealing my time with those kids. They were supposed to start forming a relationship with me today. Instead, they don't know I'm alive.

The phone clipped to my waistband blares the *Friends* theme. "Help me stop so I can answer that, will you?"

"Sure." His voice is filled with amusement, but I don't care. I'm just concerned with his strong arms keeping me from falling on my rear while I answer this call. He steadies me, and I reach for the phone.

"Hello?"

"Tabs?" My sister's trembling voice reaches through the phone, and I'm immediately on alert.

"Shelly, what's wrong?"

"I-I think I'm losing the baby and Mom can't leave Dad and I can't reach Mikey. Brian is taking me to the hospital. Can you please meet me there? I-I really need family with me."

"I'll be there in twenty minutes." I hang up and whip around to David. "I have to go. It's an emergency." Tears burn my eyes. "My little sister thinks she's losing her baby." God must be the one keeping me on my feet as I skate off the rink and hustle to the bench without waiting for an answer. My heart is in my throat.

David sits in front of me and starts unlacing one of my skates. I see his lips moving, and I assume it's in silent prayer. He wiggles the too-tight skate and frowns. "This is too small. Your feet must be killing you."

I nod. "They are. The guy didn't have the right size."

To his credit, he refrains from responding as he peels the other skate from my burning feet.

"Thanks."

"I'm going to round up the twins so we can take you to the hospital."

"There's no need for that, David." I touch his shoulder. "I'll take a cab. The kids haven't had nearly enough time to skate, and they deserve it after working so hard today."

He stands and apparently catches Rachel's eye because in a minute she skates off the ice, Jenn and Jeffy in tow. "What's going on?" she asks.

"There's been an emergency and Tabby has to leave. I'm driving her, so we'll need to leave too."

The twins send up a howl of protest. "You said we could eat at Rock Center Café."

"I know, Jenn," David says. "But some things can't be helped. We'll do it again soon. I promise."

"We're hungry, Daddy." Little Jeffy's voice is trembling.

"We'll drive through McDonald's as soon as we get Miss Brockman to the hospital."

"Look," Rachel says. "We're going to be here for a while, and I promised my nieces supper at Rock Center Café too. Why don't I look after Jennifer and Jeffy for you?"

David hesitates, and you can't blame him. Under any other circumstances I know he'd say thanks but no thanks. But a couple of things stand in Rachel's favor. She's a well-known day-time actress, and the kids already seem to like her really well. Darn it. Anyway, he looks at the kids, who apparently take this as a signal that they should begin to beg.

"Please, Daddy," Jenn pleads.

"It's really no trouble at all." Rachel's perfectly glossed lips curve into a smile. She reaches into her pocket and pulls out a card. "Just in case you don't have my cell phone number, it's on this. If you haven't called by the time we're ready to leave, I'll take them to my house, and you can collect them from there. Okay?"

She carries her card with her wherever she goes? Sheesh, I don't even have any business cards, let alone personal cards.

David takes it, and I see her do the "accidental" hand brush. Making a play for him at a time like this. No class.

"All right. You two be good for Miss Savage."

"They'll be fine." Rachel smiles down at the kids, and I swear she looks like she really does like them. "Won't you, kids?"

"Yep. Can we go skate some more?"

"Stay where Miss Savage can see you, and don't go to the bathroom by yourselves."

Rachel places her perfectly manicured fingers on his chest. His chest! "Please don't worry about them. You know I've been taking care of children all my life. Remember my six brothers and sisters? Four of them are younger than I am. I wouldn't take my eyes off those kids for one second."

I hate to be the one to say it, but she hasn't been paying attention to her nieces at all, and they're currently hanging out with a couple of boys who look slightly too old for them. "I think your niece is looking for you," I say.

She turns back to the ice, where the older of the men waves. "That's my cousin." She smiles, waving back. Then she turns to David. "Really, let me keep the twins for you. I honestly don't mind."

David gives her that beautiful smile of his. "Thank you." He pauses for one last look at his kids and holds out his hand to me. "Let's get you to your sister."

14

Shelly is still in the emergency waiting room when we arrive. Brian is sitting next to her, his hand wrapped around hers for support. He barely even looks at me when we rush in. Shelly glares.

"You said twenty minutes. It's been thirty. Do you know how long ten extra minutes can be when a woman is cramping?" She lets out a gasp and Brian's face goes pale as she squeezes the blood from his hand. I wait for the pain to subside.

"I'm sorry, Shelly. We were skating at Rockefeller when you called. David had to make arrangements for his kids." And it's not like I've never had cramps. But I know that's not what she's talking about.

Her eyes tear up. "I'm sorry I snapped. But they aren't calling me, and I'm afraid I'm going to lose the baby before the doctor sees me. Will you talk to someone?"

"We'll do our best, Shelly." David pulls me toward the receptionist, and I wish with all my heart I had Dancy's guts. Remembering how she bullied the nurse for me, I buck up and pretend I'm my friend.

"Excuse me, ma'am," David says. The receptionist totally ignores him.

I lean over the counter and wave my hand in her face. "Excuse me!"

Oh, no, she did not just raise a manicured nail at me.

"Ex*cuse* me," I insist.

"I will be with you in a minute," she says with a haughty tone that gets under my skin.

"No. You'll be with me now." I slap the counter. "My little sister isn't going to lose her baby while you finger through a bunch of stupid charts. There is a room full of witnesses who will be called on to testify in a lawsuit if you don't get off your behind and get my sister back to an examining table immediately."

The waiting room begins to rumble with support. "You tell her, baby." "Get that little girl to a doctor." The receptionist's face takes on a look of annoyed anxiety.

"All right. I'll see if we can get her in."

"Thank you," I say sweetly.

I walk back to my sister and take the seat on her other side since Brian's not budging from his position.

"Try to stay calm, Shell," I say even though I know darned well it's a dumb suggestion.

A few minutes later, the nurse comes out to the waiting area. "Dr. Wyman called. He wants to admit you for some tests. Someone will be down from labor and delivery soon to take you upstairs."

"Do you need me to sign anything?" Shelly asks, her voice teary. My heart aches for her. I can see that she's sick with worry. Her hand keeps covering her tummy as though willing her child to live.

The nurse shakes her head. "You're preregistered. We have all your information. But we'll need to see your insurance card."

"I—" Shelly looks down, and I feel her shame.

"Just bill her as a self pay. You have the address."

The nurse looks at Shelly as if to confirm. My sister nods.

"All right then."

I turn to David. "Listen, there's no reason for you to hang around. I can take a cab later, after I'm sure she's okay. Or have Laini or Dancy come get me. You've gone above and beyond the call of duty, and I appreciate it a lot."

"Can't Brian drive you?" he asks.

"Hmm?" The mention of Brian seems out of place. Like a weird dream. Not scary. Just not right, you know?

"Your boyfriend, Brian." David peers down at me as though trying to probe my soul. "The one taking such great care of your sister." Is it my imagination or is he a little offended for me? Would this be the appropriate time for me to tell him Brian is not my boyfriend, but rather a semi-stalking pain in the butt that my mom wants for a son-in-law? But the words won't form.

Instead, I give a wave. "Oh yeah. I'm sure Brian can take me home." I'm not going to mention that he must have brought my sister to the hospital in a cab or that the most he can do is share a cab ride with me—and probably make me pay for it anyway.

David's brow puckers, and I'm almost positive he doesn't believe me. But ever the gentleman, he nods. "All right. I guess I'll call Rachel and go take the twins off her hands."

"Good idea." Don't leave Hansel and Gretel in the wicked witch's clutches long enough for her to fatten them up and eat them for supper.

He turns to Shelly, who is still sitting with her feet propped up on a chair, waiting for someone to come and take her to labor and delivery. What is taking them so long, anyway? I stuff my irritation as David reaches out to her. "I'll be praying for you and your baby."

Relief slides across Shelly's face. She grabs his hand. "Thank you, David. Thank you so much. Please ask God to keep my baby safe."

"I will, honey." Is he sweet or what? I just want to grab him around the waist and press my cheek against his broad chest and not let go.

In the next minute a nurse's aide shows up pushing a wheelchair. "Shelly Brockman?"

Shelly drops Brian's hand and stands carefully. I see her grimace and my heart twists.

"Can I stay with her?" Brian asks.

"Are you the father?"

His face goes red. "No, ma'am."

"It's okay," Shelly says. "I'd like him to stay with me."

The nurse's aide gives a shrug. "I guess it's fine."

Brian turns his gaze to me. "D-do you mind?" The poor guy has such guilt in his eyes I feel a little sorry for him.

"Go. Be with her, Brian."

"I-I never meant for it to happen with us. She just . . . we have a lot in common and I . . . at the hospital when your dad was sick and then New Year's Eve. She . . ." He clears his throat.

"Brian. Really, it's okay. I'm glad you two are hitting it off."

David leans close. "Call me and let me take you home." I meet his eyes and my breath stops. The caring in his expression makes me feel—I don't know exactly because it's a new feeling—but I'd love to experience it every day of my life from a man who loves me. A man besides Dad, that is.

"Okay."

"Promise?"

"Yeah. I gotta go or I'll lose track of my sister." I give him a rueful smile. "And Brian."

He smiles back and hands me a business card. "You don't have my number."

Does everyone have business cards but me? I feel a blush. He knows I have no intention of playing damsel in distress. I've been taking care of myself for too long. Who needs to be treated with kid gloves?

"Thanks."

I hurry down the hallway just before the elevator doors close. "Hang on!" The nurse's aide scowls but pushes the open button so I can slip in. David watches until the doors close. The last thing I see is his thumb and pinky pressed like a phone receiver against his ear and mouth.

"Call me," he mouths.

Maybe having a man hover is nice every now and then. I glance at Brian, who is definitely hovering over my sister. As long as it's the right hoverer, I suppose it's okay.

Do you think God is punishing me?"

Shelly's question takes me aback, and I walk across the room and squeeze her hand. "Why do you say that?"

"You know, I was so angry that I got pregnant and that Drew ran off with his other girlfriend. At first, I really wanted an abortion. I mean, I honestly had no intention of carrying this baby. Even at my first doctor's appointment I was going to ask for the name of someone who would perform an abortion and use the money you gave me for prenatal care to pay for it."

"Shelly!"

"I know. It would have been terrible of me, but I was feeling so desperate and I—I hated this baby, Tabby. I felt like it was totally ruining my life."

Oh, sure—blame the baby. I can't find much sympathy.

Because if anyone ruined her life, she did it to herself. "What made you decide not to run off and get the abortion?" Am I naïve or what? It never even occurred to me that she might take the money I gave her and use it for an abortion.

"The doctor put the little machine on my stomach, and I heard the baby's heart beating. At first I thought it was mine. But Dr. Wyman said, 'Your baby's got a strong heartbeat.' When I realized that was my baby, I just didn't see it as an inconvenience anymore. I remembered that verse in the Bible about God knowing a baby before it's even formed inside the mother. And it was like God was telling me that He would take care of everything. That He loved this baby enough for both of us."

I don't usually feel jealous of my sister. I'm the one who always has the most going for her. The most friends, the most money, the most respect—the only thing she has more of than me is dates. And well, look what it got her. Which sort of brings me back to the point. Why does she get to be a mom before me? But then, what kind of mother would I be anyway? I pat my sister's hand. "That's wonderful, Shell. I'm so proud of you."

She smiles a truly happy smile. "Every time I closed my eyes, I'd hear that heartbeat in my mind and something started changing in my heart toward my baby. I truly love it now. I want this baby. So, do you?"

"Do I what? Want your baby?"

"Of course not." She rolls her eyes. "Do you think God is punishing me?"

"Why would He?"

"You know . . . because I wanted an abortion."

"Shelly, listen to me. I don't know why this is happening. And I don't know the end result. Only God does. But I find it very hard to believe that God would give you this love for your baby only to punish you with a miscarriage. I personally believe He's too gentle and loving for that."

"So you don't think I'll lose it?" She's looking at me with eyes as trusting as a toddler. Everything in me cries out to reassure her. I'm praying for the best.

"I don't know. But if you do lose the baby, I don't believe it will be a punishment from God. People lose babies every day for a million different reasons. Let's just keep praying, okay?"

She nods, her expression troubled. I know I didn't give her the answer she was hoping for. But who am I to try to predict the purposes of God? Guilt flashes through me. It's been a while since I've been to church. Since the morning after my first appearance back on *Legacy of Life*. And the longer I'm away from church, the less I want to go. I'm tempted sometimes to join some of the cast in an after-filming beer, but so far I've resisted. I don't want to be a stumbling block. But maybe being a Christian is more than not being a stumbling block. What if my purpose for returning to the show is more about being a light?

"Do you mind about Brian?" Shelly asks, drawing me from my reverie.

"What? You mean that he chose you?"

Her face flushes pink and she nods. "You didn't really like him much in that way, did you? It was more about Mom than Brian."

"Now, how come you're the only one who got that?"

"You've never had the look of a woman in love around him."

I give her a tender smile. "You do."

"Yeah, I guess I do."

"Brian seems pretty taken with you too."

She nods again. "We're trying not to move too fast, but you know, when it feels right . . ."

A nurse enters the room. "We're taking you down for your ultrasound."

Shelly grips my hand. "Stay with me, okay?"

Okay, Shelly, there's the fetus." Dr. Wyman is rubbing a gelled instrument across my sister's slightly swollen belly. "Do you want to know the baby's sex?"

Shelly looks at me for advice. I shrug, although I'm dying to know. "It's up to you."

She turns back to the doctor and nods.

"He appears fine and healthy to me. Can you see how strong that heartbeat is?"

He? Did he say he?

"Shell," I say, staring at my tiny nephew on the screen. "You're having a little boy."

Tears pour down my cheeks. A new love wells in me for this child. This baby that is linked to me by blood. And suddenly I understand how Felicia could love her children with her soul, even if her mind has forgotten.

It's nearly midnight by the time Shelly is settled back into her room. The doctor is pretty sure the cramps were simply first pregnancy stretching and pulling, but he's keeping her overnight to be sure. A blood test confirmed high HCG levels, and the ultrasound showed a healthy baby boy. I call my folks and give them the happy news. Brian's still hanging around and when the nurse lets him into Shelly's room, she lights up like the Fourth of July. He sits beside her bed and takes her hand, and I realize I'm watching the budding of a new relationship. I'm definitely not needed here. They barely notice as I say good night. I head down the hallway toward the elevators. As I approach the waiting area, movement catches my eye.

David?

"Going somewhere?"

"What are you still doing here?"

"What do you think?"

My stomach flips at the way he's looking at me. Intense and serious like I'm the only person in the world, despite the nurses moving up and down the hallway. I just wish . . . Oh, I don't know what I wish.

"How are Shelly and the baby?" he asks.

"They're both fine."

He nods. "Thank God," he says and meets my gaze head-on. "Is Brian driving you home?"

I shake my head. "He's staying with Shelly for a while."

His brow shoots upward. "And you're okay with that?"

I nod. "Brian was more my mom's dream guy for me than mine. I don't think she'll care which of her daughters ends up with him."

"Then I'm glad I stuck around."

"You left the twins with Rachel?" I hate the vision of him driving to Rachel's home, the twins asleep, and Rachel finagling him into staying at her house longer than is decent. But I didn't need to worry. David pushes the down button on the elevator. "They're with Nessie. She got off work right after we got here."

"Oh yeah. Nessie." His sister.

He nods. "They'll stay with her overnight."

I remain silent as we ride down the elevator together. I'm trying not to read more into this moment than the situation warrants. "I appreciate your thoughtfulness, David. But you know I'm an independent woman. I can get myself home."

The elevator jolts into place and the doors open. David presses his fingers to the small of my back and guides me into the lobby.

"Humor me. I like playing protector."

"I'm not acting very grateful, am I?"

"Nope. And after I waited around all this time, inhaling disinfectant and diseases just to see you safely home."

How cute is he? "I apologize, my knight. Thank you from the bottom of my heart for protecting me from the big bad cabbies who are just waiting to learn all of our secrets and report back to their superiors."

"What are you talking about?" He says it with a laugh, but sort of a bewildered laughter, if you know what I mean.

"Oh, forget it. Just a conspiracy theory of my mom's."

David opens the door to his Camry and waits while I slide into the soft (and cold, I might add) leather seat.

I lean my head against the headrest once I'm securely fastened into my seat belt. I feel a migraine coming on and my eyes close almost instantly.

I must have dozed off during the drive because the next thing I know, David is touching my shoulder. My eyes pop open. "Hey, are we there?" I ask.

"Yeah."

He exits the car and walks around to my side. On top of everything else, he's a gentleman. Only. Wait a sec. David obviously made a mistake. He didn't drive me to the studio to pick up Dancy's car. Instead we're parked alongside the curb in front of my apartment building.

I slide out of the car, frowning. "Uh, David. What about Dancy's car?"

"You were sleeping. I figured I could pick you up on the way to the studio. The kids have scenes tomorrow."

"But I have to be there at five in the morning. I know the twins don't."

"Let me worry about it. I'll get you there on time. I promise."

"Look. I can just take a cab. It's no problem."

He smiles at me and my stomach does a major cartwheel. "A promise is a promise, Tabby. Trust me. I'd feel terrible if you took a cab all that way."

"I'd feel terrible if you drove so far out of the way that early in the morning. You've really gone above and beyond the call of duty tonight. I can't thank you enough for driving me to the hospital."

Oh, he's giving me that look again. Like he wants to take me in his arms. And honestly? There's nothing I'd like better. But how complicated would things be if David and I started dating all of a sudden? And remember how awful I am with kids? He's got those twins who really don't like me very well. It just wouldn't work.

"Listen, David. I don't think it's a good idea for us to, you know . . ." I clear my throat because I'm not sure how to end the sentence.

"It's a ride to work, Tabby. Not a proposal. Not an affair." He steps closer and lowers his voice. "Not even a kiss."

"Right, I know that." My stomach is knotted into a ball of nerves. "I know it's not a-a you know . . ."

"Kiss?"

I swallow hard. I have to stop looking at his lips like I want to be kissed. Which I do. But that's beside the point. "Right. We're not animals. We can resist temptation."

His mouth curves into a wry smile, and I immediately know I've made a terrible mistake. "Sure. I'll do my best to resist the temptation."

Now I just feel stupid and full of myself. Obviously I've completely misunderstood David's actions. I have two choices. Hold my head up and walk off, saving myself from further embarrassment. Or do what he deserves and apologize. "I guess that did sound a little presumptuous. You've been very kind to me. Thank you. I'll definitely take a cab in the morning. I don't want to impose upon your generosity any more than I already have."

"Listen, Tabby—"

"No, you listen. It's okay. You don't have anything to explain. I'm the one who . . . well, never mind. Let's just leave it, okay?"

I just want to run up the stairs and hide my head under the covers and never ever see David Gray again.

As if he is reading my thoughts, he gives me a sympathetic smile.

"Okay, we'll leave it." He places a hand to the small of my back and walks me to the door like he can't wait to get rid of me. I don't blame him. Poor guy I've put him through a lot tonight. And as much as I'd like to linger on the step and delve into conversation, I decide to let him off the hook.

He opens the door for me and steps inside to the foyer, waiting while I unlock the inside door. I turn to him and shoot out my hand. "Well, good night. Thanks again."

He presses his lips into a grin and wraps his wonderful, warm hands—both of them—around mine, and I swear it feels almost like a hug. "Good night, Tabby."

I gulp past the sudden pinch in my throat. "Night," I croak out, rushing inside the door and up the stairs to my apartment. I can't help but turn and look back down the stairs. He's still standing there. Waiting to make sure I get in safe. He lifts his hand when he sees me looking, and regret hits me full in the gut. How come he didn't try to kiss me?

15

The phone chirps as I walk inside. The clock is ticking toward one a.m., so it's strange to be getting a call. What if Shelly's taken a turn for the worse? I make a dash for the phone before either of my friends wakes up.

"Hello?" I whisper.

"Tabby?"

"Brian. Is everything okay?"

"Yeah." He pauses. "I just left Shelly. She's sleeping."

"I'm glad you were there. It seemed to mean a lot to her."

"I think so. It actually meant a lot to me too."

I smile into the dark living room. Brian is definitely trying to drum up the courage to break the news to me.

"So, you seem pretty fond of Shelly," I say. Might as well help him out. After all, I'm about to get rid of him. And that can only be a good thing.

"You, uh, seem pretty fond of that David guy too." He sounds defensive, which raises my own ire.

"Well, it's not like it's anything big. I just went ice skating with David and his twins tonight. For research."

He gives a snort. "Research, huh? Does he know it was only research? Because he seemed pretty possessive."

"He did not seem possessive." Did he?

"Whatever. Anyway. I wanted to ask if you'd mind . . . I mean . . . well, Shelly and I have done a lot of talking lately."

Okay, time to let him off the hook and hang up the phone.

"Hey, Brian. I have a great idea. How about if you and I stop seeing each other and you date my sister instead?"

"Are you, uh, sure you don't mind?"

Is he serious? Come on. How many times have I tried to break up with him?

"I'm positive. Like I told you at the hospital, it's pretty obvious there's great chemistry between the two of you."

"I think so too." His voice sounds excited and tender and filled with awe. Methinks the boy is smitten. And thank God it's not with me.

"Good night, Brian. And good luck to you both."

Relief nearly overwhelms me as I hang up. A smile tugs at my lips.

"Bravo!" Dancy's voice in the dark scares me half to death. I jump and press my palm to my chest to make sure my heart is still beating. "Good grief, Dance, warn a girl, will you?"

"Sorry." She steps into the kitchen. "So how's Shelly?"

"Okay. They're keeping her overnight." I yawn in a big way and kick off my shoes. I open the fridge and pull out a gallon of one percent milk. I'm going to need warm milk tonight to kick in the body's natural relaxation mechanism. My body is tired, but my mind is buzzing. I smile, remembering the sight of Shelly's tiny little baby on the screen.

"What's that dreamy look about? David?" Dancy's got a one-track mind. I swear. She hates romance for herself, but is obsessed with my love life.

"No. Another young man."

She gives me a bored glance and takes the milk from me as I start to put it back in the fridge. "Brian? I thought you just turned him over to your sister. Did I hear wrong, or are you having second thoughts?"

"Neither." The microwave beeps, alerting me that my milk should be sufficiently warmed but not too hot.

"Well, then, did you meet a doctor?"

"I did, as a matter of fact. A sixty-year-old ob-gyn who introduced me to the new love of my life."

"You're driving me crazy. It's not like you to be so ambiguous."

"My nephew. My adorable, perfect little nephew."

Dancy practically drops the milk. "Shelly had the baby? Is it okay? How can it be okay? She's not quite five months, is she?"

"Relax. She didn't give birth. The doctor did an ultrasound, and we found out Shelly's having a boy."

"Well, for crying out loud. Why didn't you just say so in the first place? Are you trying to give me a heart attack?"

Other people might get defensive over Dancy's bossiness. But you know, I get her. She never had a smidge of control over her own life until she moved in with Laini five years ago, so she tends to want to run the roost, if you know what I mean.

"So you turned Brian over to Shelly. Does this mean you're going to go after David?"

I shrug as I notice a triple-layer chocolate cake and become completely sidetracked. It's been ages since I've given in to chocolate. "Did Laini make this?"

"Yeah. We're going to gain a ton if she doesn't get into school soon."

"No sense letting it go to waste." I grin and cut a thick slice of the dessert. That's the thing about Laini. She's going all domestic. Cooking, cleaning, and decorating. "Want one?" I ask.

"Of course."

We sit at the table.

"Has Laini told her mom about the design school yet?"

Dancy shakes her head. "I think she has a new strategy."

As if on cue, Laini shows up, yawning and raking her long fingers through her tangled mass of red curls. She frowns at us. "What are you guys doing? I heard my name."

I sip my milk to wash down the rich, buttery chocolate frosting. "Don't sound so paranoid. We're saying only the nicest things. Especially about this wonderful cake. Get a slice."

She wrinkles her nose. "I can't eat my own baking."

I swallow a huge bite. "Your loss."

"I was just telling Tabby that you have a new strategy for telling your family about switching careers. Want to let her in on it since you're up?"

Laini grabs an orange from the basket on the counter and pads over. She sits across from me and starts peeling. "I was thinking maybe you could come with me and let me introduce you to my grandma."

I don't see what one thing has to do with the other, but she's my friend so— "Sure, Laini. I'd be happy to meet your grandmother. I'll bring along some stuff from the studio. Mugs and T-shirts and stuff. I think we even have a duffle bag with the show's name and logo."

Laini sends me a sleepy smile. "Sounds good. She'll love that."

I nod, feeling pretty satisfied. I mean, what's the good of being a celebrity if you can't be there for your friends and their families in these situations? Making her grandmother's day will make my day. "Just pick a time."

"How about Sunday for dinner? Grandma invited us."

"I'll look forward to it."

Relief washes over her face, and she reaches onto the cake plate and fingers a bit of extra frosting. "Thank you, Tabby.

How are you going to bring it up?" She pops her finger into her mouth.

"Bring what up?" Mmm. This cake is so good—I think Laini might seriously need to consider opening a bakery instead of going into interior design.

"I thought you said you filled her in?" Laini's accusing tone is directed at Dancy.

"Nope, I said I was about to." Dancy smiles and slides a bite of the delectable cake into her mouth. "Mmm."

"What's going on, you two?" I demand around a delicious bite of my own. I think I'm truly becoming a compulsive over-eater. Freddie's going to kill me if I put on so much as a single solitary pound.

Laini glares at Dancy for a second, then turns to me. "My mother was just telling me yesterday that she's going to have to sell the summer cabin on the lake because she's having some financial difficulties. So I can't hit her up for the loan I planned on to help get me back into college."

I set down my fork and focus my attention on my friend. If anyone knows about the end of a dream, I do. "Do you need to borrow some money from me?"

She's shaking her head before I even get the words out of my mouth. Just as well. I'm not one of those rich movie actresses who make millions after all. But I'd give my last dime for my friends. I really would. "Are you sure?"

"My grandma has a lot of money. But she wants me following in Daddy's footsteps. He was her only son, after all. And I don't know if she'll loan me the money for design school."

"Okay. But I don't understand what you're asking me to do."

"Remember how I told you my grandma is a fan of yours?"

Hmm. A sense of dread is clutching my stomach, and I'm

almost unable to enjoy the last bite of my cake. Almost. I swallow and gulp down the rest of my milk. "Okay, Lane. Let's cut to the chase. What exactly am I going to do that will help your grandma pay for your classes?"

"Not pay for them. Just loan me the money. It's not like I'm asking for a handout."

"Right." Semantics.

"Oh my gosh. I've never seen more beating around the bush." Dancy stands and snatches the plates from the table. "Laini wants you to be the one to bring up the subject of her needing to borrow money."

"What?" I shriek. "You can't be serious. I can't bring up money to someone I've never even met. I'd be too embarrassed."

"No," Laini says. "You're right. Now that I think about it, it's not a fair request. It's not your problem at all."

"Oh, honestly." Dancy squirts dish soap into the sink and turns on the water. "Laini, I can easily help you pay for college. You know I have a trust I've never even touched. *I'll* loan you the money."

"No. No. No." Laini shoves up from her chair. "I can't borrow from my friends. I'd feel like more of a freeloader than I already do. It's Grandma, or I give up this silly dream and find an accounting job with one of Daddy's friends."

"Okay, I'll do it." I can't watch her give up her dream. Especially when the only thing holding her back is cash.

"Are you sure, Tabs?" Laini asks. "My grandma can be . . . harsh."

"Trust me, I have Sharon Blankenship eating from the palm of my hand. I can handle a little old grandma."

Okay, the very last thing I would call Laini's grandmother is a "little old grandma." She's more your Joan Collins type. Sophisticated, face- (and other parts) lifted—multiple times unless I miss my guess. But she is obviously delighted to meet me. Mrs. Calhoun's house is your basic upper-middle-class offering located on Lido Beach in Long Island. Two stories, columns out front, white siding, black shutters, well-kept lawn, all situated in a cul-de-sac with six other houses of similar style and quality. I can't help but think what a great place this would be to raise a family.

Mrs. Calhoun takes me into her arms as soon as Laini introduces us. "Darling!" she gushes. "How lovely to meet you."

I've had the entire cast sign her taupe duffle bag and when I present it to her, I think she might actually swoon.

She ushers us into a simple but lovely dining room. "We rarely use the dining room," Mrs. Calhoun confides. "Only on special occasions." She smiles a knowing smile.

"Thank you, ma'am. I'm honored."

"Now you two sit down while I go and bring in our meal."

Laini and I exchange a look and neither of us moves to take a seat. "Grandma, can we please help you?"

"Absolutely not. I can't allow a guest to set the table."

If she only knew how many tables I've set in my day. "We'd love to help. As a matter of fact, I insist."

"Well then, we'll do it together," she says, obviously making a huge concession. "Since you two insist." She pats Laini's cheek as she passes by. The gesture strikes at my heart. I miss Dad. I haven't been home since Shelly's hospital visit, although I've spoken with Dad every day.

I was going to take Shelly home from the hospital, but Brian did the honors and my services weren't needed. I'm starting to think that guy's around to stay. I mean, you never know, but his persistence is definitely giving me reason to hope. That persistence directed at the right woman is cute and endearing, rather than creepy and annoying, as it was when it was directed at me.

Mom's thrilled and doesn't seem to remember pushing Brian at me at all. She's acting like this relationship between Shelly and Brian was all her idea in the first place. Mom's definitely the queen of denial. Same guy, different daughter, Ma. Oh well. Other than the fact that now I have no one adoring me—and by the way, he never did give me the Christmas present he promised—I'm thrilled with the new arrangement.

We accompany Laini's grandma into the kitchen and carry back stuffed cabbages, salad, and potatoes, which Laini confides have been mashed with a blend of real butter and cream cheese.

"This smells wonderful," I say.

"Good, you need to eat," Mrs. Calhoun says. "You're much too thin."

"I have to be thin," I explain. "It's the nature of the business. They want me to lose another ten pounds, but so far I can't seem to stop eating great food like this."

She waves her hand in dismissal. "Nonsense. You stick to your guns and be a healthy girl. No one has a right to risk your health to force you to look like all those other sickly girls."

Laini's fighting back a grin; I can tell. And truthfully, I'm fighting it a little myself. I mean, this woman is talking about *me* giving in to pressure from the film and television industry? Hello? Miss Nighttime-soap-opera-heroine-from-the-eighties-look-alike. Okay, that was a mouthful, but you get my point.

Anyway, the meal is delicious. And afterward, Mrs. Calhoun brings in coffee. This is where I decide it's time to bring up the subject. "I really love what you've done to this room," I say, not so subtly.

"This?" Mrs. Calhoun looks around with a keen eye. "It's rather outdated. I'm considering a remodeling project, but I'm not sure I have the energy to mess with it."

I couldn't have set that one up better if I'd known she was looking to remodel. Sometimes things just work out the way they're supposed to. Laini nudges me with her pointed black boots under the table. I'm not sure if she's saying "shut up" or "get on with it." So I'm going for it.

"You know, Laini here has quite an eye for interior design. You should see what she's done to our apartment. Truly made it a unique blend of the three of our tastes. Well, actually, Dancy and I really don't have any taste when it comes to decorating, but your granddaughter, she's just marvelous."

Mrs. Calhoun frowns a little like she isn't sure what I'm getting at. "Well of course my granddaughter has a remarkable eye—for an amateur, that is. But of course I'll hire a professional interior designer if I decide to make a change."

"Oh, I agree one hundred percent, ma'am," I say. "But Laini is planning to go back to school for design, so maybe if you hold off for a couple of years, you'll have your very own private designer right in the family."

Laini is just sitting there like a slug, not moving, not saying anything, looking like she hopes no one speaks directly to her. Sheesh. Come on, Laini!

"Laini?" Mrs. Calhoun levels a gaze at her granddaughter. "What does this mean? Are you giving up accounting?"

Shifting in her seat, Laini clears her throat and slowly meets her grandmother's demanding gaze. "I'd like to."

"I see. And what do you think your daddy would say about that?"

Now that is just manipulation at its best. My mind conjures a combination of outrage and admiration.

"I-I don't know, Grandma."

Laini, Laini, Laini. How come I never knew she was this controlled by her need to please? I'm just about to open my mouth and save the day when Dear Old Grandma breaks into a wrinkle-free smile. (I'm pretty sure it's a smile, anyway.)

"I'll tell you exactly what he'd say, my dear." Okay, this could go either way. I watch, reserving judgment. "He'd say, 'It's about time my daughter decided to live her own life and stop allowing her mother to guilt her into a field she hates.' Your father would never have wanted you to follow in his footsteps if he knew you didn't want to."

Yeah, I gotta say, I didn't exactly see that coming. Apparently, Laini didn't either because her eyes flood with tears and laughter erupts at the same time. I've seen this sort of clashing of emotions in the movies, but truly never in real life.

"Now," Grandma says, over the brim of her china cup. "How are you planning to make this transition? Do you need some money to tide you over?"

And there you have it. Smooth as butter. When we walk away from Grandma's house two hours later, Laini has a check in hand, Grandma's blessing in her heart, and peace of mind that she's finally able to pursue her dream. I glance at my watch. Just enough time to make it back home, change my clothes, and get a cab over to Sunday night services at Tonya's church. This day just gets better and better.

Okay, I'm not attending New Wine Fellowship in a blatant attempt to see David. Tonya invited me because the drama team is performing a play she scripted. And that is the only reason I'm here. Except I do sort of wonder if David's going to show up.

The sanctuary is much smaller than the one at Eighth Street Community, but it's packed a lot tighter. The atmosphere is trendy, and I'm almost positive I passed a coffee shop on the way down the hall. A coffee shop in a church. Mom would freak. But it works for me.

Tonya seems in her element here. Not only has she written the script, but she's directing the play as well. She is absolutely glowing when she approaches me leading a pleasant-looking brunette wearing a stylish Anne Klein dress.

"Tabby, this is Greta Leonard, my pastor's wife."

Warmth exudes from every inch of the petite thirtysome-thing woman. "Tabitha Brockman. It's nice to have you visit." She winks. "I hope you won't watch tonight's performance with a critical eye. Our drama team members aren't professionals."

She knows who I am and is still smiling at me? I laugh. "Believe me, I'm in no position to critique anyone's performance. I'm looking forward to seeing Tonya's creation."

Greta turns a fond gaze on Tonya. "We've been wanting to start a drama team for two years. She's a real answer to prayer."

Tonya blushes under the praise. "I, um, have to get back to the team and make sure everyone's ready."

We watch her walk away, and Greta smiles after her. "If ever there was a girl who doesn't know her worth, it's that one. But God is already starting to give her confidence."

"I've noticed a change in her at work." I never realized I was seeing a new Tonya because she was growing spiritually. Raw pain shoots through my heart as I remember how I promised to do better too. To change. Only, I'm not sure I'm changing for the better.

"Tabby?"

Greta and I both turn at the sound of David's voice. My heart leaps into my throat at the sight of him walking up, with Jeffy in tow. Dressed in a black sports coat and a pair of blue jeans, he looks handsome and so appealing.

"Hello, David," Greta says. "I'm just getting to know Tabitha."

"Call me Tabby," I interject.

"Tabby, then." She smiles. "It was nice to meet you. If you'll excuse me, I need to get the music ready for the play."

I nod. "Nice to meet you too."

"We'll see each other again, I hope."

"Me too."

She leaves us standing there in the sanctuary, next to a row of chairs, and I'm a little at a loss. I suppose I should find a seat and not assume David's going to invite me to sit with him.

"What are you doing here?" David asks.

"Tonya invited me." Why? Doesn't he want me to be here?

"We've been coming here for a while. It's a great church."

I nod.

"Where's Jenn?" I ask.

"She's right here." Rachel's singsong voice confronts me, filling me with a knot of dread. "We had to make a little side trip to the ladies' room." She gives me a once-over, and only someone with a trained eye would notice how her nostrils flare in distaste at the sight of me even as her teeth flash with her oh-so-fake smile. "How nice to see you, Tabby. Is this your first time to our church?"

Our church?

I'm about to answer, but David takes the liberty. "Tonya invited Tabby to see her play."

"Oh, isn't it darling that little Tonya is finding an outlet for

her creativity? It's just too bad she can't get someone important to take notice and give her a real chance."

Without even taking a second to stop and think, I let out a
little laugh. "I can't imagine getting anymore important than
God."

David chuckles. "Tabby's got a point there. Maybe our idea
of important people isn't the same as God's."

Well said. I send him a nice little smile.

Color drains from Rachel's face, and I can see it's an effort
for her not to lash out. But she recovers and once again flashes
all that brilliantly expensive dental work. "You're so right, of
course. I just meant she could probably make a good living
writing scripts. I'm surprised Sharon hasn't tried to connect
the girl."

Okay, how come no one is supposed to know about Sharon
and Tonya being mother and daughter, and yet everyone seems
to know? At any rate, it doesn't matter. "I don't think Tonya
wants to write scripts for the industry," I say. "I think she really
wants to do makeup behind the scenes and use her writing for
ministry."

"Oh." Rachel seems a little at a loss for words. "Then I suppose that's what she should do."

The worship team has assembled, and I notice we're the few
people still standing in the sanctuary.

"I'm going to find a seat," I whisper.

"Tabby." David's hand grabs my elbow with a light touch.
"Sit with us." He pulls me along toward a row about a third of
the way from the front and nudges me ahead of him. I feel like
a schoolgirl as he takes the seat next to mine. I'm also very gratified to note that Jeffy and Jenn separate Rachel and David.

It doesn't take long for me to become enthralled in the story
of a young girl lost in the woods who has to choose which

forest animals to listen to and decide which trails to follow—
an allegory of how lost we are without Christ. I laugh, I cry,
and I applaud profusely at the end, along with the rest of the
congregation.

I turn to David as the lights go up. "Wow. That was really
something."

His eyes are bright, and I can tell he was moved by the allegory as well. "Very good."

"I suppose it was good, for a children's play." Pity forms inside of me as I slip my gaze to Rachel. She missed the entire
point.

When I turn back to David, his eyes are on my face. A soft
smile touches his lips. "I'm glad you came," he says.

"Thanks. Me too. I suppose I'll see you tomorrow at the
studio?"

He shakes his head. "I fly to Japan tomorrow to do some
consulting for a brokerage firm."

"Really? You're not taking the kids, are you?"

A frown creases his brow. "I wish I could. But they have
shooting and kindergarten. My sister is going to keep them
while I'm gone."

Makes sense. I try not to ask—really, I do. But the question
just flies out of my mouth. "How long will you be gone?" I ask,
sounding really needy. Cringe.

If he notices, he pretends not to. "It'll take about a week to
get the employees acclimated to their new software."

"I thought the Japanese had it all over us in computers."

He gives a laugh. "Tell that to Bill Gates."

"True. So . . ."

"David," Rachel interrupts before I can invite him and the
kids over for dinner when he gets back to town. "I think Jenn's

about to fall asleep standing up. We'd better get her home to bed."

We? Rachel's arm is placed very maternally around the little girl's shoulders, and Jenn's head rests against Rachel's waist. Rachel's eyes are hard when they meet mine. I get the feeling she's trying to send me a message.

David's face has gone red, and suddenly I feel like a fifth wheel on the family minivan.

16

Obviously David isn't the man I thought he was. I'm mad and disappointed. I wish I could go find a hole and crawl inside. Or maybe push him in. How can anyone be so dumb? Rachel's flittering around him like she's Tinker Bell and he's Peter Pan. And Mr. Clueless is falling for it—fairy dust and all.

Mr. McDreamy was gone for a whole week and just got back today and all he said was, "Hey, Tabby. Did you miss me?" when he walked on set with Jenn and Jeffy. But, oh, Rachel. Now he can't seem to get enough of telling her all about Japan and the sushi he ate. I'm so jealous. No I'm not. Well, maybe a little.

I grab a bear claw from the snack table and pour myself a cup of coffee—fully caffeinated.

I sense someone behind me, but I can't seem to find the energy to look up. And then she speaks. "Well?"

I sigh and turn at the sound of Sharon Blankenship's gravelly voice.

"Well what?"

"What are you going to do about her?"

"What can I do? Pierce her with an ugly arrow?"

Sharon laughs and puffs on her cigarette—which, by the way, are banned in the studio, but Sharon couldn't care less. She makes her own rules. I should be such a diva someday. Well, not a smoker, but you know.

"It's not about looks. And besides, you're just as good-looking as that piece of plastic."

I have no idea how I became this woman's project. But in a land called *Legacy of Life* where she's the queen and practically everyone hates her guts, I seem to be her only friend. "What do you mean, it's not about looks? And, by the way, thanks for the compliment."

"It's true. Look at David. Does he really seem enamored?"

I follow her gaze. Rachel is at his side, talking a mile a minute and he's nodding and smiling, but . . . well, maybe all that Japan talk isn't so much him offering the info as it is her asking one question after another.

Sharon states what I've just figured out. "He's focused on those children of his."

I nod. She's right.

"If you want that man, you're going to have to find a way to relate to those kids. David won't fall for the first pretty face or sexy body to strut in front of him. He's looking for a mother for his kids. Rachel has been trying to get his attention since long before his wife died. He's not interested. Now, you, on the other hand, *could* get his attention if you made a little effort in the right direction." Her gaze is focused on the twins.

I frown and turn to her. Outraged, really. "I don't want him. Why would you even say that? And I'm not looking to be a mother to anyone's children."

She gives a croaky little laugh and blows a puff of smoke away from me. "Don't hand me that, honey. You wear your heart on your sleeve for anyone to see. If David doesn't know you're crazy about him, he's blind as a bat."

Oh golly.

"Well, I don't know what you mean. Truly. I'm very happy

focusing on my career right now. I'm certainly not looking to be anyone's mother."

Then as if fate is smiling upon me, a stagehand interrupts our conversation to hand me a box of beautiful long-stemmed roses.

What on earth?

"How sweet." Sharon shoots me a patronizing little smile and moves away as Blythe calls for "places."

Thank you for backing out so gracefully. I know it must have been hard to see me fall for your sister. I'll always have a soft spot in my heart for you. Come to dinner with Shelly and me at my place? 7:00 tomorrow night. RSVP

Brian

Soft spot in his heart? Oy vey.

"Nice flowers." I look up from the card, and my stomach goes all jumpy as David's blue eyes bore into me. I feel my face warm, and I slide the card into my pocket.

"Thanks. They're from Brian."

"I figured."

He holds up the coffee decanter. "Need a refill?"

My heart is already racing—I don't think I need any more artificial stimulants. I shake my head. "No thanks."

"So, what's the occasion?"

"Does there have to be an occasion for a man to send flowers?"

David purses his lips as though he's thinking, then he shrugs. "I guess not."

"Well, since you're so curious." And since I have a sudden need to prove that I'm definitely not pining away over David

Gray. "He just wanted to let me know he is thinking of me and invited me to dinner tomorrow night at his place."

"I see." He nods and my radar picks up that he's not buying my story.

I clear my throat. "What's that supposed to mean?"

"What? I see?"

"Yeah." I know what he's thinking, and he'd better just watch it.

He turns to face me fully. "'I see' means just that. I see exactly what Brian's doing."

I lift my chin and give him what I hope is a really mean glare. "You do?" I mean, "No you don't."

Slowly, David sets his coffee cup on the table and clasps my shoulders with his strong hands, forcing me to stare up into his eyes. "Tabby, I meant Brian is doing whatever it takes to get you back. He's obviously realized Shelly isn't the one for him." His hands slip down my arms and he smiles. "And I don't blame him. You're a great girl."

I'm about to bite the bullet and set him straight when Blythe's yell rocks the place.

"Quiet on the set!"

Sharon Blankenship sashays onto the living room set in her role as Felicia's mother.

Next to me, David leans close, his lips against my ear. My heart thumps so hard, I'm afraid I won't hear what he's about to say. But I do. Loud and clear. "If you were mine, I wouldn't have let you get away in the first place."

My knees weaken. I turn to David to demand that he tell me exactly what that's supposed to mean, especially since for all intents and purposes it appears he's trying to build something with Rachel. Bringing her to church, going on little outings with Trey and Julie and Rachel—just the four of them like

Rachel did with Seth before their breakup. It's obvious she considers David the new fourth in their little two-by-two. But before I can ask him about his comment, Rachel tiptoes up to him and whispers something in his ear.

Figures. I focus my attention back on the scene playing out before me—the one with Sharon and the twins, not the one where Rachel is hitting on David. As soon as Blythe calls "cut," Jenn and Jeffy run to their dad and Rachel.

"You were amazing!" Rachel gushes to the kids.

I have to wonder how the heck she knows that since she was watching David the whole time and not the scene. Whatever. Regardless, she pulls it off because her praise lights Jenn's face like a Christmas tree and David's expression softens as he watches the two of them.

I can no longer deny that I have a crush on David. But neither can I deny that Rachel has a way that I'll never have with those kids of his. I head toward my dressing room, but first cast a final glance at the four of them. David, Rachel, Jennifer, and Jeffy. My heart sinks. It doesn't take a genius to recognize that they look very much like the perfect little family.

Brian's apartment is sparkly clean, and has no style whatsoever. He's in desperate need of Laini's touch. But I guess a single guy who works the hours Brian does isn't in need of a cozy place to come home to. Secretly, I think that's why a man decides to get married. At some point he real: life is empty and drab, and he wants a wo~ splash of color.

My stomach churns slightly as I step insid able draped in an apron and looking as domes look. Brian's face shines as his gaze rests on my sister. Has he finally come to the place where he's ready for some color?

"Mom and Dad aren't here yet?" I ask as I step in and start checking out the food preparations. Personally, I don't see how dad could be anywhere near ready to come out yet after only six weeks, but I suppose if the doctor says it's okay . . .

"Not yet." Shelly gives me a little happy squeeze. "Do you want something to drink?"

"Hot tea?" I ask hopefully. It's bone-chillingly cold out there, and I could use a little warm-up.

"Sure."

Brian moves in behind Shelly and taps her shoulder. "I'll get the tea. You two go into the living room so you can put up your feet for a while."

Hmm. Brian's sort of sexy when he gets all bossy and manly and overprotective. That's sweet, isn't it? Shelly blushes, obviously thinking along the same lines. She turns, and he kisses her upturned lips.

Uh, hello? Remember me? I feel compelled to step in.

"Okay, cowboy. Take it easy with my little sister."

They pull apart, without even the decency to look the least bit apologetic.

That was some quick work on Brian's part. Shelly's definitely carrying the glow of a woman in love. I have to say, all in all, these two are a good match. Good going, Mom. Right guy, wrong daughter. But it all worked out in the end, didn't it?

My folks show up a few minutes later, uncharacteristically tardy. Dad actually looks better than he has in a while. He's happy, thinner, and thoroughly enjoying the fact that Mom can't do enough for him—and she hasn't griped even once ce she walked through the door.

ou look very nice, Tabby," she says. And that's it. No "You're too thin" or "You're too fat"? Who is this woman and what has she done with my overbearing, critical mother? Hmm. This will definitely take a little investigation. And I know just where to look.

While Mom, Shelly, and Brian (who seems to be a permanent fixture at Shelly's ribs) set the table and whisper amongst themselves, I turn my attention to my dad.

"So, this new woman you're married to . . ."

Dad tosses back his head and gives me a full laugh. A happy, satisfied, gleeful laugh that makes me so happy, I laugh right along with him and the moment takes me back to our days watching Monty Python and the Three Stooges. "You've noticed, have you?"

"Kind of hard not to. She hasn't said a word about my new hairstyle." A little pixie cut I'm wild about with some great auburn highlights. But I know how Mom is about short hair on a girl.

"All right, you didn't hear this from me. But your mother feels responsible for this Brian upset."

My jaw goes slack for a sec. Then I realize he's serious. "You mean she thinks I'm heartbroken over Brian, and it's all her fault?"

He grins. "In a nutshell."

I give an incredulous shake of my head, my loopy earrings flowing with my movement. (And just as an aside, let me say that I'm glad big earrings are back. They make me feel powerful, yet feminine. Know what I mean?)

Okay, back to Mom and her silent guilt.

"Is it horrible that I'd like to milk this kindness from her for a while?"

"Yes. Honor your mother and father that it may be well with you. . . ."

Okay, father *and* mother.

"I'll talk to her." I give him a grin, feeling like a kid again under my father's amused expression. "Later."

"Dinner's ready," Shelly announces. "I guess Mike and Joy are going to be late."

"Oh," Mom says, "they're coming?" Her face pinches into a scowl. I knew the new her was too good to last for a whole evening.

"Yes. I thought you liked Joy."

"Well, I wouldn't say 'like' exactly. But . . ."

Poor Mom. It's hard to get past the tattoos, piercings, and salty flavor of her speech. But Joy is a hardworking college student and adores my brother. (They're an unlikely pair, but who's to say opposites don't attract?)

The buzzer goes off, and Brian pops up from his seat to let my brother and his girl into the apartment.

We actually have a nice dinner—filet of sole, braised carrots, and Waldorf salad. I settle back in my chair and start to relax, enjoying the fact that Brian has obviously put a lot of thought into this dinner.

After a nice dessert of German chocolate cake, Shelly pours decaf coffee in honor of Dad's no caffeine issue. She's a little nervous, and I can tell something's up by the way her gaze shifts to Brian as she sits and gives him a little nod.

Brian clears his throat and takes Shelly's hand across the table.

"We, uh, have an announcement to make."

Mom lets out a little gasp, and I think we all know what's coming.

Brian reaches deep into his jacket (yes, he's wearing a sports coat—who is this guy?) and produces a jewelry box. "I asked Shelly to marry me last week, and she said yes."

He opens the box and lovingly slips a respectable-sized diamond ring on her finger.

"Well, then . . ." My dad stands as one would expect of the bride-to-be's father and walks over to Shelly. He hugs her. "Congratulations, sweetie." He reaches out and shakes Brian's hand. "Welcome to the family."

And that part of the ceremony is over. Suddenly I feel all eyes on me. What? Oh, I guess since I'm the so-called jilted one, I have to give a convincing performance all about how happy I am. And not that they'd ever believe me, but I am genuinely happy for my sister and Brian.

I stand and approach my sister. She's radiant, but there's hesitation in her eyes. I smile, a genuine smile with no hint of performance. "Shelly, you'll make a beautiful bride, and Brian is one lucky guy." She falls into my arms like she's the one with dramatic flair. Hmm. Maybe I should get her an audition.

"So when is the big day?" Mike asks.

"Well, I'm looking into getting us a place to live right now. This apartment isn't big enough for a family. I only have a pull-out couch for a bed."

"I told him I don't mind," Shelly pipes in.

Brian's gaze slips over hers with all the tenderness of a man in love. "I know, honey, but I want us to start off right, and we have to think of the baby."

My dad nods in approval, and Mom is about to cry, I can tell. It's gratifying to see someone want to take care of Shelly after all the Mr. Wrongs that have come into her life.

"So where are you thinking about moving, Brian?" I ask.

"There's an old building getting a face-lift on York Avenue and Eighty-second Street. I'd like to put a down payment on the place so that as soon as they're ready, we can get married and move right in. But they're going really fast, so I need help convincing my darling fiancée here that it's a good idea."

"I just don't see how we can afford that," Shelly says. "I'll be going to school for the next four years and not contributing financially. We'll have baby expenses and child care. I just don't want us to get in over our heads."

"You're going to college, Shell?" My heart is so full of pride for this girl.

"Yeah. I'm going to be a teacher. Can you believe it?"

"That's great, sis." Mike gives her a "rock on" fist and Joy grins. "Hey, that's my major too. Are you going to teach high school or elementary?"

Somehow her soft voice doesn't fit the persona. Just goes to show you can't judge a book . . . you know.

"Elementary," Shelly says, her face glowing with confidence. "And I think we should live here and make do until I graduate and get a job."

Wow, I'm looking at her, but I can't believe this mature young woman is the same bratty little girl who used to terror-ize my Barbies and tag along after my friends and me until I had to sic Mom on her.

"You let me worry about that." Brian winks. "There are ad-vantages to being an only child of two only children. I get a trust fund when I marry."

Shelly's eyes grow wide. "Why didn't you tell me that before?"

"It was a surprise. We're having dinner with my parents next week when my dad flies in from Boston. They'll give me the check, and we can go put the down payment on our apart-ment. Unless you'd rather choose someplace else."

Shelly shakes her head. "The Eighty-second Street apart-ments are perfect. I couldn't ask for anything better."

Brian runs his hand over my sister's hair and smiles tenderly.

There's something about watching all this play out in front of me. My sister about to be a wife and a mother, living in a home of her own. My brother in love—with a hoodlum, yes, but in love nonetheless. Mom and Dad, holding hands and content.

Ahhh, love is in the air a mere three days before Valentine's Day. I'm so jealous.

Need I remind the Lord that we had a deal? I let Him run my life, and He makes all things beautiful in His time.

When, Lord?

17

The snow is coming down hard when we leave Brian's, so I cave in to Mom's request that I spend the night. It's not far from Brian's. I don't see how it could hurt. Besides, I'd love to talk wedding details with Shelly.

I'm almost positive the cabbie has never driven so much as a block in snow before because after about six near-collisions he looks almost sick when he slides the cab to a stop in front of Mom and Dad's place.

I fish around inside my purse looking for my cell phone and call my own apartment. Dancy picks up.

"I'm staying at my parents' tonight," I say. "The weather's pretty bad. Mom and Dad's was closer."

"Okay. David's called twice. Want me to give him your cell phone number next time?"

"David Gray?"

"How many Davids do you know?"

"Just him. What does he want?"

"I don't know. I didn't ask." She pauses. "Maybe he wants to ask you out."

"Fat chance." Still, at the mere suggestion my heart does some major flip-flops.

"Okay, give him my cell phone number next time he calls."

After I hang up, I poke my head inside Shelly's room. "Hey, can I borrow a pair of PJs?"

"Sure," she says, stifling a yawn. "Bottom drawer."

"Thanks." I pull out a heavy sweatshirt and a pair of lounge pants with a drawstring. "So . . ."

"Yeah." She stares at the diamond ring on her finger. "He really wants to marry me. Baby and all."

"I know. I'm glad."

She pulls her gaze from the ring and meets my eyes. "You really don't mind?" Okay, is this like the hundredth time or what? I'm starting to get annoyed at their sensitivity.

"Look, Shelly. Brian was never my type. He's Mom's type and apparently yours too. Be happy and don't worry about me. I couldn't be more pleased that the two of you found each other."

"Thanks. Turn off my light when you leave, okay?" She gives me a sleepy smile and closes her eyes, probably drifting to sleep amid thoughts of white lace and promises.

I call Jerry Gardner in the morning to let him know I won't be coming to work. "I got caught in the weather and ended up at my mom and dad's last night."

"It's okay. The twins have the chicken pox or some such nonsense, so we're going to shoot around Felicia's story line for the next few days. Why don't you take a couple of days?"

"You mean it?"

"Sure. Just be ready to work your tail off when you get back."

"Thanks, Jerry, I will."

Chicken pox? Those poor kids.

Shelly comes into the living room, her tummy preceding her.

"Wow, the baby has really grown in a couple of weeks, Shell."

"I've put on five pounds in fourteen days," she grumps. "I think I'm just getting fatter. I weigh nearly one hundred twenty-five pounds."

I oughtta slug her. I have to eat like a bird to maintain one hundred thirty. And she thinks she's fat at five months pregnant?

"How are you feeling these days?"

She shrugs and plops onto Dad's overstuffed recliner. "Not too bad, really."

Mom bustles into the room a few minutes later. "Coffee will be on in a jiff," she says. "I can't believe I slept so late. Must be all the excitement from last night."

Shelly and I exchange glances and follow her into the kitchen. "Anything we can do, Ma?"

"Get the bacon out of the refrigerator and mix up some pancake batter." She's flustered. This is something new. "I can't believe I slept so late," she says again.

Mom sets two cups of coffee on the table and a glass of juice for Shelly.

I pour a packet of Splenda into my cup and stir.

"Don't sit to drink that." Mom's nervousness is starting to be contagious. "I need help."

"I wasn't going to." I peel bacon slices and pop them onto the flatiron. They start to sizzle and smell wonderful almost immediately. Well, they smell wonderful to some of us. Shelly suddenly goes pale and makes a beeline for the door.

"I thought she wasn't supposed to get sick after the third month or so."

Mom gives me an indulgent smile. "I was always sick the whole nine months with you kids. Looks like Shelly takes after me." She pauses. "I've been watching you."

"Watching me?" Now I'm really nervous. Has Mom been

sitting outside my apartment with binoculars or something? I can't really see her doing it, but I wouldn't put it past her.

"On your show. I've had a lot of time at home lately with your dad recovering and all."

I'm stunned that my mom is stooping so low as to watch daytime television in general, soap operas to be specific. "So, what do you think of it?"

She smiles. "I'm starting to get into the story lines. Especially Felicia and Rudolph's of course. So tell me. When is Felicia's memory going to come back?"

"Mom! I can't tell you the show's secrets. I signed a nondisclosure form. They can sue me."

"Well, for heaven's sake. Who do you think I'm going to tell? The mailman?"

Guilt hits me and all of a sudden, I spill my guts. Nondisclosure notwithstanding, my mom trumps all legal contracts.

18

After helping with cleanup I suddenly get a brilliant idea. "Hey, want to look at old photos?"

"Really?" Dad asks. He knows that's about my least favorite thing to do, but for some reason all these changes have made me sentimental.

"Yeah, really." I grin at his "you traitor" expression because I happen to know he hates doing the picture album thing too.

"I love that idea," Shelly perks. "I'll help you get them down."

"What do you say, Ma?" I ask. "You up for a trip down memory lane?"

"Sounds like fun. You two get the albums."

A few minutes later Mom and Dad are happily telling stories around the pictures. Our baby pictures bring about a sigh from Shelly. "I wonder what my baby is going to look like."

"Beautiful like you," I say, feeling nostalgic, which is making me generous. I sling an arm around her shoulder, pulling her close for a second.

My parents look up from the photographs and smile. Both of them. As though I've done something wonderful. I guess it beats arguing, but you know, this baby is special, and since I stood next to Shelly's bedside and watched the baby on the screen, I've felt very "auntish" and much closer to my sister.

Shelly lets out a snort. "Look, Tabs. Remember this?"

I turn to the photo album and smile at a picture of Shelly, Michael, and me. All loaded down with chicken pox.

Mom shudders. "Three kids crying for calamine lotion around the clock. I needed a vacation after that."

"Hey, remember the grilled cheese sandwiches and tomato soup?" Shelly asks.

"Mmm," I reply. "And homemade chocolate chip cookies."

I can't help but laugh at the memory. "It didn't do a thing for the itching, but it made me feel better anyway."

"Yeah, me too." Shelly's eyes are misty. "I hope I can be as good a mother as you are, Mom."

I can't help but follow Shelly's gaze to my mom. Her eyes are swimming with tears, and it's obvious she's deeply moved by Shelly's words. She reaches across the table and pats the mom-to-be on her hand. "You'll be wonderful." I squirm a little—uncomfortable. I mean, do these two really need another bond?

I avert my gaze back to the pictures and remember that David's kids are suffering from chicken pox too. Is he rubbing them with calamine lotion and feeding them treats? Something squeezes my heart. Even though I was closer to my dad as a child, I can't imagine going through various childhood illnesses without Mom's brand of TLC. An idea hits me and true to my impulsive nature, I hop up from the table. "Well, folks. I think it's time for me to head back home."

"You don't want to stay for supper to find out Michael's big announcement?"

"Announcement?" I can't help the frown puckering my brow. "Who said anything about an announcement?"

"Well, why else would he make a point of coming over for dinner?"

"I don't know. Maybe he just wants a free meal."

"Hardly." She gives me a once-over. "You could use a hearty meal yourself. Don't you want to stay?"

"Thanks, Mom. But I have plans."

"Well, all right," she says with a sigh. "It's been nice having you home."

"It's been nice to be here." I'm about to say something about how much it's meant to spend time with her, but she points to a picture and looks at Shelly. "Look at your first birthday party. You were always such a little beauty." Oh well.

I definitely think it's time for me to go home. A whole day with the family is enough for an independent woman like me. Besides, seeing the chicken pox pictures reminds me that the twins are at home miserable and itching. I want to implement my idea before I chicken out.

An hour and fifteen minutes later, I'm sitting in front of Normandie Court at Third Avenue and Ninety-fifth Street, staring at the twenty-year-old high-rise apartment building in front of me. David and the twins live on the second floor.

You'd have thought I was a stalker when I called Jerry to ask for David's address. Quite frankly, he was taking the whole privacy issue a little far until I made a veiled threat that went something like: "You know, my throat is awfully scratchy (fake cough, fake cough). I think I might be coming down with strep throat, or possibly even mono or something. How long does it take to recover from strep? A week?"

He threatened to fire me, but we both know that's not going to happen. So with great reluctance, Jerry gave up David's privacy for the sake of production.

Next to me in the front passenger seat sits the nice big "get well" basket I put together. I take it in both hands and head for the door of the apartment building. The sixty-year-old doorman looks down his chiseled Roman nose and doesn't seem to believe I know someone that lives in the building. "David Gray," I say, trying without much success to control the hostility starting to rise at the snobbery. I mean, sure, he's just doing his job and that's a good thing. But he could do it with a little more personality and a little less attitude, if you want my honest opinion.

He comes back to me after a "private" phone call. "Mr. Gray is expecting you, Miss Brockman. Second floor, third door on the right."

My first instinct is to stick my nose in the air (much like his) and stomp off with all the I-told-you-so dignity I can muster, but I figure he's just doing his job, so instead, I slip him a couple of bills and thank him for his help. His eyebrows go up, especially when I take a Snickers bar from the basket and present it to him.

"What's your name?" I ask.

"Uh, Randall Shultz." He eyes the candy bar, and I know he wants to take it. I push it on him. "Go on, take it. I have plenty of goodies in here for the kids."

His face cracks into the first pleasant expression I've seen in the past ten minutes. "Now, that wasn't so hard, was it?" I ask. "A little smile here and there takes a good ten years off your face."

I swear he blushes and instead of frowning (and really, it could have gone either way after a comment like that one), he chuckles and the smile reaches his brown eyes.

"Thanks for the Snickers," he says. "I haven't had chocolate in six months."

"Oh my gosh," I say in mock horror. "Don't you know that chocolate is one of the essential food groups? Promise me you'll have some at least once per week from now on."

"Well, it appears my health depends upon it. You have my

word, miss." He nods toward the elevator. "Mr. Gray will be calling down asking why I'm holding up his pretty guest."

Now it's my turn to blush. Warmth floods my cheeks. "Okay, I can take a hint. So nice to meet you, Mr. Shultz."

He winks and suddenly looks very grandfatherly. "Call me Randy."

David is waiting at the doorway when I turn right off the elevator. He smiles broadly. "It really is you. I thought Randy might have been teasing, it took you so long to get up here."

"Sorry. Just having a little chat with your doorman about the importance of all the food groups."

He gives an odd little frown as he moves aside so I can step into his apartment. I am immediately struck by the cozy warmth of the place. To the right is a good-sized living room with a lovely gas fireplace and Ethan Allen furniture. "Nice place you have here. Real wood floors or laminate?" Okay, I did *not* just ask that. My nerves are getting the better of me. Calm down, Tabby.

A smile tugs at his lips. "Real oak. Want to tap it?"

"Not necessary." I'm trying to be cool, but my heart is about to thump out of my chest. "I believe you."

"Would you like to sit down?" he asks, motioning toward the beige sofa.

"Sure, thanks." I set the basket on the coffee table in front of the couch and sink into the cushions like an anchor in the ocean. I clear my throat, unsure what to do next.

Awkward silence.

"I, um, well, maybe I should go . . ."

"You just got here," David says, and I swear his voice is low and sort of husky, and I am having trouble concentrating on just why I came in the first place.

David nods to the basket. "So, what's this?"

"Oh, just a few things I thought might help get the twins through the next few days of itchy spots and fever." I grin. "It's tough being a kid."

He looks down at me with . . . oh, my . . . those eyes are incredible. David drops to the couch beside me. "Thanks," he says. "That's nice of you. I'm sure the kids'll appreciate it."

"Oh, well." I clear my throat. I never quite know how to react in these situations, and I can feel heat rise to my cheeks. "I-I just remember being sick when I was little."

So what do I do now? I've dropped off the basket, and he hasn't offered me anything to drink, nor has he called the kids in to look at the goodies I brought, so I guess he's waiting for me to take a hike.

I brace my hands on my knees and stand. "Well, I suppose I'd better be going," I say again.

He stands right along with me and is so close, I'm thinking about mentioning personal space, only—no. I like that he's so close I can smell his aftershave, can feel the heat of him. "Like I said, you just got here," he says softly. Man, his voice is so sexy and well . . . sexy. He reaches out and tucks a strand of hair behind my ear. I shudder.

"Cold?" he asks.

Um, actually, just the opposite. I swallow hard. "Yeah, a little I guess."

"Then stay. I'll crank up the fire. I was just about to pop into the kitchen and look for something to fix the kids for lunch." He unravels my wool scarf and slides it from around my neck. "Stay and eat with us."

"I'd love to." His obvious pleasure at my acceptance spurs me on and gives me the energy I need. "As a matter of fact, if you're game, I brought the perfect lunch for a winter day." I turn to the table and pick up the basket. "My mom fixed me grilled cheese and tomato soup when I was sick." I give a careless shrug. "I thought the twins might enjoy it too."

The expression on his face turns all mushy, and he reaches for me. His warm hands close around my arms, and he stares down at me. "Do you have any idea . . . ?"

My heart thumps in my chest. This is it. The moment I've been waiting for. The moment David declares it's me and not Rachel that he's truly interested in pursuing a relationship with.

"Daddy!"

Why? Why? Why?

Reluctantly he steps away. He smiles and points. "Kitchen's that way. I'll be right back."

I stare after him in bewildered silence. Do I have any idea . . . what? Frustrated, I head in the direction he pointed.

In the kitchen I find gorgeous stainless steel appliances and pots and pans that any cook would be delighted to play with.

I reach into my basket and pull out cheese, bread, butter, and a large can of Campbell's (is there any other kind?) tomato soup. I put four sandwiches together and set them all cooking on a flat skillet. The soup is warming in a pot. I pull matching plates and bowls from the cabinet and set the four-chair kitchen table.

David's voice startles me. "Who would ever believe that Tabitha Brockman, aka Felicia Fontaine, is actually a closet domestic goddess?"

For some reason, my stomach flip-flops at the words as well as the fact that he's standing inches from me, speaking over my shoulder. I have a couple of choices—slide away or turn around. I mean, come on. What would you do?

I turn, and his arms encircle me. "This might be a little too domestic for the kids," he whispers, his face close to mine like he's about to kiss me.

"I-I don't know what you mean," I say.

He presses a quick, warm kiss to my forehead and steps away from me. "I don't think it's a good idea for them to experience what looks like a mom, dad, and kids around the table situation."

Okay, but isn't he the one that asked me to stay for lunch? "Oh, sure. I understand. I'll just turn off the soup and leave."

He smiles. "I didn't mean for you to leave."

"You're confusing me." And starting to tick me off.

Walking across the room, he pulls a couple of TV trays from a wooden stand in the corner. "I'm going to take them lunch in bed. Then we—meaning just the two of us—can have a private lunch."

Oh.

I help him ladle soup and cut sandwiches corner to corner for the kids, and I have to admit, it does sort of feel like—you know—what he said. Like we're sort of a family. Only that's obviously not okay with him. Which actually sort of offends me. I mean, every time I turn around Rachel is playing the little missus, but a little soup and grilled cheese with me is too close for comfort? I'm confused. What's with the arms around me and the kiss on the forehead? *That's called mixed signals, bub*, I think to the back of his head as we each carry a tray, and I follow him into the kids' room. The spotted five-year-olds look miserable.

"Look who's here, guys," David says with what I perceive to be forced cheerfulness, as though he's trying to drum up enthusiasm.

"Why is she here?" Jenn asks grumpily.

"Be polite, honey. Miss Brockman brought you and Jeffy a

basket filled with things to help pass the time while you're sick."

Her blue eyes go wide with interest. "You did?" she asks.

"What'd you bring?" Jeffy pipes in.

"Part of what she brought is this lunch."

"Grilled cheese?" Jenn says.

Jeffy gives me a shy smile. He recently lost one of his bottom front teeth, and the gap glares. "I like grilled cheese."

My heart melts as I look into his spotted face, which, come to think of it, doesn't look as much like chicken pox as I remember from the photographs at Mom's. Still, I smile at the little boy. "So do I, especially when I'm not feeling well."

"Can we see what else is in the basket?" Jenn pipes up, absent the attitude she usually displays.

"That's not up to me, sweetheart," I say. Sweetheart? Where did that come from? I don't think I've ever called a child sweetheart, or any other term of endearment, in my entire life. My heart is pounding in my ears. What's wrong with me?

"Can we, Daddy?"

"Don't speak with your mouth full, Jenn," David says, tweaking the little girl's nose. "I'll tell you what. You two eat a good lunch and when you're finished, I'll let you see the basket." He looks from one to the other. "Okay?"

The twins nod. And it looks like they're not going to have much of a problem with their end of the bargain because they're digging in like a couple of troupers.

"Shall we?" David asks me, pointing toward the door.

"Sure."

As we walk back into the kitchen, David laces his fingers with mine. "You keep surprising me, Tabitha."

Enjoying the warmth of his hand and the way he said my full name, I'm afraid a sigh escapes me. Why do I have to be so transparent? "It was just a spur-of-the-moment idea," I admit, hoping against hope that my nerves don't get the best of me and make my palms sweat.

"Sometimes spur-of-the-moment ideas are the best," he says, stopping once we reach the kitchen, but not turning loose of my hand.

I can't help but laugh. "Tell my mom that little bit of news, will you? She thinks I'm the most impulsive girl in the world."

"Well, I think we need to set her straight about something." His husky tone lifts the hair on the back of my neck and sends a shiver of anticipation down my spine as he takes a step in my direction until we're very, very close.

"I'm not impulsive?"

"You're not a girl, Tabitha. You're a woman." He slips his arms around my waist, pulling me close against him until his face is mere inches from mine. "And I'm the one who's being impulsive," he whispers. His mouth barely brushes mine when the twins burst into the room.

"We're done, Daddy."

David steps back quickly, like a thief caught with the stolen jewels. "Already? Did you eat enough?"

"Yes, sir. I ate all of my sandwich, and Jeffy ate all of his soup."

Despite the fact that my lips are aching for the rest of that kiss, I can't help but smile.

"A deal's a deal," I murmur and head to the counter where my basket, minus the lunch fare, is still sitting. "Here you go, kids."

They pad across the room to the table, carrying the basket with two hands. I *have* sort of loaded it down. Coloring books and crayons, picture books—including *Itchy, Itchy Chicken Pox.*

And on a whim, I picked up the Disney movies *Mary Poppins* and *Peter Pan*.

"If they already have those movies, we can exchange them."

David shakes his head. "They don't, as a matter of fact. I've been meaning to start a Disney collection with the classics like these, but I never seem to get around to it."

David quickly confiscates the various candies before the kids can snatch them up. "We'll ration these," he informs the twins.

From my purse in the living room, I hear the sound of my phone playing the *Friends* theme.

"Excuse me a sec." I head into the living room and pick up. "Hello?"

"Hi, Tabby."

"Brian?"

"Yeah." He sounds—miserable.

"What's wrong?"

"I don't know . . . just seeing you last night . . ."

Good Lord.

"Look, there's nothing between us, Brian. Shelly really loves you, and I think you love her too."

"Then why can't I get you out of my mind?"

This is the same question I've been asking myself—and God—for months. Why can't you get me out of your mind?

"It's just cold feet. Nothing more."

"Do you, uh, think we could go somewhere for coffee and talk?"

"No way. You just have to wrap your mind around the fact that I'm not interested. Shelly is. So either date her or dump her, but leave me alone."

"Please." Sheesh, this guy doesn't take a hint. "I promise it won't take long."

"I can't, Brian. I'm at David's. His kids have the chicken pox."

"You're at that guy's house?"

"Yes. I brought the twins a basket."

"Trying to find a new boyfriend already?" Ah, so bitter.

"No, the twins are sick, remember? I just told you that. We work closely, and I care about them, that's all." Oh, why am I even trying to explain to him? If he breaks my sister's heart, I'll hurt him so bad.

"Well, I won't keep you then," he huffs.

"Come on, Brian. Don't hang up mad." Dead air. Too late.

When I turn around, David's standing there. "So that was Brian?"

"Yeah. Seems he's playing sister switch again." I roll my eyes, hoping he'll get the picture that I'm not interested in resuming anything with flip-flop boy.

"I see." He doesn't seem too inclined to pursue the matter. Darn it. I can't broach the topic of my nonrelationship with Brian without being way too obvious. "Did I hear you tell him the kids have chicken pox?"

"Oh, I'm sorry. I shouldn't have given out information without your permission."

"No, I don't mind, only . . ."

"What?"

"They have the measles."

"Oh, Jerry told me chicken pox." I laugh. "Oh well, if you've had one, you've had them all."

He frowns. "Not necessarily. Have you ever had the measles?"

I grin. "Nope. That's the one childhood illness I escaped—or so my mother tells me. And I have no reason to doubt her word."

He still doesn't smile, despite my efforts to pull some of that serious expression from his handsome face. He insists on being stoic. "Well, do you realize you've been exposed to them now?"

"Oh." I'm picturing myself covered in red spots. Then I get a grip. I mean really, I've reached almost thirty without getting them, how likely is it that I'll actually contract a childhood illness at my age? "I'm sure I'll be fine."

Then I remember . . . "Dancy said you called last night. Did you need something?" A date perhaps? No, probably not with a couple of sick children.

His lips twist into a rueful smile. "I was just going to ask you if you've had the measles. You were exposed to them at work this week."

Figures.

19

One bad thing about not having a boyfriend on Valentine's Day is that you have no date for the big night. And no man is going to ask out a woman who isn't his wife, fiancée, or girlfriend—or at least someone he'd like a long-term relationship with—for Valentine's Day, because it just sends the wrong message. So I'm resigned to another depressing Valentine's Day alone. I'm pretty bitter about things at the moment anyway. Brian is acting like he never tried to woo me back and is all hot to trot for Shelly again. I haven't had the heart to fill her in, and his silent pleading has convinced me that his call was simply a moment of weakness and now he's truly committed to my sister. But I'm watching him. One more slipup, and I'm spilling it to her.

The really bad news about today is that I woke up for the third day in a row with fever and body aches. I swear, if I have the measles, I'm going to kill Jerry for telling me the kids had chicken pox.

I drag myself out of bed and pad into the kitchen for Tylenol and a huge mug of green tea.

"You look like something the cat dragged in," Dancy says from the table, where she's looking very professional in her pinstriped pantsuit and brown glasses. She's reading the bestseller list in the *Times*.

"Thanks a lot," I grouch. "Have you seen my red T-shirt from Hollister? I can't find the dumb thing."

"You're not going to work, are you?"

I gulp down two extra-strength Tylenol. "Have to. Blythe threatened anyone who messes up the schedule this week. She's going to the Bahamas next week for her brother's wedding."

"Okay, I'll take you. You shouldn't have to take a cab in this condition."

Normally, I'd protest, but I'm feeling too miserable to consider it. "Thanks."

"Your red shirt is in my room. I was going to wear it yesterday, but decided to go with white."

Which explains where my white Gap T-shirt disappeared to.

Ninety minutes later I'm sitting in Tonya's chair, made up and looking like a soap queen should. You'd never know I'm running a fever of 101. Although my nose is running, and I'm starting to cough.

"You should go to bed, Tabby," she says, a worried frown creasing her brow. "Seriously. You're too sick to be here."

"I'll be sick and unemployed if I take off this week. You know what Blythe said."

She heaves a sigh. "At least promise me you'll lie down and rest between takes."

"I promise." Blood rushes to my head as I stand up, and I sit down before I hit the floor.

"Tabby, seriously. Go home. I'll tell Mother how sick you are."

"Don't you dare." Things are bad enough for me around here without Sharon going on one of her famous rampages on my account.

"All right. But if you're not over this flu in another day, I'm going to bat for you whether you like it or not."

"Okay, fine." I'm too sick to argue with her—whoever she is. Tonya has suddenly been replaced by this aggressive, bossy girl all ready to sic her mama on all the meanies trying to give me the runaround. It's endearing that she cares about me, but I truly need her to stay out of it. Between Rachel and Julie, I'm in enough hot water.

Thankfully, Freddie pokes his head into the makeup room. "Don't forget you're mine after shooting today."

"No way, Freddie. I'm sick." I'm not about to be bullied all over the gym when I can barely walk across the room without passing out.

"Don't be a wimp. You've missed two workouts this week already. How flabby do you want to get?"

I walk past him and roll my eyes. "Forget it. I'm going home to bed as soon as shooting is done for today. I may or may not get in a workout this week, but you can stop trying to guilt me into it because I'm not falling for it."

He shrugs. "It's your hips, butt, and thighs."

"Glad you remember."

"Believe me. Nobody else would claim them."

"Jerk."

"Wimp."

"Whatever."

I smile. He smiles. And we move on.

Tidbits of memory are supposed to be coming to Felicia this week, so we're showing a lot of flashback scenes. Thankfully, that means all I have to do for the most part is look reflective as the editing crew plugs in old clips of a younger version of Trey and me during the height of our love story. The twins are still on sick leave so we are filming around them and the scripts have been rewritten so they don't need to actually be here.

After the first scene, Blythe calls "Cut!" and I head for my dressing room to try to rest my aching head for thirty minutes until they call me again. Relief floods over me as I reach the door with my name in block letters.

"Tabby, wait."

Rachel. What does *she* want?

"What's up?" I ask, trying desperately to hide the fact that I could timber to the floor any second.

"David and I have a date for tonight, but his babysitter cancelled last minute. We were wondering if you could pinch-hit? We'd owe you big time."

Oh. My. Gosh. This is just so wrong for so many reasons and unless I'm misreading her face, she looks more than a little smug. And in my current feverish delirium, I'm seeing three of her, so I have a triple chance of recognizing the look. "Uh . . ." and that's about all I can pull out of my semiconscious brain.

"Hey, listen, if it's a problem, I'm sure we can postpone it. It's just that David was really looking forward to getting out after being stuck in the apartment with a couple of sick kids for more than a week. Know what I mean?"

Okay, does she not even notice that I'm at death's door here? But if I say no, what's that going to look like?

"I don't know, Rachel. Let me think about it."

Her eyes narrow. "Hey, you don't . . ." Eyes now go big— yeah, I'm not buying this act. "You don't have a crush on David yourself, do you? Oh Tabby, I'm so sorry. How stupid of me."

How could I not recognize *that* challenge? "What? Me? A crush? Of course not. As a matter of fact, I'm just getting out of a bad relationship, and I'm not even close to ready for dating." Okay, let that sink in, Miss I'm-still-married. She doesn't even have the grace to blush. Looks like I have no choice but to babysit. Otherwise, Rachel is going to spread it around that I have a crush on David.

"Okay, fine. What time should I be there?"

Her beautifully painted (and, I highly suspect, collagen enhanced) lips curve into a delighted smile. "Thanks so much. Be there at seven thirty, will you? Our reservations are at eight."

I wave her away. "Yeah, yeah. No problem. Now leave me be to rest for a few minutes or I'll change my mind."

"Okay, I'm going." She gives me a tight squeeze, then pulls back with a frown. "Hey, you feel hot. Are you sick?"

"I got overheated from the lights on the set."

Her eyes darken with what I'd think was concern if I didn't know better. "You aren't going to back out on us, are you?" See what I mean? Concern, yes. That her date might be ruined. Concern for my well-being? Not a chance.

"I already said I'd do it. So I'll do it." I slip into my dressing room and close the door in her face.

You agreed to do what?" Dancy's incredulous tone fills the car and slams into my aching temple.

"Not so loud," I grouse. "I have a headache."

"You deserve a headache." Florence Nightingale, Dancy isn't. "What were you thinking?"

"What else was I supposed to do?"

"Uh, how about tell her to shove it? You know as well as I do that David isn't interested in her as a date."

Dancy can afford the luxury of speculation because she's not the one involved here. "Oh, sure. Hey, and while I tell Rachel to shove it, how about you tell Jack Quinn the same thing?"

"Okay, okay," she mutters. "Point taken. Still, I hate for you to get walked all over, especially when you're sick."

I give a careless shrug. "At least the kids can't get the measles again, can they?"

"I don't think so."

The sun has set, but rush hour traffic feels like it will never subside. Horns blare and gas fumes reek as we sit, backed up at six in the evening.

"I have to be at David's at seven thirty," I mumble, my head pressed against the window.

"Where's he live?"

"Normandie Court."

"On Ninety-fifth Street?"

I nod miserably.

"That's not too far. We have time to go home and change into comfortable clothes, eat a bite, and still make it in plenty of time."

"We?"

"You don't think I'm sending you over there alone, do you?"

"You're the best! I'm so glad you didn't give up your car." I sigh, drifting off to sleep in the midst of the noises of the city all around me. Dancy's eleven-year-old BMW was a gift from her parents when she graduated high school. They'd like her to upgrade, but she won't think of it. She's on her own and trying to prove she doesn't need their money. She talks about the impracticality of owning a car in Manhattan where parking and traffic are a nightmare, and she's even considered selling it, but something always holds her back. My theory is that she isn't ready to completely cut the apron strings and that car is a connection to her folks. Laini's theory isn't quite as philosophical. She thinks Dancy just needs the freedom to get around on her own terms—even though she takes cabs or buses on most days.

Tylenol has made little headway on my aches by the time

we arrive at David's apartment at seven twenty. His eyebrows go up when he sees Dancy.

"I'm keeping Tabby company tonight," she says with poorly concealed hostility. "I hope you don't mind." And that's a challenge if I've ever seen one.

He gives her a sheepish smile. "The kids'll be thrilled to have two adults to hang out with."

David turns his attention to me, his expression stoic. "I was surprised you volunteered to do this," he says. "I hope you didn't cancel any plans. We could have gone to dinner another night."

I'm about to mention that I don't have anyone to have a date *with*, but Dancy's having none of that. "Well, that's our Tabby." Dancy slings her arm about my shoulders. "Generous to a fault. Although your girlfriend *asked* her to babysit. She didn't exactly volunteer."

He smiles. "Rachel's not my girlfriend. She's a *friend*, friend."

"Really?" Dancy asks with feigned surprise. "Does she know that?"

"I'm pretty sure she does," he drawls. "She's still married."

"Are you sure she remembers *that*?"

"Cut it out, Dancy." I give her a look and she drops the arm. I meet David's questioning gaze. "It's no problem, really. You should just go out and have fun with Rachel."

"But not too much fun, if you know what I mean," Dancy says in a teasing, slightly mocking tone. And . . . oh, brother . . . that's definitely a wink-wink.

I don't think David gets her at all. But I do. And she's really starting to get on my nerves. I mean, I know she's just being all protective of me, but still. Enough already.

The doorbell chimes before David can invite us past the foyer.

"That must be your married date," Dancy says in a knowing tone. I swear if she doesn't cut it out . . . Oh, I need to find a place to lie down or I'm going to die.

Of course, Dancy is right about who is at the door. Rachel appears, all smiles and cleavage. To his credit, David immediately averts his gaze from the black dress, covered (and I use the term loosely) with a faux fur cape that must have set Rachel back several thousand dollars and I know darned well isn't going to provide any warmth on a night like this. Her arms are bare, for crying out loud.

"Oh good," she says as she breezes into the room like she owns the place. "Tabby's on time."

Dancy bristles, but I discreetly touch her arm to keep her still.

Rachel takes in David's appearance and her silky eyebrows go up. I try not to be jealous, because really, who can blame her? Only a dead woman wouldn't appreciate the sight. He looks so great in a black Armani suit, his dark hair is slicked back and he smells . . . oh my gosh . . . way too good for that witch. Stop it. Stop it now, Tabby. But a man smelling of just a soft hint of Polo—it doesn't get any better than that.

Rachel smiles that fakey smile of hers and slips her clawed fingers through David's arm. "Shall we go? Trey and Julie are waiting in the taxi."

A double date with a guy like David—is she crazy? I wouldn't want to share his attention if I had the chance to go out with him.

"I just need to say good-bye to the kids first." David disentangles from her clutches and heads toward the hallway.

Rachel huffs. "Well, don't be long. People are waiting."

"Excuse us," Dancy says to the decked-out diva. "We'll just be going in there so my sick friend here can sit down." She points toward the living room and hauls me with her, leaving Rachel standing alone.

"That was rude," I hiss.

"So what? So is she."

For someone who's gone to charm school, Dancy doesn't display very good manners.

David and the kids show up in the living room a minute after we've settled onto the couch. It's all I can do to stay seated and not stretch out on the cushions.

"Hi, kids," Dancy says with a friendly grin.

"Who are you?" Jeffy asks, walking right up to her like he's never been told not to talk to strangers.

"She's my friend," I find the energy to say. "Do you guys mind if she hangs out with us?"

The twins hesitate and look at David.

Dancy takes matters into her own hands. "I brought cookie dough, and I'm ordering pizza. Now can I stay?"

The twins flash their matching gapped teeth, completely won over. Envy pulls at me. Dancy's such a natural at everything, it's not even fair.

David steps toward the couch and offers his hand. "Thank you for doing this."

I take his hand, and he frowns. "You're hot."

"Thanks," I mumble through glazed eyes. "So are you." Then I realize what he's saying, and my face goes even hotter. "Oh. Sorry."

He frowns down at me and takes a seat. His hand goes to my head before I can move. "You're burning up with fever. What were you thinking coming over here tonight?"

Ever on the defensive, Dancy jumps in the middle of the

conversation. "She was thinking that your girlfriend put her on a guilt trip and got her to babysit." She turns to the kids and gives them her broad smile. "But she was really happy to get to spend time with you two."

"Open your mouth," David instructs.

I do, only because I'm too miserable to say no.

"Uh-oh."

"Wh-what?"

"Sweetheart. I think you've got the measles. Fever, runny nose, white spots in your mouth."

"I thought the spots were on the skin."

"You'll have a rash in a few days, if that's what this is."

"David, honey," Rachel's singsong voice penetrates the living room. "They're waiting. Can we go?"

"Sorry." David stands and faces her. "I'm going to have to back out on you, Rachel. Tabby's too sick to watch the kids."

"What? Oh, Tabby, please. Are you sure you're not faking it so David can't go out with me?"

I'm going to kill her. If Dancy doesn't do it first. My friend clears her throat, a telltale sign she's about to tear Rachel to shreds with her extensive vocabulary.

"Yeah, she's faking a case of measles, you . . ." Thank goodness she stops.

"Measles?" I hate the amusement in Rachel's voice. "Our Tabby has measles?"

"She got 'em from us," Jeffy pipes up. "Don't worry, Miss Brockman. We know how to take care of you." He turns to Jenn. "Let's make her some tomato soup and grilled cheese."

My heart melts. Clearly I've been completely wrong about these two. "That's so sweet of you, Jeffy."

I meet David's gaze, and he's smiling at me.

"Listen," I hear myself saying. "You don't want to miss your reservations. Dancy's here with us. I'm not going to reinfect the kids so go and enjoy your evening, and I'll lie on the couch and rest while you're gone."

"No way," David says with a frown.

"Oh, David, please? Where am I going to find another date this late?" Rachel's whiny voice pipes up. "The kids are covered, Tabby will be asleep in five minutes, so let's go have our dinner with Trey and Julie."

"Rachel's right, David. I'll be okay. Besides, the kids want to fix me some grilled cheese and tomato soup. Are you going to deprive me of that?"

He hesitates. "All right. I suppose."

Rachel slips her hand through his arm once more. "Let's go, then. The meter's running."

I close my eyes and finally give in to my desperate need to lie down. A minute later a warm, fuzzy blanket covers me. My eyes hurt so I don't open them. But I feel a hand caress my head. "Sleep tight, Tabby," David whispers.

"Mmm . . ." is the most I can muster before sliding into darkness.

I'm floating through the air. I have no idea where I'm going, only that strong arms are around me and I'm being carried. Carried? I gasp and try to sit up.

"Take it easy, Tabby."

"David?"

"It's okay. I'm taking you to Dancy's car."

"I'm too heavy," I hear myself protest.

"Shh. You hardly weigh anything at all."

I snuggle back against his chest because it feels good to be taken care of. This moment is so surreal, I'm almost positive I'm dreaming.

"David?" I whisper through the dreamy fog.

"Hmm?"

"You're too nice for Rachel. Don't go out with her anymore, okay?"

His chest beneath my fever-ravaged head rumbles, and I wonder if he's laughing.

"Laugh if you want," I hear Dancy say. "But she's right, you know." Dancy? When did she enter my dream?

"Rachel doesn't mean to be so insensitive. She's going through a lot right now."

"Yeah, sure she is," Dancy says as I feel myself being lowered into Dancy's passenger seat. Hmm. I guess I'm not dreaming after all. Which means David just defended Rachel.

Which would be a real bummer if I weren't going to die anyway.

20

The next three days are a blur of coughing, fever, runny nose, and pain in my eyes, followed by a few more days of measles rashes—a total of ten days in all. My mother insists on being at my side and has made up a bed on the living room sofa. Thank goodness she's going home today. We've turned something of a corner in our relationship, but being cooped up with a mom for more than a week is just more than anyone should have to endure.

Blythe is fit to be tied that her filming schedule is off. But a note from my doctor is keeping me out of hot water. I mean, is it my fault I have the measles?

They've written my story line out of the show for a couple of weeks. Passing reference has been made to Felicia's desperate need to get out of town and process all the memories that are beginning to surface. How convenient for me?

But I can't lose the memory of Rachel's possessive hold on David's arm as they left for their dumb ol' date on Valentine's Day. I guess they must really be an item if he took her out on the most romantic day of the year. At any rate, he certainly didn't ask me out. Darn it.

He has, however, called me almost every day during my bout with the measles. Our conversations range from quick, "How are you feeling today?" calls to hour-long getting to know you conversations. I'm starting to think David might actually be interested after all.

"Well, I'm off now," Mom announces as I'm finishing up my breakfast. I've been so ill, I think I've actually gotten down to my size four. A tight size four, but still . . . Freddie will be proud.

"Want me to ride over in the cab with you? I know how you hate to take cabs alone."

"No. You take today to rest." She kisses me on the cheek. "I'll manage just fine."

"Thanks for everything," I say, because even though I'm relieved she's going home, she really did come through in a pinch. And when I thought I was dying for a few miserable days, I was extremely glad to be cared for by my mother's soft touch.

This is my last day off. It's Friday so of course I have the weekend. But that doesn't count because I'd have been off anyway. I decide to take a hot bath and use some of Dancy's aromatherapy bubbles. She doesn't mind. As a matter of fact, she's delighted when anyone takes on her particular obsession and soaks away tension.

I soak for a luxurious full two hours, reading *The Notebook* for the tenth time. What a love story. Will any man ever love me forever?

David's face comes to mind. David . . . beautiful eyes, tender smile. A great father. And maybe, just maybe, interested in me.

I've just dressed in a pair of Levi's jeans (which are quite loose after barely eating a bite for ten days), my white T-shirt from the Gap, and a light blue Nike track jacket. It feels great to have real clothes on instead of PJs. The sun is shimmering, and the temperature has risen to the mid-fifties. Unable to resist the call of fresh late-winter air, I pull on my Nikes, stuff my ID and a few bucks into my jeans pocket, and head outside.

After buying a soap mag from an outdoor vendor four blocks

from my apartment, I duck into Nick's Coffee and Dessert for a chai mocha latte and a slice of cheesecake.

"Hey, yo there, Tabby Brockman," Nick, the middle-aged Italian behind the counter calls as soon as I step inside. Dancy is sure the coffee shop is a front for some business even more sinister in nature, but I'm not convinced. I'd rather believe Nick is exactly what he seems—an overweight, slightly balding Italian with a great cheesecake recipe. His smile spreads across his whole face. "If it ain't our neighborhood celebrity. Where you been lately? I thought you started goin' to Starbucks or somethin'."

"Never!" I step up to the counter. "I've been sick. Measles, can you believe it?"

"Ain't you a little old for the measles?"

"You'd think." I don't even bother to be offended by the uncouth comment. I adore Nick too much. "Apparently anyone can get it."

"You ain't gonna give it to me, are ya?"

I laugh. "No. I'm past being contagious."

He's fixing my latte without even taking my order. It would serve him right if I changed it up. But then, I don't want anything else. I'm such a creature of habit.

"Been watching you on that soap opera," Nick says without looking up from the latte machine. "When are you going to get your memory back?"

"Now, Nick, you know I can't share story secrets. I could get fired."

"Oh, come on. Not even to old Nick?"

I shake my head. "Not even the man who makes the best chai mocha latte and cheesecake in Manhattan."

He flushes with pleasure and sets my latte on the counter. I dig into my pocket and pull out a twenty dollar bill. He frowns and waves it away. "'Ey now, put that away. Your money's no good today."

"Hey, thanks, Nick." I grab my drink and cheesecake and wander to my favorite corner table.

Rachel's face glares at me as soon as I open my magazine to the Who's Who and Stars around Town section. Rachel . . . and David. *Rachel Savage enjoys a romantic dinner with a mystery man. She sure can pick them.*

"She sure can pick them," I mimic bitterly.

"Did you say something?" a woman's voice asks. "Oh, Tabby, it's you."

Heat floods my face as I turn to the woman at the next table over. The woman who happens to be Greta, the pastor's wife from New Wine Fellowship. I wonder if I should say "God is good" or something. No. I mean, He is, but no.

"I've been hoping to see you again at church."

I scrutinize the comment. What's she really saying? But as I look into guileless eyes, I realize she's not trying to guilt me into anything.

"I've had the measles."

"You got them from the Gray twins?" Her eyes go wide, and then she smirks. "I'm sorry. But I don't usually associate measles with someone your age."

"Yes, well, actually my doctor says anyone can get them if they're not immune. And it's really hard on adults," I pout, "so I was miserable for days."

"I'm sorry, Tabby. I didn't mean to make fun." Then how come her eyes are still shining with mirth? "Can I join you?"

Well, I really just wanted to be alone, but she *is* the pastor's wife so I guess I should be nice. I nod, trying to drum up an enthusiastic smile. "Sure."

She hops up with all the energy I lack these days and brings her latte and chocolate éclair with her to my table. "I've been meaning to congratulate you on being back on the show." She smiles, nodding toward the magazine. "I try to watch it once a week so I can keep up with your character and the twins' story line, but I don't always get to."

My eyes go wide. "You watch the show?"

"Well, I admit, I don't much care about the other story lines. The only reason I'm watching at all is because you and the twins are in it. Don't tell anyone." A laugh escapes. "Just kidding."

I'm completely floored. I can't believe this woman who exudes spiritual maturity and confidence actually watches me on a soap opera at least once a week. She sips her drink and dabs her shiny lips with a napkin.

"Listen, I was wanting to ask you if you'd like to come share at a ladies' meeting in April."

Taken aback, I stare slack-jawed at the woman. "You want me?"

A smile lights her olive-skinned face. "Sure. You could give your testimony of how you came to know God. Talk about what it's like being a Christian in the TV industry. Especially as a soap opera star—you know what people think about those."

"With good reason, for the most part," I hear myself saying. Did I really say that?

"But every industry needs Christians. You've been placed strategically by God to make a difference in your world. It's a big responsibility—and an honor—that God trusts you enough to put you there, Tabby."

"I've never really thought of it that way."

She gives me a kind smile that reaches all the way to her eyes. "Maybe you should. David says you are a light in the place and that there is a noticeable difference on the set when you're off or if the kids are shooting a scene with someone other than you."

"He does?"

"Yep." She glances at her watch. "Goodness. Time has gotten away from me today. I have to get home and start thinking about what to cook my family for supper. Think about what I asked and let me know within a couple of weeks, okay?"

I swallow hard and nod. "Okay, I'll let you know."

I watch her walk away, laptop in hand, and something hits me.

Can I be your voice on the set of Legacy, *Lord?*

I glance back down and see the photo of Rachel and David. A sigh escapes me. It would be a lot easier if I could just be nice to everyone except Rachel. What right does she have to be on the arm of such a great guy?

I know one thing. I'm going to be at church on Sunday morning. New Wine Fellowship. I think maybe I've found the church for me. Heaven only knows what Mom and Dad will say about me switching churches, but you know? A girl can't stay tied to the family pew forever.

On Sunday, I talk Dancy and Laini into joining me at New Wine Fellowship. It's only the second regular service I've attended, and I'm energized as soon as the band starts to play. I'm caught up in the excitement when Laini nudges me. "Look who's here," she whispers.

My heart speeds up even before I see the latecomer. When I turn following Laini's gaze, I catch my breath. David's eyes are on me. I smile and somehow find the presence of mind to wave him over to an empty seat in our row.

"Where are the kids?" I whisper.

"Kids' church," he whispers back and that's all we have time for until the service is over. After the closing prayer, he turns to me. "Good to see you here."

"Same here."

"So, David . . ." I tense as soon as I hear Dancy's tone.

I think he sort of tenses too. His face takes on a guarded expression. "Yes?"

"Where's your gal pal?"

I cringe, but somewhere inside I'm grateful for a friend like Dancy who isn't afraid to say what I'm thinking. I cut a glance to David, and I'm relieved to see he's smirking. Totally not offended by Dancy's blunt question.

"If you mean Rachel, I imagine she's sleeping in."

"And where is she sleeping in at?"

Okay, besides the fact that her sentence is completely incorrect grammatically, and that's a little disconcerting coming from an assistant editor, I think that one might have been a little over the top. I step in, looping my arm through hers. "Okay, well. David, it's been great seeing you again. I'll see you on the set tomorrow."

Without even waiting for his farewell, I pull Dancy down the row, with Laini following closely behind. "What's wrong with you?" I demand when we get to the parking lot.

"Oh, don't tell me you weren't wondering how he knew she was sleeping in."

"You know what? It's none of my business. And it definitely isn't your business."

"Let's take this home, you two," says Laini, the voice of reason.

"Fine," we say in unison and actually, that's all there is to it. We never finish our conversation because my cell phone goes off the second we pile into Dancy's BMW.

David's voice greets me. "Hey, look—I'm sorry about that," I say as soon as he identifies himself.

"That's why I'm calling. Tell Dancy that I don't know where Rachel slept last night, and I'm just guessing that she's sleeping in."

My face goes hot. "Well, um, thanks for calling, and I'll certainly let her know."

"I'd appreciate it." He hangs up just like that, and I can tell he went from amused with her first question to a little ticked at the innuendo of the second. I scowl and relay the message to Dancy.

"Well, now we know, don't we?" she says without so much as the tiniest smidgen of remorse. I want to rail at her. To tell her she can't just go around insinuating that David is having an inappropriate relationship with Rachel Savage.

But you know . . . now we know.

Monday morning I wake at four a.m. to the sound of the garbage truck on the street. As if Mondays weren't bad enough. "You awake?" Laini whispers from her bed.

"What do you think?"

"I'm worried, Tabs."

Turning onto my side, I prop myself up on my elbow. "About what?"

"What if I'm making a bad decision here? Maybe I should just go back to accounting and forget about design."

Forget interior design? What was all this trouble for if she's just going to make a run for the math as soon as she gets a little nervous?

"Come on, Laini. You don't really mean that, do you?"

"I'm honestly not sure. I'm good at accounting, you know."

"You're lucky you're so good at two professions. When I lose this job on *Legacy of Life*, I'll have nothing to fall back on."

Laini laughs, just like I'd hoped. "Come on. This is about me, not you."

"Okay, so which do you want to do? Accounting or interior design?"

"Design. But I like numbers too."

Okay, that's just weird. How can anyone like numbers?

"I don't know what to tell you, Laini. Maybe it's not your career that's giving you all this angst. Maybe you need change in another area of your life."

"Listen to who's waxing philosophical," she teases.

"Listen to my words of wisdom, Grasshopper."

"You watch too many old TV shows."

"Look who's talking."

The hallway light switches on and glows beneath our door just before we hear a knock. Dancy pokes her head in. "Are you guys awake?"

"Of course."

She sighs and flops down at the end of my bed. "The Bakers are yelling again. Why don't those two just split up and put each other—and me—out of their misery?"

"Or go to counseling and work out their problems," I say.

Dancy gives a short laugh. "My parents have been in counseling for ten years and they still don't get along. They only stay together so they don't have to split the money."

I never know what to say when Dancy gets all bitter about her folks.

"How are things going at the office?" I ask. Sometimes it's better to just change the subject.

My tactic works. Dancy shakes her head. "Jack is an English egomaniac. I swear, he thinks all he has to do is walk into the office, flash that Hugh Grant boyish grin, talk in that accent—which, by the way, I'm not completely convinced is real—and everyone will just do whatever he wants. It's sickening to watch the other women in the office go la-la over him."

"Is he that cute?" Laini asks.

A careless shrug lifts her slim shoulders. "If you like that type, I guess."

Intrigued, I can't let it drop just yet. "What type?"

"You know, tall, cute, dark hair, hazel eyes, soft-spoken." Her voice has taken on a dreamy tone.

Laini is the first one to give in to laughter. Actually a little giggle. But it's enough to set me off. "Sounds like my type," Laini says. "How about you, Tabs?"

"Definitely my type too. Bring him home for dinner and let's see if he 'takes a fancy' to either of us." Of course I say "takes a fancy" in a bad English accent.

"Fine. Mock me." Dancy hops up. "Just for that, I'm taking the first shower, and I just might use all the hot water."

Our laughter follows her.

"What do you think?" Laini asks.

"Oh, she's got it bad."

"Yep, I thought so."

And if anyone can spot a girl who's got it bad for a guy—it's me.

21

Turns out, it's not hard to ignore someone who doesn't even show up. The twins are on set, back to their energetic selves, but David is nowhere to be seen. It's odd.

Rachel isn't on set today either. To be perfectly honest, that particular coincidence doesn't sit well with me, but hey, I'm not dwelling on it. I'm going to be a professional and do my job. After all, somewhere between getting into the shower (last, so my water was barely a notch above icy) and arriving on the set, I've definitely decided to move on and stop dreaming about David Gray's gorgeous navy blue eyes, or the way he looked on Valentine's Day in that suit, and oh gosh, the way he smelled. And the way his shoulder felt against mine during church. Man, how am I ever going to stop dreaming about this guy?

I swallow hard. Get a stinking grip, Tabby.

I'm just finishing up a scene with the twins, where Felicia has a rush of motherly love. She takes both children in her arms, and in an Emmy-worthy moment—if I do say so myself—allows tears to travel down her cheeks.

Even Blythe says, "Finally got the motherhood bit down, haven't you, Tabby? It's about time." From Blythe that's high praise so I walk to my dressing room feeling pretty pleased with myself.

I grab my cell phone from my purse and check messages. My heart picks up at the sound of David's voice.

"Tabby, I'm so sorry to bother you. But I have an emergency. Can you give me a call back on my cell phone?"

I dial and he picks up immediately. "Tabby?"

"Hey, David. What's up?" Okay, that was a nice blend of distant, but concerned. Nice job, if I do say so myself.

"Listen, I had a meeting with a client and he's late."

Oh, and is his name Rachel? I just can't believe him. Rachel's gone, David's gone. It's too obvious what he's really doing.

I bristle. Meeting with a client? Is that what we're calling clandestine tête-à-têtes with supporting actresses these days? "A business meeting, huh?" Sarcasm drips from my lips.

He hesitates. Ha! Caught. "Are you okay?"

"Of course I am. Why wouldn't I be?" I give a little carefree laugh. "What can I do for you?"

"Okay, look. I don't have much time. My meeting was changed from noon to three, which is terrible, because the twins have ice skating lessons at three."

I feel a premonition coming on. What am I now? Convenient babysitter whenever Rachel and David want to go off and be alone together? Doesn't he even have a clue about my feelings for him? Or maybe he does and just doesn't give a rip.

"Let me guess, you want me to take the kids to lessons and then back to your apartment."

"Would you? I'm so sorry to ask, but this meeting could mean the difference between staying independent or having to take a job I don't want."

Oh, he's good. A great liar really. "Oh, sure. No prob. We'll get along just fine. You and your, um, *client* feel free to take your time. The twins are in good hands with me."

"Are you sure you're all right, Tabby? You don't sound . . . right."

"Who me? Oh, I'm fine. Just had a very emotional scene with my children so I'm pulling myself out of it."

"Tell them I love them, okay? I'm going to call the kids' advocate on set and let her know it's okay to send the kids with you. And I'll call Randy to let you in the apartment after the lessons."

"Okay, that's fine," I say shortly because I can just imagine Rachel standing beside him, kissing his ear and playing with the black curls that cover the back of his neck. "Good-bye."

The kids and I actually have a great time at Rockefeller Center. Much nicer than last time we were here together. They hold my hand as we move through the crowd, and the feel of their tiny fingers does something I can't quite put into words.

We arrive a little while before the lesson is to begin, so the coach allows the kids to hit the ice for free skating before knuckling down for their lesson. I watch as the pair do their best to one-up each other.

"Watch me!" Jenn calls just before spinning into a single loop.

I hold my breath until she lands sure-footedly and poses with her arms in the air. "Way to go, Jenn," I call out, expelling my pent-up breath. "Look out Michelle Kwan!"

Her face glows under the praise.

"Now watch me," Jeffy calls, and he does the same jump.

"Amazing, Jeffy! You rock!"

A pleasant-looking woman moves next to me. "I don't think we've ever met," she says with a friendly smile. "I'm Erica Johnson." She points to a lovely little girl of seven or eight wearing a leotard. "That's my Angie," she says with motherly pride. "This is her third year."

"Tabby," I say. "I'm with the twins."

"Your husband usually brings them, doesn't he?"

"My . . .?" *Oh!* "Wait. I'm not—" I shake my head and open my mouth to set her straight, but she's not interested in me anymore. A small gasp escapes her as Angie goes down on the ice.

"Angie, get up some speed before you try that jump. You know you can't do a double if you're just going to drag along the ice!" She shakes her head. "I swear." Without saying another word to me, she moves away, motioning frantically for her poor kid. The woman reams Angie with a string of insults. Compassion for the child tugs at my heart, and I look away. It occurs to me that I never set the woman straight, but I seriously doubt she'll remember even seeing me.

The twins go through a series of jumps and spins, sometimes landing on their bottoms, sometimes landing the jumps. I honestly don't see how anyone can berate a child for falling. That's so . . . I don't know . . . heartless.

Finally the instructor follows the twins off the ice. He smiles at me and shakes my hand. "David couldn't make it?"

"Not tonight." I smile back and turn my attention to the twins. "You two are fabulous. Want to order pizza to celebrate a fantastic lesson?"

"Yeah!" they say in unison.

"Okay, go get your shoes on and we'll go."

"You must be David's fiancée," the instructor says. "Jenn told me they're getting a new mother."

My heart stops, and I'm finding it difficult to breathe. What if David and Rachel are secretly flying to Vegas and getting married at one of those drive-through chapels? Maybe Rachel got a quickie divorce and now they're ready to take their relationship to the next level. Oh gee. Am I ever a loser. I'm babysitting while the guy I have a crush on is marrying my nemesis.

"I'm just a friend," I say as brightly as possible.

"Oh? It must the other woman I've seen the kids with then."

A knife-sharp pain slices through my chest at the mention of the "other woman." Oh golly, I wonder who that might be.

"I'm really not at liberty to discuss David's private life," I say with a lift of my chin and what I hope is an air of indifference. After all, I really should be above idle gossip, shouldn't I?

"I understand. But please tell him not to schedule the wedding for April eighth. The children are giving an exhibition."

"I'll tell him," I say, wanting desperately to get away from the man. "Ready, kids?"

We order a thick pepperoni and cheese pizza and make it to David's apartment around five.

"Good evening, Randy," I say brightly, smiling at the doorman, who I have to say turned out to be a great guy after all.

"Good evening, Miss Brockman. And good evening to you two," he says to the twins.

"Want a slice of pizza?" I ask on a whim. After all, it's huge and there's no way we'll eat even half of the pie.

"I'd love one," he says as we head to the elevator together. Once we reach our destination and he lets us in, I hurry to the cupboard, find a paper towel, and pull out a slice of pizza for him.

"Here you go," I say brightly. "Enjoy."

"You're a nice girl, Miss Brockman," he says, accepting the offering. And as I close the door, I have to say, that's a compliment I'll cherish for a long time.

I stride back to the kitchen where the kids are waiting at the table and pull down three blue plates, setting them down along with napkins. "This looks great!"

We bow our heads and Jeffy says a simple prayer. "Thank you for the food. God bless Daddy at his meeting and God bless Miss Tabby and us here at home."

Sigh. Home . . .

The phone on the wall rings just as I'm taking my first bite. I pick it up. "Hello?"

"Tabby, it's David. How are things going?"

"Oh, we're having a great time. How about you and Rachel?"

"Rachel? How did you know . . . ?"

My stomach sinks. So I was right. The two of them are together. If not getting married in Vegas, then probably together at a hotel or something. I could just cry.

As luck would have it, Jeffy's milk glass wobbles and goes down, spilling its contents all over the table. "Hey, David, I need to clean up Jeffy's milk. Have to let you go."

"Okay, listen, Tabby. I won't be home for at least another two or three hours. The meeting got off to an even later start, and we're going to have a dinner meeting. Do you mind getting the kids something to eat?"

"Already taken care of." Does he think I'm going to starve his children just because he's off somewhere neglecting them with a lying hussy of a woman?

"Thank you. I owe you big."

Got that right, buddy.

After I clean up Jeffy's spill, the rest of my evening goes along smoothly. Amazing how just playing mother to these two on the set has awakened maternal instincts I never knew I possessed. Rachel doesn't deserve to have two kids as great as this for her stepchildren.

We quickly clean up the leftovers. Jenn and Jeffy are so cute as they dry their dishes like a couple of little grown-ups. "Good job, you two. I couldn't have done it without you."

"I like it when you come over, Tabby," Jeffy says.

"Jeffy!" Jenn's reproving tone brings a blush to Jeffy's cheeks. "I mean, Miss Tabby."

Unexpected tenderness wells up in me. "It's okay. I don't mind if you call me Tabby."

"Daddy says it's dis-re-spec-ful," Jeffy replies.

I ruffle the boy's hair. "Well, I'll talk to your dad and assure him that we've reached a level in our friendship where the two of you can call me Tabby without any disrespect meant or taken."

He frowns a little, and I realize I've completely talked over his head.

"Don't worry about it," I say. "I'm sure if I talk to your dad he'll let you call me Tabby instead of Miss Brockman. I know you don't mean any disrespect. Now, what do you want to do?"

"Will you play a game with us?"

"Are you kidding? I love games." Which isn't entirely true. But I could if given a chance to play one.

"I call *Chutes and Ladders*!" Jenn shouts.

"Sounds like fun," I say brightly, trying to talk myself into it.

And guess what? It really is fun. I'm having a total blast, even though I lose every single game, and only when I catch a wide yawn stretching Jenn's mouth do I call the playtime to an end.

"Do you take baths tonight?" I ask.

"Yes, after lessons we always have to."

"Okay, I'll run some water."

"I call first bath!" Jeffy yells. These two are apparently big on "calling."

An hour later, two very sleepy kids pad into the bedroom they share and climb into their respective twin beds.

I stand in the middle of the room and stare from one to the other, disappointed that they have to go to sleep. I'll miss them.

"Will you read us a story, Miss Tabby?"

A thrill bursts through me. "Of course I will. What should I read?"

"Daddy's reading us *The Lion, the Witch, and the Wardrobe*."

"Okay. Should I pick up where he left off?"

They both nod. "Jeffy, come crawl into bed next to your sister, and I'll sit at the end of the bed and read."

In two minutes, we're ready to begin. I open the book to chapter four where it appears David has left off and begin to read.

The twins are nodding off in ten minutes, which bums me out a little because I don't want to stop reading. I replace the bookmark and sit in the dimly lit room watching them sleep.

I'm still sitting cross-legged resting my chin on my fists watching the steady rise and fall of their little chests when David peeks into the room.

My cheeks warm as I realize I've been staring at the sleeping little angels for fifteen minutes. I slide off the bed as carefully as I can and set the book on the nightstand. I switch off the light and follow David from the room.

He softly closes their bedroom door and motions down the hall. He gives a chuckle. "When I asked you to watch them, I didn't mean you had to watch them every second."

"We just finished reading a few minutes ago."

"How were they for you?"

"Good."

"I see you got roped into *Chutes and Ladders*." He nods toward the table where I've neglected to put away the game.

"Sorry. I'll pick it up."

He puts a restraining hand on my arm. "That's not necessary."

I jerk back and clear my throat. "They ate pizza for supper. There's still some in the refrigerator if you're hungry."

"Thanks. I'm starving." He grins and yanks at the tie at his throat. He loosens it, slides it from his collar, and unbuttons his first two buttons.

"Um—no problem. The kids had baths. And they were so good at the skating rink. Did you know they can actually do single loops? They're amazing." I hear the excitement rising in my voice as his eyes squint with amusement.

"They're not exactly ready for the Olympics. But I think it's important for kids to learn a sport. It keeps them active."

I feel foolish for getting so caught up. "Yes, well. They're really good, I think. You know what else?"

"What?"

"They're smart too." I look up at him and his lips are pursed like he's trying not to smirk. "I mean really smart, David."

"I know."

He's just too calm to be grasping the enormity of what I'm telling him. "I mean, maybe they're geniuses. For instance, Jeffy read the word 'lion' and Jenn can write her full name—not just Jenn, but Jennifer. That's pretty—you know—"

"Amazing?"

He's mocking me. "I think so." I jerk my chin, realizing that I sound ridiculous to be so impressed with a couple of five-year-olds.

"I'm glad you three have reached an understanding." He smiles. "Do you want to join me in the kitchen and keep me company while I eat?"

"What would Rachel think of that?"

"I'm sure she couldn't care less." He gives me a puzzled smile. "Why? Do you think she'd care?"

I shrug. "I don't know. You're closer to her than I am."

He gives me a conspiratorial wink that I totally don't get. "Well, as one who knows her so well, let me assure you she wouldn't care if you sit and have a slice of pizza with me." He slips off his shoes to reveal dark blue socks. "You don't mind, do you? Those shoes are killers. I'd rather wear my Nikes any day."

"Be my guest."

"Oh, before I forget. How much do I owe you for babysitting and for the pizza?"

I stand slack-jawed as he pulls his wallet from his back pocket. Is he kidding me?

"Will fifty do it?"

"Fifty?"

He misunderstands my inability to form words. I'm so appalled.

He narrows his gaze. "Sixty?"

Outrage clamps my mouth shut. I send him my meanest glare, grab my purse off the counter, and whip around. I catch my sweater on the edge of the counter and it snags. Actually, snag is a mild word for the golf-ball-sized hole in the stomach of my favorite cashmere.

"Tabby, wait. I'm sorry."

"Don't worry about it. You're not the one that put a hole in it. I'm just klutzy, that's all. I'll see you and the kids tomorrow."

"That's not what I meant." He stops me with a hand on my arm.

I whip around to face him. "What then?"

"I'm sorry for insulting you. I should have known better than to offer you money."

"Yes, you should have." I grab my leather coat from the closet by the door. "And by the way," I say as I open the front door. "Don't make any *plans* on April eighth because the kids have an exhibition at the skating rink."

"Thanks. I'll remember. Be careful out there, it's starting to snow."

"I like driving in the snow."

I have trouble holding back tears as I ride the elevator down.

"How was that pizza, Randy?" I ask the smiling doorman as he tips his hat and opens the door for me.

"Hit the spot. The wife doesn't allow me to eat the stuff. Says it'll take five years off my life."

"I won't tell her if you won't." Note to self, don't offer Randy any more pizza. Could possibly be contributing to ill health and/or marriage difficulties. Although that's probably a moot point anyway because I won't be coming back to David's apartment.

I grab Dancy's keys from my purse before I step outside, then turn back and smile at Randy. "Night."

"I'll keep an eye out until you drive away."

"Thanks. I appreciate it."

I don't know how I lucked out enough to get a parking spot close to the building. I crank the engine. It makes a lot of noise, but doesn't start. Stupid eleven-year-old car! My heart picks up. This has never, ever happened before. I crank the engine again. It fires up. But before I can feel a second of relief, it sputters and dies.

I pull the hood latch and jerk out of the car. I have no idea what I'm looking for, but popping the hood seems to be the right course of action.

Help, Lord. I don't know what to do.

"What seems to be the trouble?"

Pain shoots through my head as I jump and bang on the open hood. "Sheesh, David. Warn a person! What are you doing down here, anyway? Where are the kids?"

"Sorry for startling you, I'm down here because Randy called and said you're having car trouble, and the kids are still in bed where you left them."

"Alone in the apartment? Are you crazy? Get up there before someone steals them out of their beds."

"Relax. Mrs. Rutledge, my next-door neighbor, is looking after them."

Relief floods me even as I feel a little foolish. "Sorry for overreacting."

He grins. "I liked it."

"Well, anyway. I'd better get back under that hood and see what's going on."

"Know a lot about cars, do you?" Is he making fun of me?

"Well—not really, but maybe if I . . ." I reach out to touch a black, dirty cable of some sort. But David's hand covers mine before I actually make contact with the filthy vehicle.

His lips twitch. "May I?"

"Be my guest," I say as though I'm doing him a huge favor.

"How about if you go turn the key so I can hear what it's doing."

"It's not starting," I huff. "That's the problem."

"Okay, humor me."

I jerk around to the driver's side and slide in the car. I turn the key. The car makes a valiant effort, but again sputters and dies.

David drops the hood into place and walks around to my window. I open the door. "What are you doing?" I demand.

"Tabby."

Is he trying not to laugh? I'm so glad he thinks it's hilarious.

"What?" I ask.

"I think you ran out of gas."

That is the dumbest thing I've ever heard. "Obviously you're no mechanic! Because there is no way I'm out of—" I look down at the gas gauge. *E.* "Oh."

I slide my hand over to my purse and pull out my cell phone. "Know the number of a good taxi?" I ask glumly.

David reaches out and instinctively I take his hand. He pulls me from the car. "Why don't I drive to the gas station a couple of blocks away and get you enough gas to make it to the station? Then you won't have to waste time and money taking a cab home tonight and back over here tomorrow to pick up your car."

Such a gentleman. And what a sensible solution. "Thanks. I'd appreciate it."

"Will you come upstairs and stay with the kids for me so Mrs. Rutledge can go home?"

"Of course." I mean, it's the least I can do, right? He is going out to get gas for my car. And that's when I realize, he's still holding my hand. Should I say anything?

"Are you staying, Miss Brockman?" Randy asks, and he's sort of frowning like he doesn't approve.

David drops my hand like a hot potato. "Miss Brockman is going to stay with the kids for a few minutes while I go to the gas station and fill up a gallon jug with gas for her car." He stares hard at the doorman. "That's *all.*"

Randy nods. "That's good."

David reaches into his pocket and hands me his keys. "Can you make it upstairs by yourself?"

"Yeah." I'm a little depressed now. I mean, sure I wouldn't want Randy to get the wrong idea about why I'm sticking around. But on the other hand, why did David have to be so pointed in letting the doorman know there's nothing going on between us?

What am I going to have to do to get this guy's attention?

22

W hy didn't you just confront him and get it over with?" It's been two days since my babysitting venture at David's house, and Laini has finally come back to the apartment. Dancy's so sick with the measles she's not up for a heart-to-heart, and I've been dying to talk to one of my friends about David.

"What was I supposed to say, Laini?"

"How about, 'Hey dude, how could you ask me to babysit again and go out with the woman who makes my life miserable?'"

"Dude?"

"Shut up." She tosses a couch pillow at me. I catch it easily and laugh.

"Oh well. Maybe I'm just not cut out for love."

"Me neither. Let's just live together forever and get some cats."

"Oh, and a goldfish."

"And a guinea pig named Charley."

Laughter erupts from us until reality strikes home in the form of our dear, measles-infected pal. Dancy's pale, shaky form exits her bedroom. "You guys are going to have to keep it down. My head is killing me."

"We're sorry." I understand exactly how she feels. "Go back to bed. I'll bring you some green tea."

"Thank you," she mumbles and heads back to her bedroom.

Laini coughs and I shoot around. "Don't tell me you haven't had the measles either!"

"I-I don't know."

Good grief. Looks like that so-called childhood illness is going to make the rounds in our grown-up apartment.

I give Jenn a wink and a smile just before Blythe calls "Action!"

Felicia: "I know this must be difficult, honey. But I'm sure I'll start having memories of you and your brother soon. Others are starting to come back, aren't they?" (I smile at her. She walks across the living room set where I'm sitting on the sofa and climbs up next to me.)

Amber: "It's okay, Mommy. I don't remember either."

Felicia: "I have an idea." (I smile and slip my arm around the child.)

Jenn looks up with beautiful wide blue eyes and my heart melts a little—I'm having trouble staying in the scene. I must have waited too long because Jenn bails me out with some ad-lib.

Amber: "What's your idea, mommy?" (She lays her silky head against my chest and my arms encircle her. For some reason, I'm honestly fighting back tears.)

Felicia: "What if we just stop trying to remember back then? What if I start being your real mommy right now and you start being my real daughter?"

(Jenn pulls away slowly and places one hand on either side of my face the way only a five-year-old can. Her lips tremble and her eyes fill with unshed tears.)

Amber: "I'd like that, Mommy."

I stop fighting my own tears and gather Jenn tight, even though the script doesn't call for it. I drink in the soft scent of baby shampoo and rest my cheek against her hair. Blythe calls "Cut." But neither Jenn nor I move for a second.

"Great job, sweetie," I whisper.

"You too," she says back, and I relax my hold until she's at arm's length. "Can I tell you a secret?"

I nod and wipe away a few remaining tears from her face.

"I wish you really could be my mom."

My heart squeezes and I realize something . . . I wish I could be her mom too. I lean forward and press a kiss to her forehead. "Thank you, sweetie. That's the nicest thing anyone's ever said to me. If I had a little girl, I'd want her to be exactly like you."

I want so much to ask her, "What about Rachel?" But of course, I don't go there. It wouldn't be right. And I'm not sure I have the heart for the answer.

"Come on, Jenn!" Jeffy calls. "Dad said we can have a donut."

I smile at the little girl. She grins back, and off she goes to get her cavity-inducing snack.

Well, that's that, then, isn't it? Actually, a donut doesn't sound like a bad idea. I start to head that way, still thinking about Jenn, when Julie Foster pops up out of nowhere. I stop short.

"Good job with that scene," she says grudgingly.

I almost croak at the compliment.

"Thanks, Julie. Good writing." Who am I to withhold credit where credit is due?

"Thanks."

"No problem."

And there you have it. She walks on by, presumably going to her office.

David is standing with the twins at the food table by the time I get there. I swear, I didn't see him before I decided to get my donut. I reach for one and my hand gets smacked, but not before I grab hold of the treat. "Hey!"

Freddie—of course—is standing next to me. "I saw you making a beeline and came over to save you from yourself. Put that thing down. Have you seen your butt lately?"

"Yes, and it's smaller than ever thanks to a little bout with the measles."

"Exactly. Do you want to make it stretch?"

I'm aware that David is not only listening, but laughing at my expense.

"Freddie, is this really the place to have this conversation? Save it for the gym."

"The gym? Do you even remember where the gym is, honey? I haven't seen you there in about . . . for*ever.*"

Whatever! In a split second of defiance, I put the donut to my mouth. "You can't tell me what to do." I stick my tongue out at my friend and take a huge bite. Too huge. My eyes go wide, and I'm trying desperately to chew enough to swallow.

"Oh look, little Miss Piggy," Freddie says in his mocking girlie tone. "Bite off more than you can chew?"

All the things I'd like to say fill my head, but of course I can't speak around the massive chunk of fried, sugary dough.

"Are you okay, Tabby?" David stops pretending he's not eavesdropping, and I hear the concern in his voice.

I raise my index finger and nod. But I'm really not okay. A chunk has slipped down my esophagus, and I can't breathe. Panic hits me full in the chest, and I reach out and grab David's arm.

As soon as he realizes what's going on, he springs into action, positions himself behind my back, wraps his hands around my waist, and presses on my stomach area. Once, twice, and the piece of donut flies out, whacking Freddie between the eyes.

"Ew!" he squeals.

I'm working on catching my breath when I realize David's arms are still around me. "Thank you," I finally manage.

Freddie is still freaked out about me spitting on him. He gives me a once-over to make sure I'm okay, then holds up his hand. "I have to go wash myself." He takes off before I can even apologize.

David turns me in his arms. "You okay?"

I nod and I'm about to say something like "Where'd you learn that?" or something equally asinine, when Rachel's lithe form shows up next to David, and she lays her fingers on his arm, forcing him to let me go.

"You're a real hero, David," she murmurs seductively. Why does that woman always have to butt in?

He clears his throat. "Just doing what needed to be done." His modest, slightly embarrassed answer definitely adds to his strong, silent type appeal.

"David, don't forget we have dinner at Trey and Julie's tonight. Have you thought about getting a babysitter?"

"Uh, no. To tell you the truth I forgot."

Rachel gives a little pout. "Oh, I'm so disappointed. But wait a second . . ." She turns to me then, and I know what's coming. "Tabby, do you have plans tonight?"

"Why, Rachel? Am I invited for dinner with Julie and Trey also?"

Her cheeks flush. And I decide to let her off the hook. I focus on David. "Actually, I don't have plans, and I'd be happy to stay with the kids again if you need me, David."

Rachel's face brightens. "How sweet! Thank you ever so much, Tabby."

David frowns and shakes his head. "No, Tabby. That's asking too much of you."

"Don't worry about it. The twins owe me a rematch of *Chutes and Ladders* anyway. I'm down about ten games."

"Wonderful," Rachel says and removes her hand from David's arm. "Pick me up at seven. Thanks again, Tabby. Ta-ta."

Personally, I think anyone who says "ta-ta" should be placed in front of a firing squad and forced to promise they'll never say it again. Unless they're saying it as a joke, that is.

"Tabby, I don't want you to do this." David's warm hand is on my arm, detaining me from walking away. It's all I can do to cover his with mine and revel in the touch, but apparently, Rachel is in and I'm out. So what's the point?

I lean in close to him and whisper for his ears alone. "I owe you for saving my life just now," I say. "But next time you have a date with Rachel or anyone else, I have two words for you: plan ahead. Because my babysitting services are out of business."

"Hey, I said—"

"Too late," I say. "I guess I'll see you a little before seven." I wink at the twins. "Be prepared for a *Chutes and Ladders* rematch—you're going down." They snicker. I wiggle my fingers at David. "Ta-ta, dahling."

Back in my dressing room, I find my script for the next day's scenes. I give it a once-over. "Oh no. That's not going to happen." No wonder Julie was nice to me. Nice to my face, stab me in the back. She really thinks Felicia would fall in love with her psychiatrist? No way! *No* way! I jerk to my feet and yank open my door.

When I get to Julie's office, I don't even bother to knock.

She looks up from her computer and sits back, eyeing me with a squint. "What can I do for you, Tabitha?"

I drop the script onto her desk. "What's the meaning of this?"

She flips through the pages, then meets my gaze with cool

indifference. "Which words are you having trouble with? Maybe I can help. Is it that one right there?" she asks pointing to the first page.

Okay, I walked right into that one. "Don't play coy with me, Julie. Felicia is not going to sleep with her psychiatrist."

She stands and her eyes narrow dangerously as she leans across her desk. "Felicia does what I say she does. I think you'd better remember what happened last time I decided Felicia was going to go away."

"You're seriously threatening me?"

"Call it whatever you want."

I snatch up my script and head for the door. "We'll see what Blythe and Jerry have to say about this."

"Memo to you," she mocks. "I already ran these scenes by them both before we finalized them."

"And Blythe agreed to this?"

"Thought it was brilliant."

"We'll see."

I slam out of her office and down to Jerry's. His door is closed, and his assistant isn't at her desk. I give Jerry more respect than I did Julie. At least I knock.

"Excuse me, Miss Brockman." The assistant has returned and is frowning at me. "Can I help you?"

"I need to see Jerry right away."

"I'm sorry, but he's gone home for the weekend."

I give a frustrated sigh. "Is Blythe Cannon still here?"

"I believe so. Want me to page her?"

"Yeah, if you don't mind. Tell her to call my cell phone."

The director calls me within five minutes. "What's wrong, Tabby?"

"Have you read my scenes for Monday?"

"Where Felicia and the psychiatrist . . . ?"

"Yes. That's it."

"I questioned that, Tabby. But Jerry sided with Julie. I honestly don't know what she's thinking."

But I do. I know exactly. Felicia is starting to remember the love of her life—Rudolph. And Julie doesn't want me in her husband's arms.

"Blythe. You know what's going on. You must."

"I know, but what can we do? Unless you're willing to walk and risk a lawsuit."

I groan. "The fans will be fit to be tied if Felicia has an affair. Especially now that she's starting to get her memory back."

"Oh, great scene with the kid today, by the way."

"Thanks. I've been working on that."

"It shows. Very convincing."

"I appreciate the affirmation, Blythe, but I'm still not doing this scene. I'm not doing this ridiculous story line. It's just not right. First of all, Felicia wouldn't have an affair out of wedlock just because she can't remember her husband. Her morals run too deep."

"You mean your morals run too deep."

"Okay. Maybe so. But my convictions will not allow me to do a story line where my character sleeps with someone who isn't her husband. My fans know I'm a Christian. My pastor's wife watches the show, for crying out loud!"

"Tell you what. Let's take it up with Jerry on Monday. Okay? I'll back you up."

Relief shoots through me. "Thanks."

I return to my dressing room, grab my coat, and look ahead to my evening with the twins.

23

The group around Jerry's conference table is a somber lot—myself included. Mondays are bad enough, what with the weekend over, the garbage truck waking me up at four in the morning, and just the whole thought of Monday in general. But add to it that I've been dreading this confrontation all weekend, and I really wish I could have stayed in bed. Here we are, Jerry, Blythe, a very belligerent Julie, myself, and Kyle, my agent. I need someone on my side in case Blythe Cannon bails on me.

Jerry folds his hands and meets my gaze across the sleek oak table. "What seems to be the problem, Tabitha?"

Oh boy, just like your parents, you don't want the producer calling you by your formal name in a situation like this. It doesn't bode well for what's to come.

"Well, first let me start by saying that I believe Julie is an incredibly talented writer."

Okay, Julie just rolled her eyes. Did I sound insincere? Fine, I'll just cut to the chase and forget the credit where credit is due strategy.

"I'm sure Julie appreciates your thoughts on that," Jerry says with a tight smile like he's not buying it either.

This acting ability of mine is a curse . . . no one ever believes a thing I say.

"Here's the thing. According to the script, Felicia is supposed to start having an affair with her psychiatrist. And that's just not something she would do."

Jerry draws a long breath. "I see. Correct me if I'm wrong, but doesn't Felicia do what Julie writes for her to do?" Have these two been comparing notes or what?

"She does. Yes. But I think maybe in this case Felicia needs to be allowed to stay faithful to Rudolph and not muddy the relationship with this affair. She's starting to get her memory back in snatches. Why would she just hop into bed with a man she barely knows?"

"The point is," Julie interjects, "that she doesn't actually know either of them."

"That's true, but she knows Rudy in her soul. Theirs is a love that can never be forgotten." I glance at Blythe and invite her to jump in.

Apparently Jerry picks up on my plea for help. "What do you think, Blythe?"

"Well." She looks around the table. "I think Tabby may have a point."

Julie slaps her hand on the table. "What?"

"O-on the other hand," Blythe continues, "maybe we should up the tension by allowing this relationship with the doctor to be a sort of triangle. Only maybe not lead it into anything physical."

"Of all the stupid—" Oh shoot. I shouldn't have said that out loud. That's no way to get support from these people.

"I agree," Julie says.

Uh—what?

Julie continues. "It's stupid to give them a platonic relationship. The fans have been watching tension build between Felicia and her shrink for weeks now. It's time to take it to the next level."

"No!" I say. "It most definitely isn't."

"Well, Tabitha," Jerry says, "I believe we'll go with the script as it's written."

Anger shoots through me. Have they not been listening to a word I've said? Felicia Fontaine has her faults, yes, but she is not going to turn her back on the man she's learning to love all over again and the children she loves even though she can't remember them. I can't help it. I stand on shaky legs and sweep the table with my firm gaze. "I'm not playing it that way."

"Are you saying you're going to walk off the set and breach your contract?" he asks, driving home the statement with an icy stare.

I recognize the threat, and I know he means it. "Listen, Jerry and the rest of you. I don't mean to be disrespectful or hard-headed, but the fact is this affair, thrown in out of the blue, doesn't feel right. I only want what's best for this character. And an affair isn't it. You have to consider that she has children that she loves, and she's remembering her life in snatches. It doesn't make sense to toss her in bed with another man. The fans will freak."

Before anyone can respond, the sound of "So no one told you life was gonna be this way . . ." starts blaring from my cell phone. My face goes hot. "Sorry."

I grab my purse and check the caller ID, planning to shut off the phone and call whomever it is back, but the number is my mom's. "I'm sorry. It's my mother. She hardly ever calls during the day. Something could be wrong."

Jerry stands. "That's fine. We're through here anyway."

I hate the way he said that, but what can I do about it right now?

I answer the phone, and Mom's voice greets me with a frantic tone that is completely foreign.

"Tabitha, honey. It's your sister. They've just taken her to the hospital."

I rush into the emergency room and find out they've taken Shelly to labor and delivery. David's sister is the first one to greet me when I get off the elevator on the maternity floor. "Nessie? You work up here now?" I ask.

"Just tonight. They were shorthanded. Must be a full moon or something. You here to see your sister?"

"How'd you know?"

She grins and flashes a perfectly matched set of dimples. "Michelle Brockman. And there you are. Two and two."

"How is she?"

"In labor." She stands and walks around the kiosk. "The doctor has her on IV meds to try to stop it."

"Nessie, she's only six months along."

"Don't worry. We'll put it in God's hands and pray she got here soon enough to stop things from progressing to the point of no return."

Nessie escorts me to Shelly's room. Tears are flowing down my sister's cheeks. Mom is with her, and Brian hovers nearby.

"Oh, good. You made it," Mom says.

I walk over to the bed and take Shelly's swollen hand. "How are you doing, honey?"

Her eyes fill with fresh tears, and she grips my hand as a contraction seizes her. Ouch. The girl can squeeze. The contraction doesn't last long and she loosens her hold. "Sorry," she whispers.

"Hey, it's okay. Are they subsiding at all since the doctor started the medicine?"

Brian shakes his head. "Not yet." He smooths the hair from

her forehead. "But it hasn't been long. We need to give it time to start working."

I turn to Mom. "Where's Daddy?"

"In the waiting room. Said he was going to go pray."

"That's the best thing right now. I think I'll join him."

We sit through a very intense few hours of touch-and-go, and finally around daybreak all the contractions stop. Shelly will have to stay for a couple of nights and will be on bed rest for the next three months, or for as long as she can manage to stay pregnant, but thankfully, the baby seems to be fine.

I stop by the apartment long enough to hop in the shower and pull on a clean pair of jeans and a long-sleeved T-shirt. I'm dead on my feet when I get to work. Something seems odd when I walk through the door. No one will look me in the eye, and I feel a sense of impending doom. I know we left things a bit shaky yesterday, but it seems like someone has died.

Died?

Oh please, do not tell me they've done it to me again.

I find myself rushing across the studio to find the only person who will be likely to know what is happening and who will tell me everything he's heard.

"Freddie!" I say, out of breath after my sprint across the building to the gym.

"Tabby? What are you doing here? Didn't they call you?"

My stomach sinks. "It's true then?"

"Apparently. I can't believe they made you come all the way in when they knew they wouldn't need you. How heartless can they be?"

"Pretty heartless. Remember the last time they fired me? I wasn't told until the day before they killed me off."

"Oh, honey. You think they're firing you?" Freddie gives me an eye roll. "It's all about you, isn't it?"

"What do you mean? They're not killing me off?"

"Of course not. How stupid would that be?"

"Okay, Freddie, spill it."

And like a fourteen-year-old cheerleader, he launches into all the sordid details. "Apparently, Rachel and Trey have run off together. Julie's been suspecting the two of them for a while, and that's why she decided to give Felicia a new love interest on the spur of the moment. Just in case she decided to kill off Trey. Last night, Trey told her he was leaving her and wouldn't be back on set for two months because he's going to travel to clear his head. She didn't find out until today that Rachel was his travel mate though."

"Oh my goodness. That's the most horrible thing I've ever heard."

Poor Julie! She was looking out for me and here I thought . . . I really need to learn to give people the benefit of the doubt.

"Wait! So you're saying Rachel was having an affair with Trey?"

"Hello? Where have you been? I've been saying that for the last five minutes."

"What about David?"

"David Gray?"

Freddie laughs and shakes his head. "There's no way David is going to be interested in a woman like Rachel. She's too much like that witch he was married to."

"Freddie. Don't speak ill of the dead. And what do you mean anyway?"

"Oh come on. You know, all cheap, brassy, pushy. David's not into that."

I give a sort of bitter laugh. "Oh really? Could have fooled me."

"Then you're not too hard to fool."

"Oh come on. What about all those so-called double dates with Trey and Julie . . . oh. He was a decoy." Okay, I feel badly for him for about two seconds then come back to: "He still went out with her. Do you think he knew she was using him?"

"Mr. Goody-Two-Shoes? No way. You don't know this guy very well. And here the rumor mill has been buzzing about the two of you for weeks."

"Whatever." Seriously, Freddie can be such a pain sometimes. I head to Blythe's office. "So shooting is off today?"

"For you it is. Your scenes were with Trey, who ran off with Rachel." She drops her head into her hands. "I have no idea how we're going to fix this. But you should be happy."

"Why's that?" Besides the fact that Rachel is out of David's life?

"Because Jerry told Julie to do whatever it takes to keep you. There's no telling what's going to happen with Trey and Rachel, so we can't risk losing you right now." She gives a short laugh. "I probably shouldn't have told you that."

"Yeah, probably not. I won't take advantage of the news; just don't say anything to Kyle or there's no telling how he might want to renegotiate. Did Julie call in or is she writing?"

"You know Julie. She's not going to take a day off and risk having someone else mess with her story lines."

"See you tomorrow, or whenever," I say. She waves me away as her phone rings.

On impulse, I knock on Julie's door. "What?" she hollers.

Oh boy. This was a bad idea.

I poke my head in.

"Come to gloat?" she asks, sarcasm dripping.

"No. I came to see if you want to go out to breakfast with me. I'm headed to the café on the corner."

"I don't need your pity."

"Good. Then come with me and let's talk about what we're going to do with Felicia."

"You want to brainstorm?"

"I'm not a writer, but I have an instinct about my character."

"Okay, fine. But this doesn't mean I believe you about that Christmas party."

I sigh. I guess I'm going to have to let that one go.

She grabs her purse. "But thanks for getting me out of here."

Laini, Dancy, and I are sitting around the table trying out Laini's latest creation: stuffed crab casserole—don't ask. It looks incredibly messy, but tastes surprisingly good.

"So, Trey and Rachel just . . . took off?" Laini asks. Apparently she escaped our measles epidemic because after a couple of days of treating a cough with Robitussin, she's fine. Dancy's still a little shaky, but definitely on the mend.

"What are they going to do about Rudolph and Felicia?"

I shrug. "They can't kill him off, although that's what Julie's really pulling for. Trey has three days to check in. If he doesn't, they'll bring in a replacement. As a matter of fact, I think they're eyeing Kirk Cameron for the role."

Laini gasps. "Mike?" Everyone's heartthrob from the eighties sitcom *Growing Pains*, she means.

"You have got to stop watching so much TV Land."

"So," Dancy says around a bite. "Have you heard from David?"

I shake my head. "Can you imagine a woman dumping David for Trey? I mean really. It's just gross."

"Are you going to call him?" she presses.

"Of course not. What would I say?"

"How about . . . what's the deal with your dumb girlfriend running off with a married man?"

I roll my eyes. "I'm so sure I'm going to ask him that."

"Well, the least you can do is call him and offer your sympathy." Laini jumps on the bandwagon. "After all, you two have sort of become friends."

"Oh, all right. Fine."

I shove up from the table and grab the cordless phone to dial David's number. The phone rings, once—twice—and on the third time his answering machine picks up. I wait for the beep. "Uh, hey David, it's, um, Tabby. I heard about Rachel and just wanted to tell you how sorry I am that she did that to you. I hope you're not feeling too badly. I'm sure there are plenty of other fish in the sea for you to choose from." Oh, good grief. I did *not* just say that. "Well, I guess that's all. Have a good evening and . . . well . . . good-bye."

"That was painful," Dancy says.

"Who asked you?" I dive into another spoonful of crab casserole. "Is there dessert?" I ask, needing something to take away the humiliation of that message I just left.

"Sorry. No time. I was researching design schools all day. Only had time to whip this casserole up real quick."

"Who wants something from Nick's? I need cheesecake and a latte."

Dancy tosses me her keys and gives me her order. I head out to the sidewalk. The street is well lit and I decide rather than risk losing Dancy's parking place, I'll simply walk the few blocks to Nick's.

"Hey there, Tabitha!" the Italian calls out when I walk inside. "What are you doing here so late?"

"I need cheesecake to numb my emotional pain."

"Sit down and tell old Nick all about it."

"Oh, you don't want to hear my troubles."

"Are you kiddin' me? I'm a very sensitive guy. Just ask my wife."

Nelda looks at him askance. "Yeah, you're a regular Dr. Phil."

"Don't tell me that. You know I hate that guy."

I can't help but grin at this couple who have been married for thirty years.

Nick brings me my chai mocha latte and a slice of cheesecake. "Come on, Tabitha. Spill it."

"There's been some trouble on the set of *Legacy of Life*. I'm not sure what's going to happen. They're talking about recasting the character of Rudolph."

"Best thing that could happen. That guy's a putz."

"You think so?"

"Sure. He don't have a face anyone can believe."

"What do you think of Kirk Cameron for the part?"

"The kid from that show? Now there's a face you can trust. That all that's buggin' you?"

"No." I sip my latte, enjoying the warm sweet taste of spice and chocolate. "Well, there's this guy."

"I knew it."

I cradle my latte and stare at the already receding foam on top. "Yeah, well. He doesn't see me the way I see him. And besides, his girlfriend just dumped him and ran off with a married man."

"That's harsh." Nick shakes his head. Then he meets my gaze. "Does he know you like 'im?"

What am I, in junior high? I shrug. "I don't know. Probably."

"Well, if he ain't flattered, he's a putz too."

I can't help but laugh. "Nick, how come they don't make guys like you anymore?"

"God broke the mold, sweetheart. Didn't he, baby?" he calls to Nelda.

"Sure. And a good thing too. Who else would want him?"

Nick gives me a wink. "Don't let her fool ya. She's crazy about me."

"She'd be crazy not to be."

I order for Dancy and Laini, and Nick heads behind the counter. Again, he won't let me pay.

The bell above the door dings just as I'm getting ready to leave, and I suck in a sharp breath. "David? What are you doing here?"

"Your roommates told me where you were." He's looking at me with such intensity I'm about to drop what I'm carrying. "I got your message, but I didn't really understand it."

"Oh."

"This guy botherin' you, Tabitha?" Nick calls.

"He's okay, Nick. We're just leaving."

"This the guy that just got dumped?"

"Uh, yeah."

"No!" David says, stepping to the counter. "I didn't get dumped."

Nick gives him a scrutinizing squint. "You mean your girl didn't run off with some other guy?"

"She did too!" I follow David to the counter. "I had breakfast with the wife of the man she ran off with. They're getting ready for a trip."

David scowls but directs his comments to the big Italian behind the counter. "I'm not denying that Rachel ran off with Trey. I'm just saying she was never my girlfriend. You've known all along about my history with Rachel. She's only a friend. And honestly—she was my wife's friend."

I snort. "Oh please." I stare at Nick. "Then why did he take her out on Valentine's Day? You don't ask just anyone out on the most romantic day of the year. It's reserved for someone special."

"I didn't ask her. She asked me. I turned her down, until you volunteered to babysit. Then I didn't have another excuse."

My eyes go wide. "Oh? She said you wanted me to watch the kids."

"Well, I didn't. The last thing I wanted was to go out with Rachel. She isn't my type."

"'Ey," Nick butts in. "What's your type?"

David jerks his head at me. "She knows."

"No I don't."

David takes the packages from my hands and sets them on the nearest table. He slips his arms around me before I even know how to react. "Yes you do."

"He's for real," Nick says. "Look at his face."

"Wait a minute. What about Rachel?"

"Would you forget about her? She wasn't my girlfriend."

"What about the night I took the kids to lessons and you had a"—yes, I succumb to air quotes—"*business meeting?*"

"What are you saying? That I faked the meeting and had a secret rendezvous with Rachel?"

"If that's not what happened, then explain why you said, 'how did you know' when I asked how your evening was with Rachel?"

"Good grief. You honestly thought I asked you to pick up my kids, feed them, bathe them, and put them to bed, so I could meet Rachel?"

I give a miserable nod and his expression softens.

"Tabby, I was having dinner with potential clients who were looking for a new software analyst. That's what I do. While I was waiting for them to show up, Rachel came into the restaurant. She sat with me and ordered a drink. When Trey showed up, it was all too clear what was happening and that I was their cover. Do you have any idea how many double dates I was forced to endure before I put a stop to it?"

"Then how come you never asked out Tabitha?" Is Nick still here?

"At first she had a boyfriend. Then I realized she was struggling with my children. And any woman I become involved with has to have the capacity to be a mother."

"What are you sayin'?" Nick says, sounding downright insulted. "Tabitha's gonna be a terrific mother."

"I know." David tightens his hold and smiles. "My children love her already."

"I'm pretty crazy about them too, David."

"I'm pretty crazy about you," he says softly.

"You are?"

"He is, honey," Nelda says from the kitchen. "I can see it in his eyes. And Nick's right. That's a face you can trust."

"There you have it," David says. "What do you say? Want to give us a try and see what happens?"

Is he kidding me? I can't speak. All I can do is nod. David dips his head and finally, finally, finally, his lips close over mine in a kiss that was definitely worth waiting for.

Epilogue

All right, let's see . . . so to recap what has happened in my life during the past six months. Well, I have a boyfriend. Yes, a boyfriend. A very cute one who loves to spend time with me and never cancels dates unless he absolutely has no choice. And have I mentioned that he kisses like a dream?

And you know it's David. We're a couple. People lump us together that way. David and Tabby. "Let's see if David and Tabby would like to come along with us." Or, "Darling, do you think David and Tabby might like to have supper with us on Saturday?"

It's such a wonderful thing to have a real relationship.

What else? Oh, I've gained two adorable possible stepchildren-to-be. David hasn't actually mentioned a ring, but I'm hoping after he sees me today in my maid of honor gown (size six) for Shelly's wedding, he'll no longer be able to put it off. I'm actually hoping for a Christmas wedding—although that might be pushing it a little, considering this is already the beginning of September. So maybe I should stop thinking of poinsettias and consider lilies instead. Oh! And lavender bridesmaid gowns. No. Dancy would kill me. She's already said no fuchsia, lavender, or pastels of any kind. Which really doesn't leave me much choice for summer colors. But I did promise, and a promise is a promise. Besides, she's having such a wretched time at work with her British jerk of a boss that I really don't want to add insult to injury anyway. So I guess I'll go with the black and white wedding theme. That's classic and elegant and who wouldn't love that?

Oh, Kirk Cameron turned us down for the role of Rudolph, so Jerry cast a relative unknown. And he's fantastic. Fans overwhelmingly prefer him to Trey. Apparently they say he has an honest face.

The wedding coordinator gives me the signal that it's my turn to walk down the aisle. I crank my head forward and kiss my nephew's head. I'm carrying him instead of a bouquet. Shelly absolutely refused to get married without her son by her side and Brian agreed. Of course Brian agrees with anything Shelly says. I swear I've never seen a man so in love. Well, except for David. My boyfriend. Oh, did I already mention I have a boyfriend? I have a real, live boyfriend.

So I'm carrying my darling nephew, Frankie, down the aisle. People are smiling of course. His chubby legs are kicking as I hold him face-first to show him off. And he's squealing with all the excitement of the day. My gaze finds David's, and he looks a little shell-shocked. Yep, I think this might have done the trick.

Jenn is the flower girl and Jeffy the ring bearer. When I get to the front of the church, I stop next to Jenn. She looks gorgeous in a miniature bridal gown. Her blond hair is curled into ringlets and piled on her head. She takes my breath away. Jeffy is standing like a gentleman in his pint-sized black tux. Oh, what's he doing? Eyeing the communion bread and licking his lips. I only pray he keeps his fingers off the loaf.

Shelly is a vision walking down the aisle on Dad's arm. Dad. Those Weight Watchers points are paying off. What a transformation. He's a nice, healthy two hundred pounds, which, at six foot two, isn't bad. He's just ten pounds from his goal weight.

His diabetes is under control, and he's stopped taking blood pressure medicine altogether.

My gaze falls on David, but he's not looking at the bride. His eyes are fixed on me, and the expression of love absolutely takes my breath away.

"I love you," he mouths. I feel my cheeks warm, and I smile at him. And since no one else is looking at me anyway, I go ahead and mouth "I love you too" back at him.

My eyes get misty as I watch my little sister become Mrs. Brian Ryan. (What were his parents thinking?)

By the time the ceremony is almost over, my arms are about to fall off. To finish off the wedding, Shelly reaches over and takes Frankie from my arms. Together, she and Brian dedicate him to God and promise to raise him to love and serve the Lord.

Oh! Did I forget to mention that? My sister and Brian have started attending my church, where I've become quite the celebrity since I gave my talk at the ladies' meeting. Mike and Joy are still hanging out with my parents at their church. Joy prefers a more traditional service. How crazy is that?

I still don't know if I'm making much of a difference being a Christian in the soap opera industry. I mean, Freddie's still gay, and Julie has moved on to yet another relationship. Tonya is still bullied by her mother, who still smokes three packs of Winstons per day. Some days I think I should just give up and go back to wearing the bunny suit. But on those rare occasions when God opens a door and I'm allowed to share His goodness with someone, I know I'm there for a reason. To be salt and light.

We turn as the preacher introduces the new married couple and I wait, expecting to follow the bride and groom down the aisle to the receiving line. Only I see Shelly give David a nod, and my boyfriend stands and walks to the front. He drops down on one knee in front of me and holds up a case with the most fantastic engagement ring I've ever seen. Is he kidding me? I glance over at my sister. "Are you okay with this?"

Her eyes are filled with tears. "It was our idea. Would you give the man an answer?"

The wedding guests laugh. I turn back to David with a teasing grin. "He hasn't exactly asked me a question yet."

A smile tips the corners of his lips. "Will you be my wife?"

"And be our mom?" Jeffy and Jenn take up positions flanking their dad.

"Yeah," Jeffy says. "We really want you to be our mom."

I'm sorry, but that's just the best proposal a girl could possibly get. I drop to my knees in front of my little family-to-be. I touch their pudgy cheeks (the twins' of course; David's cheeks are chiseled). "I love you too. And nothing would make me happier than to be your mom."

I reach up and touch the precious face of the man I love. His eyes are misting and tears travel down my cheeks. "Yes, I'll marry you."

The wedding guests applaud as David slips the ring on my finger and kisses me. A sweet kiss, filled with promise and love.

One thing is for sure, this is far better than winning an Emmy.

But you know . . . if they offer me one, I'm not going to turn it down.

Author's Note

Dear Readers,

Broaching the topic of daytime soap operas in any sort of positive light is a little tricky for a writer of Christian fiction. Some Christians are strongly opposed to daytime serials due to content issues. But I fully believe that God has placed many actors and actresses in the studios for His purposes just like most other fields. In Catch a Rising Star, I've tried to show Tabby as a character who wants to make a difference in the field she loves—acting. We see her stand up for her principles more than once, as I'm sure actors and actresses are given the opportunity to do daily while walking out their faith in an industry where Christians are rarely, if ever, celebrated.

I hope you enjoy the fun and imperfections of this character as much as I have enjoyed discovering her in my head and heart. I hope to see Tabby truly make a difference in her world as we catch glimpses of her in coming books in the Drama Queens series. Stay tuned!

God bless you abundantly above all you could ask or think. Until we meet again,

Tracey Bateman

READING GROUP GUIDE

1. Tabby plays a soap heroine. What do you think about a Christian taking a role on a soap opera?

2. Should Christians watch soap operas? Why or why not? By the same token, are secular movies or TV shows really any different from today's daytime television dramas?

3. Tabby's relationship with her mother seems volatile at best. How could she have done things differently to smooth things out?

4. Should parents try to push their kids into relationships with the potential mate they think would be a good fit? Do you know of instances where it has worked out? What about instances where, as in the case of Brian and Tabby, no love connection occurred?

5. Should single people actively search out dates and potential mates? Or should they wait contentedly for God to bring the right person?

6. How did Tabby's faith play out on set? Should she have been more open? Less? In her attempt to be salt and light in her world, do you think she succeeded?

7. Tabby starts out really disliking children and even gets off on the wrong foot with David's kids. But in the end, she grows to care about them a great deal. Can you think of an instance where your first impression of someone was wrong and your heart eventually changed? What does that say about giving people the benefit of the doubt to begin with?

8. Shelly is pregnant out of wedlock. And yet she and Tabby and their brother were raised in a Christian home by Christian parents. Does it make a difference how you raise your kids if they're ultimately going to do whatever they choose anyway?

9. Tabby's relationship with her dad is close and tender. Why do you think it's so vastly different than the relationship she has with her mother? What could Tabby have done differently?

10. Tabby and her two best friends support each other through all of life's struggles. What are your thoughts on female relationships? Is it possible to have close friends in a group setting without gossip and hurt?